Jan glared at Doug

"Don't you have any idea what you did to me?"
she demanded.

She stood up, facing him, her fists clenched.
Her cheeks were flushed, her breath coming
fast. "Damn you," she said. "All those years
you never gave me so much as a second thought,
did you? You walked out of here and never looked
back. Do you know how much that hurt? Did
you know that all our classmates called me
'Doug MacKenzie's leftover girl'?"

Jan pounded her fist on the wooden surface of
the table. "Didn't you know that by coming back
here you'd stir things up all over again?"

Doug's voice was so husky he could hardly
speak. "I had no idea," he said. "God, Janny,
what can I say to you?"

"Nothing," she said. "It's too late. It was too late
a long time ago."

The Leftover Girl is Meg Hudson's eighteenth Superromance novel. The author tells us that working on this book was a pleasure for her. "I enjoyed being around Doug and Jan and the twins," she writes. "I genuinely like them, and I hope our readers will share my enthusiasm." Meg Hudson makes her home in Massachusetts.

Books by Meg Hudson

HARLEQUIN SUPERROMANCE

Don't miss any of our special offers. Write to us at the following address for information on our newest releases.

Harlequin Reader Service
P.O. Box 1397, Buffalo, NY 14240
Canadian address: P.O. Box 603,
Fort Erie, Ont. L2A 5X3

The Leftover Girl

MEG HUDSON

Harlequin Books

TORONTO • NEW YORK • LONDON
AMSTERDAM • PARIS • SYDNEY • HAMBURG
STOCKHOLM • ATHENS • TOKYO • MILAN

Published August 1991

ISBN 0-373-70465-8

THE LEFTOVER GIRL

For Joel and Jill,
with love

PROLOGUE

THE ELLIS FALLS BOARD of Selectmen met with the public on Wednesday mornings at ten o'clock, in the large, corner office on the ground floor of the Town Office Building.

The selectmen, their secretary and the town manager, sat behind a long wooden table. Folding chairs, borrowed from the nearby Heatherton Funeral Home, accommodated the public. The chairs never seemed to wind up in straight rows, which made it difficult to weave past them without being noticed. Especially if you were a selectman, and already fifteen minutes late for the meeting.

As Janet Grayson edged along the wall to her place next to Chairman of Selectmen Bartlett Folger, she knew all eyes were upon her. She was also aware of Selectman Folger's disapproving glance as she sat down beside him, and she muttered, "Sorry."

Glancing up, she met the indulgent gaze of Tom Prentice, the town manager. She fought back a stab of annoyance. She didn't need special consideration because she was the only woman on the board. Further, Tom had asked her out a couple of times lately, and she didn't want an other-than-business involvement with him.

Jan broke the eye contact with Tom and, looking around the room, noted that most of the people here today were senior citizens. That was fine, she liked having older people involve themselves in local government. But she doubted if any of those present had been required to cope with two teenagers, a chocolate business, three cats and a capricious beagle, before setting out this morning.

The same could be said about the other members of the board. Two were retired, two were still in business, and all of them were old enough to be her father.

Bartlett Folger said, "To bring you up-to-date, Mrs. Grayson, Mrs. Newman has been telling us that a local landscaper has been dumping brush into the marsh across the street from her property. As we all know, that's against the conservation laws. Our marsh areas are few enough, and those that remain are important bird sanctuaries..."

Bartlett never lost the opportunity to make a small speech. Jan sat back, listened to him droning on, and felt the tension slowly ebbing out of her. Slipping on her town official's hat was always a welcome change of pace.

The board allotted exactly two hours for the weekly open meeting with the voters, then went into executive session. Today, once the public had been excused, Bartlett Folger said, "We have only one important matter on the agenda this morning. Now that the Memorial Day weekend is behind us, we need to get on with plans for the Fourth of July."

Herb Flynn, who ran the Valid Value hardware store when he wasn't being a selectman, glanced up in surprise. "That falls to the Board of Trade, doesn't it?" he asked. "The parade, anyway? And the fire department'll handle the fireworks. If I'm remembering right, we voted a fair bit of change for fireworks at the town meeting."

"Yes," Bartlett Folger said, looking pained. As a retired banker, Bartlett considered spending town money on such frivolities as fireworks a deplorable waste.

He continued, "We have a different situation, this Fourth. It has been suggested that we combine the traditional celebration with a 'welcome home' reception to be held in the high-school gymnasium."

"Who's coming home?" Herb Flynn asked.

Tom Prentice answered that one. "Ellis Falls' most famous son," he said. "Douglas MacKenzie is returning to his roots here in western Massachusetts to write a book. He's coming back after a twenty year absence—during which I'm sure every one of you has spent a good many hours watching him on television. The Board of Trade has asked him to act as Grand Marshal of the parade, and he's accepted. But certainly the town also will want to honor him. I've suggested to Bartlett that we hold a welcome-home reception in the high school gym, open to everyone."

Herb Flynn said something in answer to that, but Jan didn't even hear what it was. She felt giddy and tried to tell herself it was because she'd forgotten to eat breakfast. But honesty compelled her to admit that lack of food didn't have much to do with this sudden light-headedness.

Douglas MacKenzie, coming back to Ellis Falls after all these years?

Two decades flashed by, like a video tape being rewound. Jan saw herself walking down Catherine Street in the moonlight with Doug MacKenzie. It was just about this time of year, but it was unseasonably warm. A Saturday night, the two of them had been to the movies together. As they came within the shade of a maple tree, just leafed out, Doug stopped, put his arms around her and kissed her, and Jan could taste a hint of buttered popcorn on his lips.

She was upset, terribly upset, because Doug had just told her he'd decided to accept his uncle's offer to put him through college. Doug's father had died five years earlier. This uncle was his only brother. His gesture, Jan had to admit, was generous. But, it had a catch to it. It meant Doug had to go to California and live in his uncle's home while he attended UCLA.

The continent that would stretch between them seemed vaster than the universe to Jan. She remembered looking up at Doug and blinking back her tears. "If you go out there," she said, "I'll never see you again."

"Nonsense," Doug chided. "I'll write you every day. I'll call you up every week. You can come out for some of the holidays, I'll come East other times..."

He paused and reached for a strand of her dark copper hair, then curled the silky lock around his finger. Jan nestled against him, rested her head on his shoulder.

They stood like that for quite awhile, locked in an embrace, the moonlight splashing through the maple leaves. Then Doug suddenly stepped back, and Jan saw him tug at the brand-new gold class ring that glinted on his finger. A minute later, he was pressing the ring into her palm, and folding her fingers around it.

"There," he said. "To remember me by." He saw the tears she could no longer hold back and protested, "Hey, stop worrying, will you? You're my girl, remember?"

She thought about that now, and smiled grimly. She had been his girl, all right. And she had become his leftover girl.

Twenty years ago come August, Doug had gone off to California. And, except for a couple of postcards Jan had never heard from him since.

CHAPTER ONE

"IT'S GOING TO RAIN," Vicky wailed, "and our float will be ruined."

"Do you always have to be so negative?" her twin brother demanded. Chet was fastening the brass buttons on his band uniform tunic, swearing under his breath because the buttons were slightly too big for the buttonholes.

"Who's being negative?" Vicky challenged. "Look out the window, then tell me it's not going to rain. Which is rotten luck," she added, "because this year's parade is important. Do you know who's going to be Grand Marshal? And one of the float judges after?"

"Yes, I know who's going to be Grand Marshal and one of the float judges after," her brother mimicked. "I'm beginning to wish he'd stayed in China or Afghanistan. Or was it South Africa he was reporting from the last time?"

Jan, overhearing the twins as she dressed—their voices did carry!—was inclined to agree with her son. Douglas MacKenzie's homecoming was threatening to spoil the town's Fourth of July celebration. Everyone was so bent on honoring the returning hero that the usual festivities—like games for the kids on the school athletic field and hot dog roasts before the evening fireworks—were being bypassed. The big event, aside from the parade, was going to be the welcome-home celebration in the high school gym. The women's auxiliaries of the Rotary Club, the Kiwanis Club, and the Lions Club had combined forces not only to decorate the gym lavishly but to prepare refreshments that would outdo a city caterer.

Was this what Douglas MacKenzie really wanted? Jan wondered. Was he coming home after twenty years because he thirsted for some grand scale local lionization? She would have thought that a man returning to his hometown in order to settle in and write a book might prefer a bit more privacy. Maybe even a dash of real solitude.

Jan listened to her almost-seventeen-year-old twins bicker about the weather and the parade as she tugged a red-and-white-striped top over her white skirt. She wished she'd bought the top a size larger. It wasn't really tight, but it was a shade snugger than most of the things she wore. She fastened on some strands of red, white and blue beads, then reached for her white straw boater and set it squarely on her head. The straw boaters, banded with red and blue ribbons and trimmed with red, white and blue rosettes, had been Bartlett Folger's idea, and all the selectmen were wearing them.

Jan wandered out into the living room, and asked a rhetorical question. "Ready, kids?"

Chet had just finished buttoning the tunic, and he stared at her blankly. He still needed to comb his hair; he still needed to put on his socks and shoes. Jan looked around and wondered where he'd put the shako that went with the uniform. The tall black cone trimmed in white, with a bright red plume—Ellis Falls High's colors—was nowhere to be seen.

Chet, she thought, slightly annoyed with him, was awfully absentminded lately. Sometimes she had to speak to him three times before he'd look up and answer. It didn't take much intuition to sense that something was bothering him. She just wished she knew what it was. Chet, until recently, had always been so open with her. More so than Vicky, who tended to keep her secrets to herself.

But Jan's annoyance faded as she looked at Chet standing there in his band uniform, and she felt a surge of love and pride.

Jonas had died when the twins were only four— after a losing battle with a terrible, virulent type of cancer. Maybe because she was, essentially, the only parent her kids had ever known, Jan had always felt a special obligation to them.

Though they were twins, they did not look alike. Chet, tall and exceptionally well built for a boy his age, had Jan's dark copper hair, brown eyes and rather square face. Vicky took after Jonas in looks and coloring; she had blond hair and gray eyes. She was on the short side—five-three, to Jan's five-six— and she had a terrific figure. It followed that she was extremely attractive to the boys in her school. Too attractive, Jan sometimes felt.

Vicky was wearing a very short-skirted red-white-and-blue cheerleader's costume, with white socks and white sneakers. She looked distractedly at her mother. "I can't find my pom-poms," she complained.

Jan decided that maybe Chet wasn't the only twin who was getting absentminded. The pom-poms were fashioned from paper strips and they looked like big red-white-and-blue shaggy chrysanthemums fastened to the ends of long sticks. They were so large it would be impossible to lose them.

"Maybe you left them in your bedroom?" Jan suggested.

Vicky shook her head. "I checked."

"Well, maybe they're in the bathroom."

"Mother..." Vicky warned.

"She probably left them at school," Chet said. "Mom, have you seen my shako?"

"You probably left your shako at school," Vicky snapped.

Jan, ignoring the twins, marched out to the kitchen. As she'd suspected might be the case, the missing items were on the kitchen table, evidently having been deposited there when both Vicky and Chet had taken time out to go to the fridge in search of a snack.

She marched back to the living room, holding the shako and the pom-poms. "Know that old saw about losing your head if..." she remarked. Then she said briskly, "Come on, kids, we've got to get this show on the road."

THERE WERE DARK CLOUDS hanging over the Berkshires, and the sky looked like oyster stew. Jan had listened to a weather report earlier, and the meteorologist had said the rain was going to hold off until late that night. "Expect to hear thunder after midnight," he'd predicted.

Even a weatherman could sometimes be overly optimistic, Jan thought. As she climbed the steps into the reviewing stand and took her place next to Bartlett Folger, she cast another glance at the heavens. If the upcoming stormy weather held off until the parade was over, it would be a miracle.

She could hear the roll of drums, the blasts of trumpets and the clear, higher tones of the clarinets coming from the direction of the high school, and she shivered. She'd been so busy the past few weeks that, most of the time, she'd been able to stave off an attack of nerves when she thought about seeing Doug MacKenzie again. But, this was the zero hour, and she wasn't ready for it.

The parade route stretched from the high school, at one end of town, to the Legion Hall, at the opposite end. The reviewing stand was midway along the route. Someone had come up with the brainstorm of borrowing Mel Higgins's old white Caddy convertible for the Grand Marshal to ride in. Everything would halt while the Caddy pulled up in front of the reviewing stand, where the Grand Marshal would get out and join the selectmen to review the floats, which would then begin passing by.

Jan knew the schedule by heart. But now as she saw the band approaching, the drum major striding out in front, baton twirling, it fully hit her that within minutes Douglas MacKenzie would be sitting in this same reviewing stand with her. Which, she told herself, was no cause for hatching out a swarm of butterflies. Doug was part of a very distant past.

Since he left town, you met and married a wonderful man, whom you lost much too soon, Jan reminded herself. *You gave birth to two great kids. You took your grandmother's recipe for Chocolate Fantasies and converted it into the basis for a business that now fills coast-to-coast orders for very special chocolate confections. You're thirty-eight, and you've*

*led a full and satisfying life, if not always an exciting
one. When you've seen Doug MacKenzie on TV these
past few years, he's seemed like a stranger. Or,
maybe, a cardboard cutout of someone you knew a
long time ago.*

*It's not like your girlhood knight in shining armor
is about to appear, riding in a vintage white Caddy.
As far as you're concerned, Doug's armor tarnished
a long time ago....*

Jan saw the front bumper of the Caddy carrying
Doug MacKenzie come into view behind the band,
and she choked up with suppressed laughter.

Suppose, after all this time, he didn't even recognize her!

THE BAND MARCHED by the reviewing stand, and Jan
momentarily forgot all about her incipient encounter
with Douglas MacKenzie when she saw her son. Chet,
marching tall and straight as he blew his shiny brass
trumpet, looked magnificent. Jan felt a wave of
emotion, and wished for an intense moment that
Jonas could be here to see the way his son was growing up. Jonas would be as proud of Chet as she was.

Then, right behind the band, came the white
Caddy, top down, and she saw the Grand Marshal
sitting on the edge of the back seat. He was wearing
a white suit, a bright blue shirt and a red tie. He'd
been given one of the same kind of boaters the selectmen were wearing, and he was waving it at the
applauding crowd. He looked terrific, almost as
young as he'd looked twenty years ago. That same
thick dark hair. Those same chiseled features, aug-
mented by a deep, even tan that even the sun wor-

shipers here in Ellis Falls couldn't compete with, this early in the summer.

The Caddy pulled up in front of the reviewing stand, and Doug MacKenzie got down adroitly from his perch. He bounded up the short flight of wooden steps, and Jan, watching him, had to admit that he still had a lot going for him. There was an aura of virility about him, a sexiness and an air of self-assurance, plus a high-voltage smile that could have melted a glacier.

Bartlett Folger, beaming for once, extended his hand in greeting. Douglas MacKenzie clasped Bartlett's hand, said something not quite audible, and moved smoothly into place, standing in front of the chair to Bartlett's right.

Jan was standing in front of the chair to Bartlett's left, and she felt as if her white pumps had been soldered to the spot. She heard Bartlett make the introduction, heard him say, "Mrs. Grayson, Mr. MacKenzie," but it took a moment for her to get the courage to look up.

The blue blaze she encountered was only too familiar. But what she hadn't expected to see in those eyes was shock, deep and unadulterated.

The smile was wiped clean from Doug's face and he looked dazed as he said, "Janny."

"Hello, Doug," she managed, and was spared further conversation because the band started playing, drowning out anything she might have said. The parade began to move again. The floats slowly passed by, and finally the one Jan was looking for approached.

Vicky was the focal point of the float. She was standing on a revolving platform as she put all the bounce and energy she had into her cheerleader performance, her pom-poms jouncing wildly as she twirled around. Other girls pirouetted around the base of the revolving platform in much the same manner, but they were eclipsed by Vicky, both because of her superior position—she was higher up than anyone else—her enthusiasm, and her shining blond prettiness.

Jan heard Doug say to Bartlett Folger, "Good-looking girl, isn't she?" and she smiled to herself. How would Doug react if he found out the teenaged girl he was admiring was his high school sweetheart's daughter?

The last of the floats passed, followed by a series of fire engines from Ellis Falls and neighboring communities, all honking their horns at a decibel level that threatened to split eardrums. The dignitaries began to leave the stand and head for their cars to drive over to the Legion Hall grounds for the judging. Jan had parked her car about fifty feet from the stand, and made a beeline for it, looking neither to the right nor the left. She doubted Doug was apt to ask her for a ride over to the Legion Hall. Bartlett Folger was undoubtedly planning to chauffeur the returned hero himself. But, she didn't want to take any chances. She still needed a little more time before facing Doug alone.

So far, the rain had held off, but the swollen clouds looked darker and more ominous than ever. Jan took a shortcut over a back road to the Legion Hall. She parked at the edge of the lot in the rear of the building, then strolled across to the field where the floats were lined up waiting for inspection.

Vicky was standing in a group with some of her classmates, but she detached herself and came over to her mother. "Mom," she asked, keeping her voice low, "do you think our float has a chance at the prize?"

Though the cheerleaders' float had exhibited more enthusiasm than any of the others, the rest of the floats were far more elaborate. Jan was about to sidestep a direct answer when her daughter plunged on to another subject.

"Isn't he absolutely gorgeous, Mom?" Vicky asked, her gray eyes shining.

There was no need for Jan to ask her who she was talking about.

"I've always thought he was the handsomest man on TV, but in person he's dynamite," Vicky said. "When we went by the stand and I saw you practically sitting next to him, I was green. Didn't you get goose bumps all over, Mom?"

Sooner or later, the truth was going to come out. Jan decided she might as well start telling her daughter some of it.

"Vicky," she said, "Douglas MacKenzie isn't exactly a stranger to me." She drew a deep breath. "We went to school together," she confessed.

Vicky looked at her mother as if she suspected Jan might be having delusions. Then, she accused, "How come you haven't said anything all this time?"

"There wasn't anything to say," Jan managed feebly.

She saw Douglas MacKenzie approaching the floats, accompanied by Bartlett Folger, the other three selectmen, and Tom Prentice. "See you later, Vicky," she muttered, and reluctantly joined the group. Right now, judging the floats was an official duty.

Doug gave her a rather lopsided smile, but he didn't say anything. Jan was getting the impression that seeing her had thrown him a curve. Evidently he hadn't expected to find her still living in Ellis Falls.

She kept as much distance from him as she could, as she moved along the line of floats with the other judges. Rose Ladue, the selectmens' secretary, tagged along, noting each judge's rating. Tom Prentice was empowered to cast a deciding vote in the event of a tie.

Vicky had returned to her post on her float. Though Doug gave her a friendly grin, Jan had to allow him points for honesty when he muttered to Rose, "I'd give it a four."

The judging finished, the floats were awarded first, second and third place prizes in their respective categories. And the last of the third place prizes had just been given out when the heavens—patient all this time—opened up.

Thunder rumbled, lightning streaked, and the rain began to fall in torrents. People fled in every direction, and Jan headed straight for her car.

It didn't take much to turn earth to mud up in this mountain country, and the heels of her white pumps began to sink into the mire, making it difficult to run. Maybe, she thought later, if her pace hadn't been slackened by the forces of nature, Doug MacKenzie never would have caught up with her. As it was, the sound of her name being shouted carried over the pelting rain and the intermittent growl of the thunder.

"Janny, wait up, will you?" Doug bellowed.

No one else had ever called her Janny.

Jan didn't wait. She didn't have to, because Doug caught up with her and they covered the last several feet together.

By the time she got inside the car, Jan was soaking wet. She looked across at Doug, and saw he was just as wet as she was. He was also luckier. Somewhere, he'd dispensed with the white ribbon-trimmed boater. She'd still been wearing hers when the rain struck, and the ribbons had been anything but dye-fast. The colors had run, so the red and blue was streaked across the red and white stripes of her top, and the escaping colors were making blurry little stripes of their own down the front of her white skirt.

She'd intended wearing this same outfit to the reception. Now she realized she couldn't. Nor could Doug arrive at the affair being held in his honor looking three-quartered drowned.

Jan said reluctantly, "I guess we'd better head for my place and dry off. Everyone's going to be late getting to the high school anyway."

As she spoke, she wished the guest of honor hadn't chased after her to hitch a ride. There had been a number of other cars parked closer to the floats. Bartlett Folger's, for one. Bartlett accepted the choicest parking spaces as a perk of his official position.

She was aware of Doug's eyes on her as she drove, and that steady blue gaze made it difficult to concentrate. Finally she asked, "What is it?"

He said slowly, thoughtfully. "I was thinking what a long time it's been."

He didn't seem to expect an immediate reply from her, and she didn't give him one. Driving in this downpour was taking her full attention anyway. The trip to her house, which should have taken ten minutes, stretched closer to twenty. And it wasn't until she turned the corner into her street that she remembered the twins wouldn't be coming home before the reception. They planned to go to friends' houses to freshen up, before moving on to the high school gym.

Jan stole a glance at the man at her side. He was staring out at the falling rain, seemingly immersed in his private thoughts.

She wondered how it must feel to come back to the town where you grew up, after a twenty year absence. Doug, when he'd left Ellis Falls, had not been the favored son he was today. A lot of the local people had put the MacKenzies on the wrong side of the tracks.

Her own family had not been happy about her going around with Doug, Jan remembered. She'd always felt her parents had been relieved when time went by, and Doug faded out of the picture.

But now he was back again. And for the first time in twenty years, she was alone with the man who had walked out of her life when he was a boy and had quickly forgotten she ever existed.

Right now, was Doug looking so preoccupied because he was remembering things he'd given little, if any, thought to over the course of those two decades?

Jan wished she could read his mind.

CHAPTER TWO

DOUG WAS STILL STARING at nothing in particular as Jan pulled into a driveway by a large white-frame house set well back from the road. But his vacant expression was deceptive. His mind was racing, and his emotions were churning in a way he never would have expected.

He'd been so totally unprepared for this encounter with Janny Phelps. Mrs. Janet Grayson, he corrected himself. Now he cursed his impulsiveness in making the decision to return to Ellis Falls to write his book.

Why hadn't it occurred to him that Janny almost certainly would have married long before now? And that she might very well still be living in this town where they'd gone to school together? Somehow—though he couldn't precisely have said why—he had expected she would have left Ellis Falls, by the time she was out of college, anyway, and gone on to greener pastures.

Were there greener pastures? Doug had been just about everywhere and he knew right now he was in danger of sentimentalizing, but Ellis Falls, thus far, looked awfully good to him.

He watched Janny take the key out of the ignition switch, saw her grimace as she looked out at the rain, which was still coming down in torrents. Then she said, "Now's as good a time as any, I guess."

She raced up the front walk of her house, Doug following close on her heels. She unlocked the front door, then started switching on lights as soon as she was inside. The afternoon had turned deep gray.

"This way," she told Doug, and made straight for the kitchen. She tossed the streaky boater into the sink, and slipped off her soggy pumps. Turning, she saw Doug standing in the middle of the kitchen floor, a sheepish expression on his face.

"I'm afraid I'm dripping," he apologized.

He was, indeed, dripping. They were both dripping. An involuntary smile curved Jan's lips. If she could have worked out the least romantic scenario possible for a reunion with the high school sweetheart who'd abandoned her two decades ago, this would be it.

"I'll get some towels," she said, and hurried to the linen closet off the downstairs bathroom.

She returned with an armful of large, fleecy towels, handing some of them to Doug, keeping some of them for herself. For the next few minutes they worked on trying to get as dry as they could—which was not nearly dry enough. By then, Jan was shivering.

"I think we'd better take a hot shower," she said, then wished she could rephrase the suggestion. She went on hastily, "The shower's in the upstairs bathroom. Why don't you go first? Do you think it would be safe to put those clothes you're wearing in the dryer?"

"It'll have to be," Doug said. "Otherwise, they're going to be holding a reception without a guest of honor. The stuff I brought with me is all at the Ellis Falls Inn.''

''I could drive you to the inn and you could get some dry things,'' Jan offered.

''We'd just get soaked all over again. It's coming down harder than ever. No, I'm willing to trust your dryer... if you could loan me something to put on in the meantime.''

Jan nodded and this time made for Chet's room. She returned with a bright green terry robe. ''I think it will fit,'' she told Doug. ''The bathroom's at the top of the stairs. I'll put on a pot of coffee while you're showering.''

For the next fifteen minutes Jan tried not to think about Doug MacKenzie taking a shower in her upstairs bathroom. But she couldn't block out a picture of him in the shower stall... and the picture was a shade too vivid for comfort. He was bigger and better developed now than he'd been at eighteen; but even at eighteen he'd had a terrific physique, and she'd been very well acquainted with it. Doug had been her first lover—her only lover to date except Jonas.

She and Doug had learned about making love, together. At least they'd learned the basics. There'd been none of the nuances, the fine points. Those came later with Jonas, who was six years older than she was and knew a great deal about how to satisfy a woman. She and Doug, in contrast, had been like eager puppies....

Her thoughts were punctuated by a familiar, high-pitched moan, and a series of impatient meows. She'd put the cats and Floppy, the beagle, out on the back screened porch when she left earlier, and now they

were clamoring for attention. Jan let them in, glad to
have some extra business to occupy herself with while
Doug MacKenzie finished showering. A few minutes
later, when he walked into the kitchen wearing the
green terry robe, she was instructing the three cats to
share the meal she'd put out for them, and mollify-
ing the beagle with some dog biscuits.

She turned from the animals to pour out freshly
brewed coffee for Doug and herself. She still felt
chilled to the bone, and sipped the hot coffee appreciatively. Doug followed suit, but after a moment he
said, ''If you'll direct me to your dryer, I'll start my
clothes tumbling.''

She hesitated, then said, ''You'd better let me do it.
I know my machine's idiosyncrasies.''

Doug nodded and handed her his damp clothes
bundle. Jan went downstairs to the laundry room and
separated the items. She hadn't expected Doug would
include his underwear—which was silly of her. Had
she expected him to put it on wet? But there it was,
and there was something unexpectedly intimate about
handling his cotton jockey shorts.

She stopped back in the kitchen just long enough
to report that she was going upstairs to shower. The
bathroom was warm and moist. Steam clouded the
mirror over the sink. Jan was very conscious that she
was following closely in Doug's footsteps as she
slipped out of her clothes, and got into the shower
stall. She lathered herself with soap, let the hot water
cascade over her clammy skin till she felt warm again.

She thought about putting on a robe and checking
on Doug's clothes, but then she decided to dress first.
She chose a two-piece deep blue silk outfit that em-

phasized enough of the patriotic motif of the day. She was a bit tired of looking like a human American flag.

When she returned to the kitchen Doug was sitting at the table holding Abigail, the oldest of the three cats. He looked as if his thoughts were at least a million miles away as he stroked the cat with a tenderness that was not lost on Jan. She couldn't remember Doug ever having a pet of his own when they were growing up, though he'd always loved animals.

Floppy, the beagle, was sitting at his feet, begging for her share of attention. Doug yielded, reached down, and caressed her amber velvet ears. The other two cats were still eating the last of the food Jan had set out for them.

The small scene looked so...domestic. Doug glanced up, caught her eyes, and smiled. "Quite a menagerie you have here," he remarked.

"Yes. The beagle supposedly belongs to my daughter, Vicky," Jan said. "My son, Chet, brought home Puff and Huff, the two gray cats, when they were kittens—they were born in a friend's house and were destined for the Animal Rescue League. Abigail—the tortoise one you're holding—arrived on an afternoon very much like this one, and we couldn't bear to turn her away. We ran a 'Found' ad in the paper, but no one ever claimed her."

Jan tossed the last words over her shoulder as she moved toward the stairs leading down to the laundry room, where she took Doug's clothes out of the dryer.

"At least you won't look completely crumpled," she said, as she returned to the kitchen. "I smoothed out your suit, and actually it doesn't look half bad—though I suppose it could do with a touch of the iron."

"It's fine," Doug said, taking the clothes from her. He was looking her over as he spoke, and he added, "You made a remarkable comeback."

"What?"

"Well, you went upstairs looking like you'd just swum the English Channel, and here you are ready to play fashion model."

She laughed. "You always did exaggerate," she said unthinkingly.

She had not meant to make any allusions to the past and she regretted this one as soon as it escaped her lips. But Doug let it go by without comment. He glanced at the clock and said, "I suppose I'd better get my act together."

"Yes," Jan agreed, "or you'll be keeping your public waiting."

He gave her a quizzical glance, but didn't comment. Instead, he said, "Be back in a minute," and he was, in not much more than that.

"Everything came out fine," he reported, "except my shoes still squish."

"Too bad I couldn't put them in the dryer." Jan handed him his red tie, which she'd dried separately. "There's a mirror in the front hall," she told him.

"Don't need it," Doug said, and proceeded to knot the tie perfectly right where he stood.

Jan had wondered if Doug might not have become pretty conceited over the years with all the fame and attention that had come his way. Now, watching him, she still wondered. A man who was willing to tie his tie without looking in a mirror was either so self-confident he couldn't make a mistake, or else he had a certain quotient of modesty and humility about him.

Which was it with Doug?

JAN FOUND a big umbrella for both of them, and they
dashed for the car. They said very little to each other
on the drive over to the high school. Again, Doug
seemed preoccupied, and Jan imagined he must be
thinking about all the faces from his past he was
about to encounter. In some ways, this was a trium-
phant return for him, but in other ways the homecoming must be stirring up some painful memories.

He'd been thirteen when his father died after a long
illness. His mother had been married three times—
enough to raise eyebrows in Ellis Falls, especially back
in those days. Doug had been the child of her second
marriage. When her third husband left her, Doug's
mother had gone on welfare.

The MacKenzies had lived in a rented house down
toward the old railroad station. That whole area had
been razed five or six years ago to make way for a
shopping mall. But before then, Mrs. MacKenzie had
left town—with a man, people said—and she'd not
been heard from since.

Remembering all those things, Jan glanced at Doug
and thought he looked rather grim. Was he, perhaps, having second thoughts about coming
"home"?

She decided to pose the question. "What made you
choose Ellis Falls to write your book in?"

He looked startled and it took him a second to
wrest his attention away from whatever he'd been
thinking about. Then his lips twisted wryly, and he
said, "I guess I thought people wouldn't pay as much
attention to me here as they do most places. I guess I

thought I'd still be 'the MacKenzie boy,' nothing more, nothing less.''

As she smiled, he nodded. ''Yeah, I know. I begin to see it was wishful thinking. But I honestly did think people here wouldn't take that much notice of me. And, I hope that that's what will happen, once this 'welcome-home' celebration is over.''

''I don't know,'' Jan said. ''People in Ellis Falls do watch TV, Doug. You're as much of a celebrity here as you are anywhere. You may be pretty much in demand during your stay here.''

He shook his head. ''I can't let that happen. I need peace and privacy and I still think—hope—I can get it here.''

''Well, good luck.''

''You don't think it's possible?'' he asked. ''I hope you're wrong, Janny.''

She didn't comment.

The rain was slackening somewhat as they pulled up in front of the high school. They shared the umbrella's protection as they walked rapidly to the gym. Jan had intended to separate from Doug at that point, but someone took the umbrella out of Doug's hand before he could turn it over to her, someone else propelled the two of them forward, and it became too late for her to retreat gracefully.

To her chagrin, she and Doug made quite an entrance, walking into the high school gymnasium with half the town already assembled there.

The music director had kept the band intact, damp uniforms and all. Now, as Doug walked through the door with Jan at his side, the band broke into the strains of ''Hail To The Chief.''

Doug murmured in a low tone meant for Jan's ears alone, "I didn't know I'd been elected President of the U.S.A."

She didn't respond. The one thing she'd been hoping was that Ellis Falls' citizens might have forgotten that she and Doug once had been paired together. But now—talk about giving the tongues of the local gossips a chance to wag!

The committee in charge of the reception had agreed that it should be kept informal. Nevertheless, an impromptu speech was expected of Doug, and he made it standing on a hastily constructed platform.

Jan, watching him, thought that he accepted the limelight as naturally as if it were sunlight. He spoke with an ease she envied, affected no postures. He joked, he laughed, he made light of himself and his celebrity status. Then he wound up by saying, "It's good to be home again," so simply and so eloquently that even Jan felt a lump in her throat.

The lump dissolved when her sleeve was tugged and she turned to see Vicky looking up at her excitedly. "Mom," she said, "you walked in here with him. Where did the two of you come from?"

"I gave him a lift," Jan replied.

"Well, you certainly took your time getting here," Vicky said.

"Vicky, it was pouring. My clothes were soaking wet. I had to go home and change," Jan explained patiently. "I take it you went back with Cathy to her place and got dried off?"

"Yes. Poor Chet...there was nothing much he could do about that uniform. We didn't dare put it in the dryer. He must feel like a wet rug by now."

The band had dispersed. Jan saw several boys and girls in uniform circulating, but she didn't spot Chet. Jim Farrish, one of the trombone players, came over looking for Vicky, and she went off with him to get some refreshments. For a minute, Jan was alone in the middle of the gym. Watching the people milling around her, she felt like she was looking at an animated Norman Rockwell painting. The clusters of red-white-and-blue balloons suspended from the ceiling, the red-white-and-blue streamers, the banners printed with Welcome Home Doug MacKenzie in big red-white-and-blue letters; it was such a slice of American life.

"Jan."

Nancy Ellis appeared beside her so quickly, so quietly, that Jan was startled. Nancy was wearing a bright red dress that was perfect with her dark hair and eyes but also accentuated her skin color, which right now was too pale.

Funny, how looking at someone in an unfamiliar setting could make you see them so differently. She'd never before noticed the dark shadows under Nancy's eyes, or that look of—unhappiness? Was that the way to define Nancy's expression?

She and Nancy ordinarily saw each other every day. For the past five years they'd been partners in Chocolate Fantasies, Inc., the company named for the marvelous confection Jan's grandmother had invented, the recipe for which she had then passed on to her granddaughter.

Jan thought of herself as the stay-at-home part of the business. Nancy—since the business had begun expanding so satisfactorily—did a fair bit of traveling, acquiring orders from exclusive Albany, Hartford and Boston stores. This coming fall Nancy intended to make a pitch for some accounts in Manhattan. Meantime, business came to a relative standstill during the months of July and August, since gourmet chocolates, such as they produced, were too perishable to ship well in hot weather.

Nancy had completed her last road trip of the season a week ago, bringing back a satisfactory batch of early fall orders.

Had Nancy been pushing herself too hard?

Concerned, Jan asked, "Are you okay?"

"I'm fine," Nancy said, a shade too quickly.

"Where's Bob?"

"Chatting with the guest of honor. Incidentally I've been hearing that you and MacKenzie knew each other pretty well when you were both in high school."

So, the tongues had started to wag. "That was a long time ago," Jan said. She was spared further explanation as one of the Kiwanis wives zeroed in on her.

"Janet," she was asked sweetly, "do you suppose you could pour coffee for a while? We're really swamped."

Jan went and took the indicated place at the refreshment table, glad to have something to do.

DOUG MACKENZIE felt as if his face had been frozen into a permanent, phony smile. It wasn't the first time he'd had that feeling, but this wasn't what he had come back to Ellis Falls for.

He'd shaken innumerable hands at this point, had people whom he vaguely recognized—twenty years could effect a lot of physical changes—and people whom he didn't recognize at all tell him they never failed to watch him on TV. A fair number had asked for his autograph and proffered a paper napkin or a scrap of paper plus a pen with which he could sign his name; and that had dismayed him. He'd been trying to get away from celebrity status and it looked as if he'd run into it, head-on.

As he had told Janny, he could only hope the tumult would soon die down, so he could get started on his book.

The idea for the book had been brewing ever since he had covered the spring of '89 student revolt in Beijing for his network. He had watched youth speaking, shouting and dying in the effort to achieve democracy, and he had been deeply moved. He—who never cried—had cried on the inside as he watched the massacre in China. And, though he had gone on to another part of the world to carry on with the news analysis and reporting for which he had become famous, the Chinese students lingered in his mind and heart.

Their stand, in his estimation, emphasized the vital role of youth in shaping the world's history. He thought of young people he'd seen everywhere, ready to stand up and fight and die for the things they deeply believed in. Even when he did not share their beliefs he deeply admired the courage of their convictions. And he wanted to address his book to literate young people—like the Chinese students to whom he intended to dedicate it. At the same time, he wanted to spell out to people of all ages the message that today's youth were to be listened to. For the hope of the future lay in their hands.

A lofty aspiration, Doug admitted. But he was committed to writing this book as he'd been committed to few things, and he had quickly found a willing—eager—publisher. Then he had convinced his network to give him a leave of absence. And then he had made the decision to come back to Ellis Falls.

Now he listened with one ear to what a portly man in a gray business suit was saying to him while his eyes roved the gym, searching for Janny Phelps. Mrs. Grayson.

He supposed that terry robe she'd loaned him belonged to her husband. The thought gave him an odd feeling. He wondered where her husband was? All the time they'd been in Janny's house, he'd been expecting the man she'd married to show up. Then, she'd spoken about her kids. A girl, who was the owner of the beagle, a boy who'd brought home two of the three cats. He wondered how old the kids were and where they'd been while the parade was going on?

During the float judging procedure he'd been made aware that Janny was a member of the Ellis Falls Board of Selectmen. The thought brought a smile to his lips. Janny, in politics? It was the last pursuit he would ever have expected her to follow.

His eyes suddenly stopped roving because he'd located Janny standing behind one of the refreshment tables pouring coffee. He quickly excused himself to the portly man in gray and headed in her direction.

"Suppose I could have a cup of that brew you're serving?" he asked her.

Jan filled a plastic cup with coffee. As she handed it to him she said, "The crowd's starting to thin out. We can make an unobtrusive exit pretty soon, if you like, and I'll drive you over to the inn."

He had to ask the question. "What about your husband? Is he here, Janny?"

After a slight hesitation, Jan said quietly, "My husband's dead, Doug. Jonas died thirteen years ago."

He stared at her. "But you said you have two kids..."

"I do," she said. "Twins. Chet and Vicky are almost seventeen."

He continued to stare. "You," he finally managed, "have teenage kids?"

She had to smile at the incredulous note in his voice. "Yes."

"Janny," he protested, "you're not old enough..."

"Oh, yes," she said. "I'm old enough. I was twenty-one when I had Chet and Vicky. An adult, even in the eyes of the law."

"What I'm saying is..."

"I think I know what you're saying," Jan said steadily. "But...a lot of time has passed, Doug. Twenty years is a long time. A lot has happened, there've been a lot of changes. Nothing remains static, even in places like Ellis Falls."

"Yes," he said, his eyes still fixed on her face. "Yes. I see what you mean."

"The fireworks have been canceled," she went on, abruptly changing the subject. "So, just give me the word when you want to leave. Then I'll round up the kids and we can scoot out of here."

Doug couldn't remember ever feeling more ill at ease. "Janny," he said, "the inn's out of your way. There's no reason for you to drive me over there. I can call a taxi."

She laughed. "There's still only one taxi in Ellis Falls," she said. "That's one thing that hasn't changed. Henry Banks runs it and he usually puts the cab in his garage and closes the door in weather like this."

"In that case," Doug said, "I'd as soon leave now."

Jan reached for her handbag and slipped him her car keys. "Why don't you ease out of here?" she suggested. "I'll get the twins and join you as soon as I can."

She didn't want to make a public exit with him, Doug could see that. He smiled ruefully. Janny knew her town, knew how quickly the gossip mills could start grinding.

A few minutes later Doug slipped out through a side door and noted that, thankfully, the rain had finally stopped.

As he waited in her car for her, he thought about Janny and wondered what she'd say if she knew how often she'd crept into his thoughts over the years. There had been other women along the way. No lasting relationships, though. He supposed he'd become something of a rolling stone. He'd shunned serious commitments. Also, his work caused him to move so frequently. He was always traveling, going where the action was. It was difficult to form permanent friendships, to say nothing of deeper liaisons.

But in so many places...Beirut, Rome, Nicaragua, Peru, London, Moscow, wherever...Janny had edged into his dreams at the times when he was the most alone.

Now, he reflected on the important part she had played in his life when they were growing up. They'd shared so much...beyond the physical.

He flinched when he thought of the potent physical attraction that had caused them to play around as they had. It shocked him to think what babes in the woods they'd been, where sex was concerned. And it suddenly occurred to him that he could easily have become the father of a child two or three years older than Janny's twins.

How fatherhood at that early age would have altered his life! Brooding about what might have been, Doug wondered whether the alteration would have been for better, or for worse.

With her husband, with her kids, Janny obviously had made a very full life herself. His life, in contrast, suddenly seemed pretty empty.

CHAPTER THREE

VICKY CLIMBED into the back seat of the car and Chet slid in beside her. Jan got behind the wheel and made over-the-shoulder introductions. The car was parked under a streetlight and when Doug turned around to acknowledge the introductions he got a clear glimpse of Vicky's face.

"Well," he said. "The cheerleader on the revolving platform."

Vicky beamed. But then she said, "We didn't win any prize."

"If it had been a talent show," Doug said solemnly, "you'd have come in first."

Jan could have throttled him. Vicky already got more than enough adulation and attention from boys and she didn't need that kind of flattery.

The Ellis Falls Inn was a big, rambling place on the outskirts of town. Jan drove through the gates, negotiated the curving driveway and pulled up in front of the main entrance.

Doug immediately suggested, "Would you guys care to come in for something to drink, or maybe an early supper?"

"Thanks, but we should get home," Jan answered. "Chet's uniform still hasn't dried out. Anyway, it's been a long day, and you have some settling in to do."

Vicky piped up, "We'll take a rain check."

This time, Jan could have throttled *her*. But Doug merely smiled and said, "You're on."

He hesitated, with one hand on the door handle. "I wonder if I might enlist your help about something?" he asked Jan.

"What?" she ventured cautiously.

"I need to find a place to live for the next six months. Preferably a place with a fair amount of seclusion. I thought maybe you might be able to put me on to something—or might know someone who could."

Vicky answered before Jan could speak. "Mom has a cottage for rent," she said.

"Oh?"

Jan said quickly, "I don't think Doug would be interested in our cottage, Vicky."

"I don't know about that," Doug said. "How big is it, and where is it?"

"It's two bedrooms, living room, kitchen and bath," Jan said, "but there's nothing fancy about it."

"I'm not looking for anything fancy. Is it a summer cottage, or heated for year-round use?"

"It's heated," Vicky informed him before Jan could speak.

"Where is it?"

"On the grounds of our place," Jan said reluctantly. "You couldn't see when we drove over to the house, it was raining so hard. But my house is at the dead end of Sandisfield Street and I own quite a bit of land around it."

"Ten acres," Vicky volunteered.

Jan decided the next time she took her daughter anywhere she was going to bring along a muzzle. She could imagine how Vicky would love to gloat to her friends that Celebrity Douglas MacKenzie had rented her mother's cottage for the duration of his stay in Ellis Falls. She could imagine how people who'd known Doug and her twenty years ago would react to that. And she didn't want any of it.

"Might I stop by and take a look at your cottage tomorrow?" Doug asked her.

"Doug, I really don't think you'd want the place," Jan said quickly. "It's true that it's heated, but I've never rented it for year-round occupancy, just to people who wanted some summer vacation time in the Berkshires."

Vicky again interceded. "Mom had a rental," she told Doug. "The same people from New Jersey—Mr. and Mrs. Alsop—who've been coming here for years. But Mr. Alsop had a heart attack a couple of weeks ago so they've had to cancel out."

Jan's lips tightened. "As it happens, Vicky," she said, "I think Ruth Mason has another rental for me. I'm to check with her tomorrow."

"This is a real-estate agent you're talking about?" Doug asked.

"Yes."

"I suppose her clients would have priority?"

"Yes."

"Could I look at the cottage anyway?" Doug persisted. "The people your agent has in mind might renege."

Doug knew he was in danger of making a pest of himself with Jan, but the thought of renting a cottage right on her property was a very appealing prospect.

He'd keep to himself, of course, if she'd agree to rent to him. He wouldn't take advantage of their former friendship; he wouldn't intrude on Jan's space. But . . . being so close would give them the chance to get to know each other again. And, Doug was discovering, that was a chance he wanted.

"Mom," Vicky said, "if you're going anywhere in the morning I plan to be home. I could show Mr. MacKenzie the cottage."

"Suppose I stop around about ten?" Doug suggested smoothly, and made his exit before Jan could think up a reason why that wouldn't be convenient.

As they drove back across town to Sandisfield Street Jan said irritably, "You had no right to do that, Vicky. I don't want to rent the cottage to Doug MacKenzie, so you've put me in a difficult position."

"Why wouldn't you want to rent to him?" Vicky was being very logical. "He said he's going to be around six months. Renting the cottage for six months would bring in a nice piece of change."

"Maybe Mom has her own reasons why she doesn't want to rent the cottage to Mr. MacKenzie, Vicky," Chet put in. "You should have laid off."

"Why in the world *wouldn't* she want to rent to him?" Vicky asked again.

Jan wondered if maybe her daughter was being a shade too ingenuous. Maybe Vicky already had heard some twenty-year-old gossip. A couple of her friends were children of Doug's and her high school classmates.

She didn't pursue the matter. Though it was still early, this really had been a long, full day. What she wanted most was to get home, get her clothes off, maybe make a cup of hot cocoa and then curl up in bed with a good book.

It was a while before she had some time to herself. First, there were the animals to be tended to. Jan started ladling out dog and cat food. Vicky decided to take a bubble bath, saying that she was going to soak for hours because she felt cold right through to her bones and had been most of the day.

Looking at Vicky's abbreviated costume, her mother didn't wonder at that. She'd been thinking lately that it was way past time she and Vicky had one of those proverbial mother-daughter talks. Like it or not, she was going to have to sit down with Vicky soon and have a serious talk about sex. She just hoped she could carry it off. She usually wasn't reticent about discussing anything with Vicky. But sometimes she wondered if they were on the same wavelength.

She was also beginning to think she needed to talk to Chet. She'd been at both the twins for weeks about college applications. They'd be graduating from Ellis Falls High next June; it was none too early to start planning where they wanted to go from there. But Chet had so far disregarded the college catalogs Jan had sent for. And, lately, he'd been so vague and withdrawn, which was very unlike him.

Jan sighed. There were moments when it was difficult to be a single parent.

Chet appeared from wherever he'd been and headed for the upstairs shower. He reappeared fifteen minutes later wearing the green terry robe Doug had been wearing a few hours earlier.

He was carrying his damp band uniform and he complained, "The wool's beginning to smell musty."

"Hang it out on the back porch," Jan instructed. "The air will freshen it. Put it far enough back, though, so it won't get wet if it starts to rain again."

"Okay," Chet agreed, then turned to ask, "What's for dinner?"

Jan hadn't even thought about dinner. There'd been a lot of food at the reception. She'd assumed that Chet had eaten his share of it. Now she asked rather wearily, "Are you really hungry?"

"Starved," Chet informed her and went out to the back porch with his uniform.

Jan gave Chet an impromptu supper of bacon, a mound of scrambled eggs and a stack of toast, plus a couple of cups of cocoa. Vicky reappeared while he was eating and deigned to have some scrambled eggs, but avoided the bacon, toast and cocoa. Vicky was at a highly diet conscious stage. Evidently she felt she had to compete with her friends, some of whom Jan privately thought looked anorexic—though chances were they were merely going around hungry half the time in the effort to keep off the pounds.

She could sympathize with Vicky. Jan had never had a real weight problem. She was naturally curvy and couldn't imagine herself being any other way. But Vicky was shorter than she was. If she gained even a few more pounds, she'd look plump. And being thin was so much more important to young women than it had been when Jan was in high school. Even so, she worried about the gaps in Vicky's diet.

Chet ferreted ice cream out of the freezer, once he'd finished eating everything else in sight, and made what he called a Goober sundae by pouring maple syrup over the ice cream, then sprinkling the syrup with peanuts. He never gained an ounce, but then he used up a lot of calories by working out at the gym. He was also on the basketball team at school, swam like a fish, played tennis and was seldom idle.

It was almost nine by the time the twins and the animals settled down, and Jan finally had the chance to make a cup of cocoa for herself, and head for her bedroom.

As she undressed, she heard thunder rumbling again. Today, there'd been one spate of stormy weather after another, yet there was a certain comfort to snuggling under a couple of blankets—unusual for the night of the Fourth of July—and hearing the patter of rain on the roof.

She was reading a book full of intrigue and suspense and she'd been eager to get back to it. But now she found herself holding the book and staring into space instead of focusing her attention on the printed words.

This had been such an unusual day. The reunion with Doug had gone differently than she'd expected it to. She'd intended to preserve a certain degree of aloofness, but—due in part to being caught in a torrential downpour together—it hadn't worked that way. She thought of Doug, holed up in his room at the Ellis Falls Inn. His suite, not his room, she corrected herself. Bartlett Folger had told her they'd booked the best suite in the place for Doug. Ordinarily it was used as the bridal suite.

Jan had to chuckle, thinking about Doug occupying the bridal suite in solitary splendor. Then she had a sudden vision of him in Chet's green terry robe, and she felt as if a knot was tightening in the middle of her chest.

It would have helped if he'd reappeared in her life looking world-weary, dissipated, jaundiced. Instead, he was even more attractive at thirty-eight than he'd been at eighteen.

Doug at eighteen. Jan suddenly got out of bed, went over to her closet and, standing on tiptoe, reached for a box in a far corner of the top shelf. She tugged the box down and took it over to the bed, telling herself all the while that she was being very foolish.

She should have thrown out the contents of this box a long time ago. Yet she'd kept it hidden all during her marriage to Jonas, and subsequently she'd guarded it from the potentially prying eyes of either Vicky or Chet.

It was crazy to open the box now and to indulge in a nostalgia trip. The past was the past. It couldn't be resurrected; for that matter she wouldn't want to resurrect it. Too many good things had happened to her since she'd last seen Doug MacKenzie.

Nevertheless, she lifted the blue cardboard cover of the box, which once had held the dress her mother had bought her for the high school senior prom, and stared down at the miscellany it contained.

There were two gardenia corsages, now withered and brown, each with a long, pearl-topped pin sticking through its stem. Doug had given her one of the corsages when he'd taken her to the junior prom, another when he'd taken her to the senior prom. Ever since, the scent of gardenias had evoked an instant image of him.

There were letters that Doug had written her when they were in school. Notes he'd slipped her in class. A couple of little "prizes" she'd saved from Cracker

Jack boxes, the contents of which they'd consumed at Saturday night movies. A scattering of snapshots. The program from a high school football game. And, the yearbook. She thumbed through the pages of the yearbook and found Doug's class picture and remembered that he'd been voted the one most likely to succeed.

There was a lace-edged handkerchief. She'd cried into it after she kissed Doug goodbye the night before he left town. That was really a maudlin touch! There was even a faint trace of lipstick on the handkerchief. And then there was a small, white box and inside it, Doug's class ring wrapped in tissue. Elastic bands had encircled the shaft of the ring so that it would fit on what Jan had considered the proper finger of her left hand on which to wear it. She'd meant, in fact, to take the ring to a jeweler's and have it cut down to fit properly but—thank God—she'd somehow never done that. As it was, she had worn Doug's class ring as if it were an engagement ring. Which was what she'd considered it to be. The tangible evidence of a pledge between the two of them. Never verbalized fully, she realized now. At the time, she hadn't thought that what there was between Doug and herself had needed to be verbalized.

She'd worn his ring much too long, she remembered. Replaced the rubber bands more than once. Until time passed—again, too much time—and one day she'd taken it off and put it away with the other things, and never looked at it again until now.

There was a further assortment of other odds and ends, and she could remember only too well the sentiment attached to each one of them. And there were the two postcards he'd sent her from California. Her last communications from him.

Jan picked up the first. Doug had written it about a week after his arrival in L.A. It showed a picture of the University of California's Westwood campus, and he'd scrawled, "This is where I'll be going to school. Pretty neat, huh? Janny, do you miss me half as much as I miss you? Every day I wish you were out here. We could borrow my uncle's car and take a whirl down to Disneyland. I've already seen all kinds of things out here I want to show you one of these days.

"Gotta run, Janny. I love you, I miss you."

The card was signed simply, "Doug."

The second card had been mailed shortly before the Thanksgiving holiday. Evidently, by then, Doug was already fully into the college swing. He wrote:

"Everything's going great at school. Met a lot of neat people, work a lot, but there's time to play. Not enough time to play, maybe, but time. Hope it's going that way for you. You've never said if you decided to go to U. Mass at Amherst or if you're waiting till next semester, or what?

"Upcoming turkey time makes me think of New England. I'll miss all the old traditions.

"More later," the writer promised. Then, again, simply signed, "Doug."

Jan had answered his cards. She, in fact, had written Doug consistently, and she'd made no secret of her feelings. Funny, he never responded in kind. Reading the two postcards in retrospect, it was as if she were hearing the message that, by then, he was already running scared when it came to any real commitment to the high school sweetheart from whom he was now separated by the better part of three thousand miles.

In the letter that was to be her last letter to him, Jan had told Doug that she'd shelved college plans, for the moment, even though—as he already knew— she'd been accepted by U. Mass and a couple of the other places to which she'd applied.

She *had* sent Doug a Christmas card. Much too sentimental a Christmas card, as she recalled it. She hadn't received one in return. Maybe Doug just hadn't gotten around to sending out cards that year— none of their classmates had mentioned hearing from him. Maybe her card had harped on a note he thought better to ignore. Maybe, by then, he'd decided there should be a clean break between them. Who knows? Maybe he'd even felt he was being kind to her, let- ting her off the hook so finally and completely.

Impatient with herself for ever having gotten into this, Jan returned the box to its place on the shelf and got back into bed.

She switched off the light and stared thoughtfully into the darkness. Might as well face up to the fact that it wasn't going to be easy having Doug around town for six months, she told herself. Especially if their paths crossed very often, either by accident or design.

Thirteen years was a long time to have been a widow, and seeing Doug again had already stirred up emotions she would rather have remain dormant. She'd dated several different men over the years since Jonas had died. Living in a small town like Ellis Falls, though, she'd been careful about whom she dated and where they were seen because she didn't want gossip starting that might affect her kids. Also, none of the men she'd gone out with had ever come to mean enough to her to even consider a serious involvement. Maybe because she'd been so busy with the twins, and the chocolate business and—more recently—her selectman's post, there hadn't been much time nor energy left over.

But now she was suddenly aware of how much she wanted a man's arms around her. She wanted to feel masculine flesh touching her flesh, she wanted strong hands to explore her body, then linger in those private places that were such sources of delight....

Someone? Or Doug MacKenzie?

Jan lay in the darkness listening to the rain and wouldn't let herself answer that question.

VICKY, who usually loved to sleep late whenever she had the chance, was dressed and down in the kitchen by nine-thirty the next morning. Jan had gone out to check on her small vegetable garden and was at the sink washing some of the lettuce she had just picked. She saw that her daughter was garbed in a full-skirted, pale yellow cotton dress that enhanced her blond coloring. She had even taken time to put on makeup. She was wearing just a touch of blush, lip gloss and a deep gray shadow that brought out the silvery color of her eyes.

Vicky took a carton of yogurt out of the fridge, spooned some wheat germ on top of it and then sat down at the kitchen table. Holding her spoon poised in midair, she asked Jan, "Weren't you going somewhere this morning, Mom?"

"Not that I can remember," Jan answered, turning her attention back to washing the garden dirt out of the lettuce. Then the reason for Vicky's query struck her. Doug MacKenzie had said he was coming by at ten o'clock to look at the cottage.

Jan turned away from the sink, dried her hands on a dish towel and faced her daughter. "Look, Vicky," she said, "I know you promised to show Douglas MacKenzie the cottage, but it isn't available."

Vicky frowned. "You mean you've rented it since last night?"

"Not exactly," Jan admitted. "But Ruth Mason's clients have priority."

"Maybe Mrs. Mason doesn't have any rentals for you," Vicky suggested.

"I plan to check with her this morning."

"Why don't you call her? She'd be in her office by now."

Jan capitulated because it seemed the easiest course to take with Vicky.

Ruth Mason answered on the second ring. "Jan," she said, "I was going to call you today. The people I had in mind for your cottage opted to take a vacation in Quebec instead. So far, I haven't been able to come up with anyone for July. But I'm sure we'll have no problem getting an August rental."

"That's okay, Ruth," Jan said hastily. "I'll get back to you."

She turned to find Vicky watching her. Jan drew a deep breath. She'd never in her life told a deliberate fib to either of her children and she was damned if she was going to start now—Doug MacKenzie or no Doug MacKenzie.

"All right," she said, feeling an edge of desperation that was reflected in her voice. "Ruth doesn't have anyone at the moment. But she's sure she will have."

"Why wait, Mom?" Vicky asked. "Could be this just isn't a big year for the tourist business in an off-the-beaten-track town like Ellis Falls. Maybe this is the year everyone's heading for Cape Cod or Martha's Vineyard or somewhere more exciting."

"Maybe," Jan conceded.

She'd never been overly concerned about renting the cottage, even though the rentals did bring extra money which she always put in the twins' college fund. The cottage had been on this place when she and Jonas bought it. It had been badly run-down, but after a time they'd fixed it up because her parents needed a place to stay after selling the big family home on Greylock Street. Her mother and father had lived in the cottage for several months, while making a decision about whether or not they wanted to move to Florida permanently. Florida had won out.

Subsequently, it was Ruth Mason who'd suggested that some extra money could be made from renting the cottage to carefully selected tenants. The idea had made sense.

Vicky said, "Mom?"

"Yes."

"Mom, you're daydreaming. It's five minutes to ten. Mr. MacKenzie will be arriving any minute. Are you going to show him the cottage, or shall I?"

"Neither of us is going to show Doug MacKenzie this cottage," Jan said bluntly. "I told you last night I don't want to rent it to him and that still stands."

"So," Vicky said slowly, "then it's true."

Jan put the lettuce, which had been dripping in a colander, into a plastic bag and put the bag in the vegetable tender in the fridge, gritting her teeth as she did so. She knew exactly what Vicky was getting at.

Parents talked too much in front of their kids, she thought bitterly.

Vicky repeated her statement, rephrasing it into question form. "It is true, isn't it?" she asked.

Jan's mouth tightened. Exasperated, she asked, "Just what is supposed to be true?"

"You had a—a relationship with Douglas Mac-Kenzie when both of you were in high school."

Jan said nothing. She wished Chet were here because she knew he'd take one look at her face and tell his sister to lay off. But Chet had left the house over three hours earlier. He had a summer job with a landscaper and worked weekdays from seven to four.

Vicky also had a summer job, working for Chocolate Fantasies' shop down on Main Street. But, this time of year, the shop was open only in the afternoons.

Jan was wondering just what she should say to her daughter when they both heard a car door close. One of the kitchen windows faced the driveway that ran along the side of the house. Jan went over to the window and peered out. Doug MacKenzie was emerging from a bright red sports car and sauntering toward her back door.

He hadn't forgotten that it was a custom in Ellis Falls—as it was in a lot of places in New England—to go to the back door when you were calling on someone, unless you were approaching people you didn't know.

Vicky, at Jan's elbow, said, "Wow, what super wheels!"

As she spoke, she was moving away from the window, heading toward the door, and she was out on the porch before Doug got to the top of the back steps.

"Hi," she greeted him enthusiastically.

"Well, hello," he said, smiling at her.

Jan, still standing by the window, didn't say anything.

Doug knew the moment he walked into the kitchen that something was wrong.

He watched as Janny collected herself and said, "Hi, Doug. Would you like some coffee? I can make a fresh pot."

"No, thanks," he said quickly.

He caught the glance that passed between Vicky and her mother, and it was clear to him that he'd walked in on some kind of serious private discussion.

"Look," he said, feeling as if he were treading on egg shells, "maybe I've come at a bad time. There's no hurry about this. The inn has given me the bridal suite, would you believe? Complete with complimentary breakfast. So I'm not exactly suffering."

He was hoping to coax a smile from Jan, but he didn't. Even Vicky looked rather grim. It occurred to him that the discussion he'd interrupted probably involved him.

He'd come here this morning hoping to convince Jan that if she rented her cottage to him he wouldn't become a thorn in her side. He had so much work to do that it was going to take every minute of the six months he'd allotted himself to accomplish it. Just the task of assembling all his research notes before he began to write was going to be enormous....

But, he had to admit in all honesty, he didn't intend to work twenty-four-hour days. He'd let his thoughts drift toward the evenings, and though he had no intention of imposing on Jan, it had occurred to him that maybe he could take her—the kids, too, for that matter—out to dinner occasionally. Or, maybe they could go to the movies, or share a good TV program. Just now and then. He'd even been picturing a few evening card games, maybe especially next fall and winter, when it would be dark and cold out and they could set up a card table in front of the fireplace in Jan's living room....

Vicky spoke, and she came directly to the point. "Mom," she asked pointedly, "do you want to show Mr. MacKenzie the cottage, or shall I?"

Doug had the feeling a gauntlet had just been thrown down on the kitchen floor and he wondered whether or not Jan was going to pick it up. He caught the annoyed glance she shot at her daughter, heard her sigh. But then she said, "I'll show the cottage, Vicky. I'm sure your bed still needs to be made up, and your room tidied."

Doug followed Jan out the kitchen door, across the porch and down the steps. Her back was ramrod straight as she led him along a path that passed a small vegetable garden, then curved across an expanse of open field toward a stand of pines, mixed with oaks and maples. The cottage was nestled at the edge of the woods a couple of hundred feet from the house. It looked like something out of Hansel and Gretel. Doug could picture smoke curling out of the chimney on a cool day and he knew this was exactly where he wanted to be.

But Jan paused on the wide, stone slab in front of the door and turned to face him. There was more than a hint of defiance in her voice as she said, "I'll show the cottage to you, Doug, because I said I would. But before I do, I want you to make me a promise."

"What kind of a promise?" he asked, curious.

"I want you to say the cottage won't be suitable for you," Jan said. "That's what I want you to tell Vicky. I'm not trying to be dishonest about this. Believe me, the cottage isn't suitable for you. And having you live here on my property," she finished, a swift rush of color tingeing her cheeks as she spoke, "certainly wouldn't be suitable for me!"

CHAPTER FOUR

JAN OPENED THE DOOR to the cottage and went inside before Doug could answer her. As he watched her, she moved around the living room drawing up shades and opening windows.

"It smells musty in here," she said wrinkling her nose. "I should have aired the place out. I intended to, but then when the Alsops had to cancel..."

Jan was fiddling with bric-a-brac as she spoke, her nervousness very apparent. Doug's eyes followed her, and he'd seldom felt more baffled. Her attitude didn't make sense to him. What was she afraid of? Local gossip because the two of them had dated in high school?

That was ridiculous. They had been eighteen when he'd left for California. Now they were mature, responsible adults. And, if Jan wanted a chaperon, should she rent this place to him, she had two built-in ones. Chet and Vicky.

Doug forced his eyes away from Jan and looked around the living room. He immediately fell in love with it. The walls were pine paneled, and one of them was centered by a big stone fireplace. The furniture was maple. The couch and chairs were well-used and comfortable, with bright floral-patterned covers that matched the curtains. Janny had said the place wasn't fancy, and that was true. Rather, it was simple and homey. Exactly what he was looking for.

He followed Jan, who had gone into the first of the bedrooms and was opening windows. There was a big double bed in the room, an armchair by the window in which one could spend quiet hours reading, and a maple chest big enough to accommodate all of his personal belongings.

The other bedroom was somewhat smaller. But the light in it was good. If the twin beds could be moved out and a desk and maybe a studio couch brought in, it would be a perfect workplace for him.

The kitchen was painted yellow. The equipment was not state of the art, but the stove and fridge looked in good shape and there was plenty of counter space. In the bathroom there was a shower rather than a tub... which would do just fine.

The air drifting in the opened windows carried the scent of pine. Doug sniffed deeply and felt himself relaxing. He'd been tense for such a long time. But this, he knew, was a place in which he could unwind.

He wanted this cottage—and suddenly he wished it didn't belong to Janet Phelps Grayson. Because it appeared she had no intention of renting it to him.

Jan had offered no tour of inspection. He had merely followed her around. Now they were back in the kitchen, and she fussed with a couple of pot holders hanging on a hook by the stove.

Doug broke the silence and felt as though he was shattering a thin glass wall. "I really like this place," he said.

Finally, Jan turned to him. "Please, Doug," she protested wearily.

"Please, what?"

"I don't know why you seem so determined about this," she said frankly. "There are certainly other properties around town for rent. We do have some tourist business in Ellis Falls, but not that much. As you may remember, most of our summer people are people who own their own places here and come up from the city for the whole season. Anyway... I'd be happy to put you in touch with my friend Ruth Mason. She'd be glad to help you out."

"I don't want to be helped out, Jan," Doug told her. He knew she was going to think he was being stubborn. But he truly felt that this cottage was right for him. He needed to make her understand that here he'd be both physically and mentally at ease. Here was the place he could write his book.

Words usually came easily to him—words he was going to speak to an invisible television audience, anyway. Now he struggled, wanting to say the right thing but finding this kind of direct communication very difficult.

"I feel I could work here," he finally managed. "The atmosphere's right. That's very important to me."

There was no friendliness in Jan's expression. "I should think you could find any number of places where you could work," she said.

"It's not that simple." Doug ran his fingers through his hair. Somehow he was going to have to make her understand his viewpoint.

"This place... it just feels right," he said lamely.

"Doug," Jan said, "I've heard about artistic temperament, but I've always thought it was restricted to fiction writers and musicians and painters. You're a highly competent journalist. You deal with real life all the time.''

"The book I'm going to write is extremely personal and emotional, Janny,'' Doug said. "I want to tell what I've seen in Beijing and other places where youths have tried to make important changes in the tenor of life. Even more, I want to tell what I felt. If you call that exercising artistic temperament, okay. Regardless, I need the right kind of place to work in, the right kind of solitude.'' He finished quietly, "I won't get in your hair.''

He moved over to one of the armchairs and sat down, facing her. After a moment, Jan followed suit, choosing a straight-backed chair. Doug didn't have to be told how much she wanted to get this meeting over with; the desire to escape radiated from her.

The tension that had begun to evaporate in Doug started to build again. A muscle in his cheek twitched as he surveyed Jan, and wondered just what in hell was the matter with her. She was treating him as if he were a pariah, and he didn't think he deserved that from her.

"You asked me why I decided to come back to Ellis Falls to write my book,'' he said finally. "I gave you part of the answer. But there's more to it than that. When I lived here in Ellis Falls—as you well know—my family wasn't exactly in the social register. As yours was. Even before my father died, I wouldn't say we were welcome in the best places. After he died, things only got worse. The whole town was down on my mother. Admittedly she made a mess of her life and that didn't get better either. She died a few years back in the mental hospital where I'd had to place her.

"Anyway," Doug continued, "all things considered, I suppose anyone might, indeed, wonder why I chose to come back here. But you see, Janny, regardless of anything else, Ellis Falls is home to me."

His smile was whimsical. "I guess maybe I half expected to find Ellis Falls like the legendary Brigadoon, where the town and its people only come to life once every hundred years so no one ever ages, nothing ever changes," he confessed. "When I came into town yesterday, it didn't look like that much had changed either. I noticed the new shopping center outside town, the new supermarket. But Main Street at a quick glance looked pretty much like it did when I left here."

"Ellis Falls has stayed pretty much the same, I guess," Jan admitted. "The population has hovered around five thousand for years. Kids come to the high school from all over the countryside, so an addition, you may or may not have noticed, was built four years ago. We get some winter as well as summer tourist business now because skiing has been developed in a couple of mountain areas near here. The hospital has a new wing. It, too, serves the whole countryside."

Doug smiled. "You sound like a selectman," he told her.

"I am a selectman, Doug," she said rather testily. "I ran for office because I felt a relatively young voice was needed on the board. Also, a woman's voice. I'm the first woman ever elected to a selectman's post in Ellis Falls. The board is only part-time now, incidentally. We have a town manager, that's new since your time. He's a trained professional, so having his expertise when we need it is very valuable."

"That's interesting," Doug said gently. "But... we're getting away from the main issue."

Jan sat up even straighter. "Doug, I don't want to rent to you," she said flatly.

She tried to soften the statement by adding, "I've never rented the cottage for a long period of time. Just a couple of months, in summer. Ruth has suggested that I might get winter rentals from skiers. But, frankly, I'm so busy with my business—except for the months of July and August—that I haven't been interested.

"I admit everyone can use extra money," she went on. "I put the cottage rental money into the twins' college fund, but actually Jonas provided for their education with the insurance he left us. So, sometimes renting the cottage is more of a bother than it's worth."

Doug listened to her, discouraged. She'd said in the first place that she didn't want to rent to him. And that, he thought grimly, was exactly what she meant.

Why didn't she want to rent to him? He had only the fondest memories of his relationship with Janny. Leaving her to go off to California had been one of the hardest things he'd ever had to do. He smiled rather wistfully. He'd had a crazy dream, at the time, that he'd go forth into the world and find fame and fortune, and then he'd come back here and scoop Janny up on his symbolical white horse and carry her straight to paradise... wherever that might be.

Problem was, neither fame nor fortune had come that easily. It had taken time, and all the effort he could muster, to establish his place in a profession where it was difficult to even get near the ladder, let alone start climbing it. After that, the internal competition made it a challenge to hang on to the rung you were on, then climb up to the next one. It was a long while before he could stop worrying about his status in his profession. Until then, it had never occurred to him that maybe a person actually could go home again. That thought hadn't struck him until quite recently. And, by then, Janny Phelps was pretty much a sweet memory.

His smile grew even more wistful as he thought about that memory. They had been such kids, the two of them. He had long since put their high school romance into what he considered the proper perspective, and he'd assumed she'd done the same thing. But now it hurt a little to remember how replete their experience had been with the sweet-sad pain of first love.

Also, their relationship had been overwhelmingly romantic. A memory to be cherished forever—even though as time went by certainly neither one of them could seriously have believed it might have endured if he hadn't left Ellis Falls to go west to college.

Could they?

Rather, could Janny?

Was he being obtuse? Did this woman, looking at him as if he were an absolute stranger, have something against him? The Janet Grayson he'd seen in operation thus far seemed to have made a very good job of her life. It was tragic that her husband had died when he did and left her with four-year-old twins. And, a surprise to think she hadn't remarried since. But she was a successful businesswoman, a politician, the mother of two great kids...

Why the hell wouldn't she rent her cottage to him?

Their eyes met. Jan said, "I'm sorry, Doug."

"Are you?" he asked her. His voice—usually so well modulated—rasped slightly.

He stood, suddenly restless, and walked over to a window. The sky had grown very dark, and as he watched, he saw lightning cut a jagged scar against the charcoal clouds. Then thunder growled, the sound vibrating in the stillness.

"Looks like this must be the summer for thunderstorms," Doug observed, turning and facing Jan again.

"We always have our share of them, this time of year," she reminded him.

"Yeah, I guess so," he agreed, memories of long-ago midsummer afternoons surfacing. He glanced at his watch. "I'd better get going," he announced.

"Where are you going?"

"Back to New York."

He saw Jan's eyes widen slightly, but she simply asked, "Why?"

"Why am I going back to New York? Well, I think I'll ask the network to cancel my leave of absence for the time being. Maybe I'll take the Northern Ireland assignment they've been trying to get me to accept. They want me to spend some time in Belfast and surroundings, then do an in-depth report on the current situation."

"Am I right in feeling this sudden change of plans is coming about because I won't rent my cottage to you?" Jan asked, her voice as expressionless as her face.

Doug didn't answer.

"Your silence sort of says it all," she informed him. Then she demanded icily, "Don't you think you're being childish, Doug? It seems ridiculous to me that you're trying to give me a guilt complex because I'm exercising my own freedom of choice.''

"I'm not trying to give you a guilt complex, Janny.''

"The hell you aren't,'' she answered, with a sudden fire that surprised him. "I can just see what my kids will say. 'Mom, you made Mr. MacKenzie leave town.' Why are you doing this?''

Doug couldn't remember ever seeing her so angry.

He said slowly, "I guess I'm exercising some of that artistic temperament you spoke about. In other words, I'm acting like a spoiled child. Forgive me, Janny. The last thing in the world I want to do is lay any guilt trips on you.''

Though he didn't feel much like compromising, the fact was—Doug acknowledged honestly—that Janny had the right to rent her cottage to whomever she pleased, or not to rent it at all. If she chose not to rent it to him, that was her own business.

"Look," he said, "call your real-estate agent when we get back to your house. Maybe she can come up with something for me.'' Doug was already moving toward the door as he spoke. His sudden capitulation had an unexpected and admittedly paradoxical effect on Jan.

"Wait a minute, Doug," she said. She'd already warned herself that if Doug was going to be around Ellis Falls for six months there was no way she was going to be able to avoid encounters with him. Now she remembered he'd promised he wouldn't get in her hair if she rented the cottage to him. She had her own work to do anyway, and she could take some steps to jazz up her social life as well so that she'd be going out in the evening more than she did now. Which, she admitted, would be good for her.

If she filled her days and nights sufficiently, there would be no reason to worry about having Doug so near. Matter of fact, there might be an advantage to having him on her own turf. That way, she could at least avoid unexpected meetings with him. Maybe her thinking was hazy, Jan conceded, but right now it would do.

"I'll rent the cottage to you," she said abruptly. "Provided, of course, that the terms are satisfactory to you."

Doug drew a deep breath. "I'm sure the terms will be fine," he said, and let it go at that. He was not about to chance another change of mind on Janny's part.

THUNDER RUMBLED as Doug and Jan walked across the field to her house, and the first raindrops began spattering down just as they got to the back steps. They'd barely made it into the shelter of the porch before the heavens opened up and unleashed a drenching load.

The kitchen was empty, but Jan could hear Vicky's voice and knew she was on the living-room phone talking to one of her friends. She'd often thought she should try to clock the number of hours Vicky spent on the phone some week.

She glanced at the kitchen wall clock. Too early for lunch, but she wanted something. "I'll make coffee," she said.

Doug pulled out a chair and sat down at the kitchen table. Immediately, Abigail, the tortoise cat, appeared and he picked her up, settled her in his lap and began stroking her.

As Jan poured out coffee grounds and measured water she knew Doug was watching her, which made her intensely self-conscious.

What must he be thinking about her? She'd just done such an about-face she couldn't blame him if he considered her a stereotypical fickle female. That wasn't a correct evaluation, but at the moment it would be hard to refute it.

Vicky came into the kitchen and, before she noticed Doug at the kitchen table, began, "Mom, I was talking to Jim and he's driving into Boston this afternoon. He wants me to go along. We can take in a movie tonight, then drive back right after it."

"You have to work, Vicky," Jan reminded her daughter. "Anyway, this isn't exactly ideal weather for a trip to Boston."

"Jim has a couple of things he has to do," Vicky said. "That's just the point, anyway. No one's going to come into the shop in weather like this. So, why open it?"

"Tourists tend to shop around in bad weather because there's nothing else to do," Jan said, wishing that Doug weren't hearing this conversation. She knew Vicky. In another minute, her daughter was going to make her out to be a slave driver. "Rainy days are good for candy sales," she concluded. "And, we have a certain obligation to keep the shop open the hours we say it's going to be open."

Vicky started to protest, but then her eyes fell on Doug and she swiftly changed her tone of voice. "I didn't know you were here, Mr. MacKenzie," she said, flashing him a dazzling smile. "Did you and Mother settle things about the cottage?"

"Yes," Doug said, and gave her an answering smile. "Looks like you and I are going to be neighbors."

"Great!" Vicky exclaimed. "That'll be just super. I'm glad you got Mom to change her mind."

"So am I," Doug said softly, his eyes on Jan again.

Jan didn't answer. Floppy had just appeared from the direction of the living room, yawning, and she paused to give her a dog biscuit. Then she busied herself with putting china and spoons and cream and sugar on the table and, next, brought over a carafe of hot coffee and sat down herself.

"Mind if I join you?" Vicky asked.

"Do you want a cup of coffee, Vicky?" Jan didn't mean to sound so stern. But Vicky seldom indulged in coffee; in her opinion caffeine was bad for the complexion.

"No," Vicky said, "I just wondered when Mr. MacKenzie will be moving in."

"Your mother and I have a few details to iron out," Doug said.

The kitchen door opened and Chet came in, followed by Huff and Puff. His T-shirt and jeans were soaked. He looked as wet as she and Doug had looked yesterday, Jan thought. The two gray cats were pretty sodden, too, and they sat down and started licking their fur, almost in unison.

"Hi," Chet greeted Doug, then immediately went to the fridge, got out a carton of milk and drank thirstily. Turning, he said, "Mr. Brett told us all to go home. Looks like it's going to rain all afternoon, so there was no point in our hanging around." Chet decided, "I think I'll see if there's a sci-fi movie or maybe a horror story on TV."

"Great," Vicky said disgustedly. "You get to lounge around all afternoon while I have to go to work in another hour. Mom, are you going to drive me in?"

Thus far, Jan had circumvented either of the twins having their own cars, a situation that they sometimes protested loudly.

"On the other hand," Vicky said, "maybe Jim could drive me downtown before he takes off for Boston."

"I'll drive you, Vicky," Jan said.

"Why don't I take you?" Doug suggested smoothly. "Your mother and I have a few things to go over, but then I'll be free."

"Great," Vicky said, her smile returning.

Chet started ambling toward the living room. Jan said, "Chet, you are going to change out of those wet clothes, aren't you?"

"They'll dry out," Chet said.

"Chet," she urged, "for heaven's sake go put on something dry. You might change, too, Vicky. I doubt you'll want to wear that dress in this weather."

The yellow dress Vicky was wearing was one of her best.

"And I'll drive you," Jan added. "I have some errands to do in town anyway."

Vicky shrugged and followed Chet out of the room. Jan smiled a tight smile. "Teenagers," she said. "Sometimes it's hard to set them in motion."

"Yeah, I can imagine." Doug refilled his cup with coffee as he spoke. Then, as he stirred sugar into the dark brew, he said rather hesitantly, "Jan, if you don't mind my asking—why did you change your mind about renting me the cottage so suddenly?''

"I realized I was taking the whole situation too seriously and building up needless obstacles.''

"Well, then . . . thank you.''

Jan nodded. Then asked, "What are these details we need to settle? The rent's four hundred a week in season, but obviously I won't expect you to pay that much when you're taking the place for six months.''

"I'd be glad to pay it.''

Jan shook her head. "No. Let's say six hundred a month from now till early January. That would cover the six months. You'll be responsible for the utility bills, of course. There's an oil furnace.''

"You don't have to cut the rate for me.''

"I'm not. I think that's a fair price for such a long rental.''

"Okay, if you say so.''

"Ruth will draw up a lease,'' Jan said, trying to be very businesslike about this. "Is there anything else?''

"Yes. If it would be okay with you, I'd like to move the furniture—most of it—out of the second bedroom so I'll have room for a desk, a couple of file cabinets and a table to put a printer on. Would that be all right? There's a storage place in town, isn't there, where I could have the things stashed while I'm here?''

"That won't be necessary,'' Jan said. "There's a barn back of the garage I use mainly for storage. Chet can get a couple of friends to help, and you can move the furniture. Sunday would be a good time, when Chet doesn't have to work.''

"Fine.''

"Do you already have the office furnishings you need?"

"No."

"You might get better prices in Boston," Jan said, "but I think you could find what you want over in Pittsfield."

He smiled slightly. "I was thinking of Pittsfield," he said.

"I forgot you know this area as well as I do."

"Knew it," he corrected. "It occurs to me maybe there've been more changes than I thought."

It was an oblique remark, but Jan let it pass. She had a few things to do before she drove Vicky into town. Also, she needed a little time in which to put her thoughts together and adjust to this idea of Doug MacKenzie becoming her tenant.

She imagined her preoccupation showed. Because Doug said, "I'd better be getting along."

The rain was still coming down in torrents. "I can loan you a slicker," Jan offered.

"Thanks, but I'll just make a dash for it."

At the door he said, "I'll give you a call before Sunday, to be sure the moving detail's okay with Chet."

"It will be fine with him."

Doug looked at her thoughtfully. "Shouldn't he, maybe, be consulted about that?" he suggested.

"I'll ask him."

Doug nodded, and a moment later Jan, watching from the kitchen window, saw him streak across to his car. She knew he'd flown into the Springfield airport where a limousine had picked him up. So, the red sports job must be a rental.

It wouldn't be too practical in a Berkshire winter.

Jan took the coffee cups she and Doug had used over to the sink. That last remark he'd made about Chet kept coming back to haunt her. She hadn't intended to imply that she made Chet's decisions for him, but she supposed that was the way it had sounded.

Well? Did she still tend to make decisions for Chet and Vicky, as she'd needed to do when they were younger? She was thinking only of them in anything she did or said that concerned them. She worried about them; she couldn't help it. Being their only living parent entailed a double responsibility.

True, all of that Jan mused as she dashed some detergent into the cups, then ran them under hot water and stacked them in the dish rack. But it was also true that the twins were seventeen, or would be very shortly, and the time was fast approaching when she was going to have to let go of them.

Jan thought back to when she'd been seventeen. She and Doug had made love for the first time the summer after their junior year in high school. Till then, they'd managed to contain themselves. But there came a moment when their bodies couldn't tolerate caution any longer.

They'd been knowledgeable, but not as knowledgeable as today's kids. That first time, they'd been lucky. But then Doug had said solemnly that one or the other of them had better take some precautions. Jan, unable to even think about approaching her mother on such a subject, had left Doug in charge of birth control.

Now she wondered what would have happened if, that first time, they hadn't been lucky? She was sure

Doug would have married her—but would their teenage marriage have worked?

He would have had to give up going to California to college. He would never have become a famous television personality. She would never have married Jonas. By now she and Doug would have a twenty-one-year-old son or daughter. There would be no Chet and Vicky.

When she started to think about what might have been, the possible consequences became overwhelming.

Jan forcibly put her thoughts aside and went to the foot of the staircase. "Are you ready?" she called up to Vicky. "We'd better be heading for town."

CHAPTER FIVE

NANCY WAS IN THE OFFICE at the shop when Jan arrived with Vicky. She was on the telephone and she looked harassed.

Hanging up the receiver, she said, "Some people don't want to accept the fact we don't operate at full production in the middle of the summer. You'd think they'd understand that chocolate is perishable, and that it is senseless to ship our chocolates in hot weather. The quality suffers, the flavor suffers."

Nancy was shuffling some papers on her desk as she spoke, so Jan had a good opportunity to study her. She didn't like what she saw. Her partner was losing weight she didn't need to lose, for one thing. And she was very tense.

Nancy had been dedicated to the business ever since the two of them had decided to go into partnership five years ago. By then, Jan had been making her "chocolate fantasies" herself, and selling them to local and area outlets. She'd made the candies in her own kitchen, and even her two kids had gotten sick of the smell of chocolate. Nor had she blamed them. She'd once been a chocoholic herself. Now, it was ages since she'd taken a bite of one of her own confections.

She said carefully, trying to keep her tone light, "Nancy, methinks maybe you could do with a short vacation. If you want to take off for a while I see no problem.''

"No?'' Nancy asked skeptically. "So who's to monitor the kitchen help, and the summer sales force? We agreed to each go on a half workweek through the summer. That means it takes the two of us to keep things going.''

Chocolate Fantasies was employing only a skeleton crew this time of the year in the large kitchen at the back of the shop, where the candy was made. The "summer sales force'' was even smaller.

Leona Martin, a widow who'd wanted something to do, had proved to be the perfect person to put in charge of the shop during the summer season. In fact, Leona was so good—and enjoyed her job so much— she was now working for Chocolate Fantasies year-round.

A retired schoolteacher, she tended to treat anyone under thirty as if they were one of her pupils. Nancy and Jan were both amused at the way Leona gently bossed around the teenagers who worked in the shop with her, and got away with it.

In July and August, with Leona presiding every afternoon, only two teenagers were employed as salespersons, and they worked alternate afternoons. Vicky was one, her close friend Cathy Ferguson was the other.

Now Jan said, "Look, Nancy, I can come in every afternoon to be sure things are going smoothly, and keep the paperwork up-to-date at the same time. Our fiscal year ended June 30. I just have to finalize some records, then I can turn the books over to the accountant. I think,'' she concluded, "you need a vacation, and I wish you'd take one.''

Nancy looked up, her dark eyes sharp. "What makes you think I need a vacation?"

It was not like Nancy to sound so suspicious without cause. But nothing about Nancy's behavior right now was "like Nancy." Troubled, Jan decided on a direct approach. "Nancy," she asked, "is there something wrong?"

"Why do you ask that?"

Nancy's and Jan's desks faced each other. As she said, "I wondered, that's all," Jan pulled out her desk chair and sat down. She was remembering that Nancy would soon be forty-two. Maybe her behavior could be attributed to an early onset of menopause... but she doubted it.

She remembered the way Nancy and her husband, Bob, had moved in separate circles at the Fourth of July reception for Doug. Could Bob and Nancy be having marital troubles? They had always seemed to be the "perfect couple." This was the second time around for both of them, and Jan had always assumed they'd both profited from their previous mistakes.

Bob came from the Ellis family for whom Ellis Falls was named. There were currently four lawyers in town, and he was undoubtedly the most successful of them. Bob was a big man, outwardly affable and easygoing. Sometimes Jan felt his casual manner was a facade. As a selectman, she came in contact with him every now and then in connection with town affairs, and she knew that his mild manner hid a razor-sharp mind.

She'd often thought Bob and Nancy proved that opposites really do attract. They had met at a political rally in Boston, several years ago. Nancy, newly divorced, had been trying to find something to do with her time, and she'd volunteered to help out in the current gubernatorial campaign. Bob loved to tell the story of the gorgeous brunette who had approached him and insisted he wear a button, touting his own candidate. He'd given Nancy a hard time, pretending that he was an Independent, not committed to either party. So, Nancy had gone all out to convert him.

Bob, by then, had been divorced a couple of years. His first wife was a Washingtonian whom he'd met while attending Georgetown University Law School. She'd abruptly gone to the Virgin islands for a divorce, the middle of one winter. Jan recalled how the rumors around town had spread thick and fast. It was said that Bob had been playing around with his secretary. Actually no one ever found out for sure what had precipitated the divorce.

Nancy and Bob hadn't waited very long after their initial meeting to get married. That was eight years ago, Jan remembered. She'd just been getting started with her candy business. Three years later, she and Nancy had joined forces. Nancy, who'd been in business in Boston before her first marriage, had a certain aggressiveness about her that Jan knew she lacked, and a lot of innovative ideas. Thus far, they'd done very well together. They were totally dissimilar in personalities—again, maybe it was a question of opposites attracting. Whatever, Jan couldn't imagine having a better business partner.

Nancy said suddenly, "Jan, stop looking at me like that. There's nothing wrong with me."

Jan wished she could believe that.

"I admit I've been . . . out of sorts," Nancy said. "It's nothing important, though, and I don't want to take a vacation. On the other hand, if you'd like to get away for a few days I can handle things.''

Jan repressed a smile. Nancy never seemed to realize that—once away from business—the two of them led very different lives. Right now there was no way she could leave town and go anywhere, especially with the kids out of school.

''Let's play it by ear,'' she compromised.

''You shouldn't be in here today anyway,'' Nancy reminded her. ''This is supposed to be your day off, remember?''

Jan threw up her hands. ''I'll leave, I'll leave,'' she said with a laugh. ''Actually I drove Vicky over, and I have a few errands to do in town. Then, I will need to get home. I have a selectmen's session tonight, and that always means an early supper. Nancy...''

Nancy looked up.

Jan said, ''Don't hang around here any longer than you have to. It's still raining out, it's a miserable day. Why don't you go home and curl up with a good book?''

Nancy gave her a strange look. ''I'd rather stay here,'' she said. ''There are a few fall orders I want to recheck.''

Only when Jan was at the door, did Nancy say, ''Jan...stop worrying about me.''

Jan turned. ''I'm not worrying about you.''

''I think you are, and there's no need,'' Nancy said. ''I'm fine. I haven't been sleeping too well lately, that's all, and maybe the lack of sleep's catching up with me. I need to make a couple more phone calls. Then—'' Nancy managed a faint smile ''—maybe I will go home and curl up with a good book.''

Again...Jan wished she could believe her.

THE NIGHTS when the selectmen were to hold hearings on various town issues were always hectic ones in the Grayson household. The selectmen's sessions began promptly at seven o'clock, and the selectmen were required to get to the town hall fifteen minutes beforehand. That meant an earlier than usual suppertime.

Vicky's stint at the shop was over at four, and she had told Jan earlier that Jim Farrish was going to pick her up after work and bring her home. Jan, driving home herself, had felt vaguely uneasy about it. She liked Jim, it wasn't that. He was a friendly, good-natured boy, and he came from a solid family. His father was in the real-estate business in town. But Vicky had been seeing a lot of Jim lately, pretty much to the exclusion of anyone else, and Jan disliked the idea of her going steady. Maybe because she knew what going steady in high school could lead to!

Chet and a classmate had gone into town this afternoon to catch a rainy-day matinee at the movie theater. It was the classmate who had the needed "wheels," as Chet had pointedly mentioned.

Jan had warned both twins to be back early, since this was a meeting night. By five o'clock, she had a tuna-noodle casserole and a tossed salad ready to go on the table, but the twins were still absent. After waiting a few minutes, she put the casserole back into the oven to keep warm and the salad into the fridge to keep cool, and went to change her clothes. By a quarter of six, she was back in the kitchen again, and there was still no sign of the twins.

Chet walked in as the grandfather clock in the living room chimed six, and by then Jan was annoyed.

But Chet immediately apologized and that, as usual, disarmed her.

"Mike and I went over to the pharmacy for a soda after the movie, and the place was mobbed," he said. "Thought we'd never get waited on. Then, we ran into a couple of kids we knew..."

Chet was opening the oven door and peering in at the casserole as he spoke. "Where's Vicky?" he asked.

"Somewhere between here and Chocolate Fantasies, I would presume," Jan said tartly.

"Mom..."

"Yes?" Jan was getting the salad out of the fridge.

"Don't be too rough on Vicky," Chet said. "She's got her own problems."

Jan stared at him. "What do you mean, Vicky has her own problems?"

"No big deal," Chet said quickly. "It's just that she has to sort a few things out. Make up her mind about a few things. I don't mean to be a pest about this, but it would help if we both had wheels."

Jan couldn't see the connection between Vicky having "problems" and owning her own automobile. But she only said, "I can't afford for each of you to have a car, Chet. We've been over that. You know the score."

"Maybe Vicky and I could share a car."

Jan had to smile. "You're telling me the two of you could work out a mutually agreeable schedule?"

"I think we could."

"I don't," Jan said frankly. "Especially during the school year, it seems to me you'd both want the use of a car at the same time...a lot of the time, anyway. All that means to me is that we'd have a lot more arguments around here than we do now.''

''I'm not saying we'd never argue about who was to have the car,'' Chet said, being equally honest. ''But I think we could work it out between the two of us. The thing is...''

''Yes?''

''Well, you were so insistent on both of us taking driver ed, and getting our licenses. Why—if you never want us to drive?''

Jan didn't answer him. She couldn't bring herself to tell Chet the truth—which was that she had a real fear of either he or Vicky driving in the vicinity of Ellis Falls. Once out of town, many of the roads were steep and winding. When she and Doug had been seniors in high school, one of their classmates had been killed, driving on one of those roads on a rainy night. His parents had given him a car as an early graduation present.

He was not the only teenager who had died on area roads. A couple of years ago, the young son of the local bank president had lost his life when his car had gone out of control on a mountain road and he had plowed, head-on, into a tree. Jan had gone to the funeral, and it still haunted her.

She knew she shouldn't allow her fears to influence her children's lives to an undue extent. Chet was right...she had insisted on the twins taking driver ed and getting their licenses, so they were qualified to drive. And, now and then, she did let one or the other of them drive her car when she was with them.

It was true, though, that she couldn't afford to finance cars for both of them. Chet had suggested that if she could get up a down payment, he could make monthly payments by saving up the money from his summer job, and then working extra after school and on Saturdays the rest of the year. But Jan doubted he'd have enough to make payments on any decent car, and she wasn't ready to commit herself to filling in the gap.

She glanced at her watch. Six-fifteen, and Vicky still wasn't home. She took the casserole out of the oven, and said to Chet, "We'd better go ahead and eat."

It was a silent meal and, for Jan at least, a very hasty one. Vicky still hadn't returned by the time she had to leave the house. She drove faster than she should have, and it was almost seven at that when she reached the town hall. As she parked in the lot at the back of the building, she felt frazzled.

There were several issues coming up at the meeting that were of concern to Ellis Falls' citizens. That meant there was bound to be considerable discussion over them, and Jan reminded herself, as she sat down with the other selectmen, that she was going to have to keep a tight rein on her patience.

Bartlett Folger cleared his throat, rapped his gavel and announced, "The meeting is open."

He cleared his throat again. "The first item on our agenda tonight deals with the matter of the carnival scheduled to be held the first week in August on the old fairgrounds," he said. "It would appear we've run into a problem. A number of trailers have occupied the fairgrounds for the past four summers, with the approval of the Board of Selectmen. The trailer owners have obtained proper permits and licenses to occupy the property, and now they say they will be seriously inconvenienced if they are required to move elsewhere for the week the carnival is to take place.''

A hand shot up from the audience. ''Mr. Chairman?''

Bartlett Folger nodded gravely. ''Mr. Baker?''

Jan sighed. Abner Baker was one of the biggest floor-holders at meetings of any sort. He loved to hear the sound of his own voice. At this rate, they'd be here all night.

She settled back, determined to keep calm. Then, glancing across the audience, her gaze suddenly meshed with that of a man in the third row.

Doug. Jan couldn't believe what she was seeing. Doug MacKenzie, at a meeting like this?

He grinned. She found herself smiling back at him, and suddenly she felt better. Also, she became motivated to put her best foot forward in her official capacity, so she sat up a shade straighter and paid attention to what Abner Baker was saying.

''Fact is,'' Baker stated, ''this carnival is for the benefit of the Future Club, and you know what that means. All the money raised will go toward the future of our kids here in Ellis Falls. That's what it's all about, isn't it? Today's kids are tomorrow's future leaders?

''Not only that . . . towns like Ellis Falls need a summertime carnival. Remember when you were kids and the carnival came to town? Remember the rides, and the cotton candy and the stuffed animals you won on the games? Hot dogs on a summer night, going through the Tunnel of Love with your best girl . . . hey, that's a part of living we shouldn't let go by the boards,'' Baker said, and the audience laughed appreciatively. ''As far as the trailers go, no reason why they shouldn't get a change of scene for a week, is there? If they temporarily locate in a place that's even better than where they are now?

"The Mountain Club, of which I am president, is volunteering free land space to the trailers for the week the carnival's here," Abner Baker announced triumphantly. "They can use our campgrounds up on Deep Pines Lake. We'll even help get 'em moved."

Abner Baker sat down to a round of applause.

"The board will take your offer under advisement, Mr. Baker," Bartlett Folger said stiffly. "We will notify the Future Club within the week as to whether or not we can issue them the necessary license to hold the carnival."

Jan spoke up. "I'm for taking a vote right now, Mr. Folger," she said, as she stood, "so the members of the Future Club will know whether or not to proceed with their plans. The first week in August isn't that far away. Also... let me say that I go along with Mr. Baker. The carnival will not only benefit a very good cause, but it will add a little sparkle to the summer scene in Ellis Falls. I remember carnivals, when I was growing up here. They were a part of vacation time. It's several years, now, since we've had a carnival in town...and I think we're ready for it. I, in fact, would like to see this become an annual event. Not necessarily always benefiting the same organization, but benefiting some worthwhile cause."

Jan received her round of applause, and as she sat down she couldn't help glancing toward Doug. He met her eyes, nodded approvingly and gave her a thumbs-up sign.

Bartlett Folger reluctantly called for a vote on the carnival issue, and the result was affirmative.

The board moved on to the next issue on the agenda, which dealt with some criticism the selectmen had been receiving because they recently had voted to switch the town insurance from their present carrier to another Massachusetts insurance association.

Jan had been asked to explain the rationale for this, but as she got up to speak she became so conscious of Doug's presence she wasn't sure she could get a word out.

Her voice trembled slightly as she began, "We're changing our insurance to save the taxpayers—to save you—a considerable sum of money. We took the action upon the advice of the town's insurance advisory committee, which is headed by Robert Ellis, whom I am sure you all know. The change will save you approximately forty-six thousand dollars annually. Also, if we insure with this company now, we will be eligible for a dividend next year.

"The bid of the company we've chosen definitely is superior," Jan continued, now in command of the situation. "They cover more than one hundred small towns throughout the state, and they do not deal with communities whose population exceeds fifty thousand people. We think that makes them especially right for us. We can expect considerably more attention than we've been getting from our present carrier. So, in your interest, we felt there was only one way to go. Any questions?"

To Jan's surprise and relief, there were no questions to be fielded and she sat back down again. Herb Flynn whispered, "Nicely done," and she smiled at him, pleased. It had taken the other selectmen a while to accept having a woman on the board, but finally they'd come to treat her as a real member of the team.

The meeting was over at nine-thirty. As Jan picked up her briefcase and handbag, Tom Prentice appeared at her side.

"Great job you did on the insurance, Jan," he complimented her.

"Well, you briefed me."

"Only to a point. You did your own homework, as you always do." He hesitated. "How about stopping off for a cup of coffee somewhere?" he suggested.

Tom was a nice man. He'd been in town about four years, and his wife had died not long before that. He was in his late forties, a shade overweight, a comfortable person to be around. Jan happened to know that Rose Ladue—the selectmen's secretary—had her eye on him, and she wished he'd return Rose's interest. As it was, she hated to be put in the position of constantly discouraging him. But—because he was such a genuinely nice person—it would be wrong to encourage him. She recognized his loneliness and could empathize with it. But she had an idea Tom was looking for another mate, and she wasn't interested in him.

She opted for a harmless fib. "I wish I could, Tom. But I have to get home."

A couple of minutes later, Jan cut out the back door of the town office building and headed across the lot to her car, thankful that the rain had stopped.

Midway along, she was halted by a, "Hey, wait up there!" and she turned to see Doug coming across the lot toward her.

He caught up with her, and he said, his expression serious, "You were very good in there, Janny."

"Thank you."

"It's fascinating to see politics on the real grass roots level," he said. "It gives me a good feeling. Makes one aware that at the bottom of a structure that sometimes seems to be pretty unwieldy, we have a very good base. And will have, as long as people like you devote themselves to the public interest."

He took her arm. "I'd like to talk to you," he said. "I was going to suggest we go over to the inn. They have a pleasant lounge, and it's never very crowded."

"That would be nice... another time," Jan said, after only a second's hesitation. "This has been another long day, Doug. I really need to get home."

"I won't keep you long," Doug promised. "Problem is, I suppose you have your car with you and I have mine. How shall we work out the logistics?"

She had turned him down, yet he was taking it for granted she'd change her mind. She could see that Doug had grown very accustomed to getting his own way... yet he was so very disarming, smiling down at her as if she'd said yes in the first place.

"Doug..." she began.

"Please, Janny," Doug said. "This is important to me."

"Can't it wait, whatever it is?"

"For my peace of mind, no."

"All right," she said reluctantly. "But it really will have to be brief. I'll follow you to the inn. No sense in my going in your car. You'd just have to bring me back here."

He didn't comment on that, and a couple of minutes later Jan followed the sleek red sports car out of the parking lot.

The moon was trying to break through the clouds, causing the clouds to look as if they'd been edged with silver. The air was soft, scented with the perfumes of summer. Jan felt a stirring, a twisting inside her; a longing.

She had a lot of friends in Ellis Falls, some of them people she'd known all her life. She and Nancy had become close. She loved her kids, and most of the time she felt they had a very good rapport. But it would be folly not to admit there was something missing in her life.

Most of the time, she was too busy to dwell on the lack. But Doug's reappearance in town had made her sharply aware of it, and she didn't thank him for that. There was no sense in denying to herself that he stirred her—he stirred her far too strongly. He made her want things she couldn't have, and her common sense told her she'd be crazy to become involved with him, even if he wanted to get involved with her. He was here on a temporary basis, he'd made that clear. The first of the year he'd be off again, seeking out the world's trouble spots.

She'd been left by Doug once before...and she had no intention of giving history a chance to repeat itself.

JAN HAD BEEN to a couple of civic luncheons recently at the Ellis Falls Inn, but it had been a while since she'd visited the lounge. She saw that the spacious room had been redecorated in soft pastel hues, and that the lighting was nicely subdued. Music filtered from a band playing in the main dining room, where there was a small dance floor.

As Doug had said it would be, the lounge was un-crowded. The few couples occupying banquettes were immersed in themselves. The room had an intimate ambience that could become insidious ... if one were in the mood for intimacy. Jan stiffened her spine, and reminded herself that she was not in the mood for in-timacy. Just because she was a little tired, a little de-pressed, concerned about both her kids and Nancy, didn't mean that she should let herself go soft all over.

Doug suggested, "How about a drink?"

She nodded. "A glass of white wine would be nice."

He gave their order then sat back, softly tapping the edge of the table with his fingers, keeping time to the music.

"Remember this song?" he asked. "Goes back to our time."

Jan had already identified the song. "Brown-Eyed Girl," by Van Morrison. She and Doug had danced to it at their senior prom.

"What was it you wanted to talk about?" she asked, deliberately trying to break any mood that might be developing.

"Us," Doug said.

"Us?"

"I have a question I have to ask you," he admit-ted. "The main reason, I might add, why I wanted to talk to you tonight. This is something I think we should clear up before I move into your place. Janny ... just what is it you have against me?"

CHAPTER SIX

"WHAT DO I HAVE against you?"

Jan echoed Doug's question. Her hand trembled as she set the wineglass back down on the table, and fought for composure. What did she have against him? How could he possibly be so obtuse?

Didn't he realize he'd walked out on her twenty years ago and—except for a couple of hastily scrawled postcards in answer to the impassioned love letters she'd written him—had never tried to get in touch since? Didn't he realize that, if hearts really could be broken, he had broken hers? He must have heard *something* from their other classmates. She remembered he'd had one especially close friend in school, Joe Morgan. Joe had moved away from Ellis Falls years ago. But if he and Doug had been in touch in the early days certainly Joe must have passed on the current gossip to him. Doug must have heard that there'd been a lot of talk after his departure, and Jan had been dubbed Doug MacKenzie's "leftover girl." She'd certainly heard the gossip, and how it had stung! Doug had done a real job on her ego.

Mixed feelings surged. Some of her twenty-year-old pain resurfaced. The words escaped before she could stifle them. "I can't believe you've become so insensitive," she accused.

"Insensitive?" Doug seemed genuinely astonished.

"Coming back here as you did," Jan went on, as if she hadn't even heard his query. "Didn't you ever stop to think that people would remember..."

To her surprise, she saw Doug flush. And she suddenly realized that what she'd just said was reminding him not of herself, or their romance, but of his own status here in town when he'd left.

The MacKenzie boy from the other side of the tracks.

She started to say something by way of explanation then decided that explanations were better left unvoiced just now. To go into anything further she'd have to reveal far more of her own feelings than she wanted to reveal.

As she began to cool down, Jan was exasperated with herself for having let Doug get under her skin so easily. It seemed painfully obvious that where their past was concerned he had buried any guilt over what he'd done to her, or else had actually forgotten his own promises and his failure to keep them.

Maybe, because Doug had suffered a lot of unhappiness with his family in his growing-up years, he had—whether consciously or unconsciously—been determined to put his past behind him once he got away from Ellis Falls. And she'd been part of that past.

Whatever...this was the here and now, and Jan was damned if she was going to let this man upset her life. She'd experienced many difficult situations, and she'd pulled through them. She could live with Doug MacKenzie inhabiting her cottage for six months and pull through that, too. In fact, maybe having to suffer his presence on her premises from now through the rest of the year was exactly what would enable her to wash the memory of him out of her hair, for once and for all.

"Look, Doug," Jan said, sighing. "I have nothing against you, really. It's just that I've had a lot on my mind lately. The twins. My business. My responsibilities as a selectman. Speaking of which," she finished, putting her napkin on the table and easing out of the banquette, "I really must get along home. Tomorrow promises to be another long and busy day."

Doug seemed to accept her explanation. He nodded, called for the check and they left the lounge.

Jan tried to say good-night to him at the door of the inn, but he took her arm and said, "I'll see you to your car."

They were at her car and he was opening the door for her when he said, "Would you mind if I start moving in on Saturday? I talked with Chet, and he's not working this Saturday. He said he could get a couple of his friends, and they could help take the bedroom things out to your barn."

"When did you talk to Chet?" she asked curiously.

"I called your house before I headed over to the town hall," Doug said. "Vicky told me where you were...."

So, Vicky had made it home by what ordinarily would be "suppertime," after all.

"Actually it was Chet who suggested Saturday," Doug went on. "He said he and his friends could help me out Sunday, too, if there was more to be done. Incidentally, I hope you didn't mind my showing up at the meeting tonight. I wanted to see you in action, Janny.''

"No," she said, "I didn't mind."

"You handled yourself extremely well."

Jan didn't answer that. She eased past Doug and got into the car, much too conscious of his proximity. He looked good. He smelled good. If he'd opened his arms to her a second ago, it would have been very easy to go into them—despite her mixed feelings about him.

Doug closed the car door, then stood back and said, "See you Saturday."

The day after tomorrow. She had approximately forty-eight hours, Jan thought, to get a much, much firmer grip on herself. She nodded, and drove off into the night.

SATURDAY WAS BRIGHT and beautiful, a perfect summer day. The sky was a clear, freshly washed blue; no clouds to wrinkle it. The sun was benevolent; golden warmth, without searing heat.

Doug appeared at the house shortly after nine o'clock. Jan was in the laundry room down in the basement, transferring a load of wet clothes from the washing machine to the dryer when she heard Floppy barking a welcome. She went back up to the kitchen, to find Doug sitting at the kitchen table, watching Chet polish off a second bowl of cereal.

He stood quickly when he saw her, "Hope I'm not too early," he said.

"No, not at all," Jan managed. Doug was dressed for the task at hand, today. He was wearing snug-fitting jeans and a blue T-shirt and a pair of scruffy running shoes that looked as if they might have kicked around the world with him. He was so damned masculine, Jan thought, and because of that he made a woman aware of her femininity even when he wasn't trying.

She became conscious of the old white shorts she was wearing, and the faded pink shirt, and she inadvertently touched her hair, knowing it must be a mess. Also, she didn't need a mirror to tell her that her face must be shiny, and she hadn't put on any makeup.

Chet pushed back his chair and stood up, grinning at Doug as he flexed his arm muscles. "I'm ready if you are," he announced. "Mom, when Mike and Al get here tell them to come on out to the cottage, okay?"

"Okay," Jan said.

Doug followed Chet, but he turned before he went out the kitchen door to say, "You're sure you don't mind if I move things around?"

"Not at all," she said. And, determined to play the part of a good landlord, added, "If you need anything, let me know."

She wasn't prepared for the look Doug gave her. Inscrutable . . . yet still loaded. For no good reason at all, she was flushing as she poured herself a cup of coffee.

Vicky appeared, wearing a long white nightgown that made her look like an angel in a Christmas play. She stretched, yawned and said, "I thought I heard voices."

"You did," Jan told her. "Your brother and Doug MacKenzie were here. They've gone out to the cottage to start moving some things."

"I'll go put something on," Vicky said immediately. "Maybe I can help."

"Vicky, I'm sure Doug has all the help he needs," Jan said. "Mike and Al are on their way over. The four of them should be able to make do."

"I'm sure they could always use an extra pair of hands, Mother," Vicky said. Then, she compromised. "Okay, I'll boil some eggs for egg salad. If you're not using the car, I can go over to Spencer's Market and get some other fixings for sandwiches."

"Sandwiches?" Jan asked blankly.

"Mummy, you can't expect those guys to work all day without a break for something to eat," Vicky told her.

Unfortunately that made sense. Jan had not thought about feeding Chet and his friends at lunchtime today, to say nothing of Doug MacKenzie. Vicky was right.

"You can take the car over to Spencer's," she told her daughter. "No detours, though, okay?"

Vicky's expression was pained. "Why would I detour?" she asked. "I have things to do here."

"I'd say you detoured Thursday night, Vicky."

Vicky sparked defensively. "I got home about five minutes after you left. Ask Chet."

Jan didn't want this to turn into an argument, but she had to say, "Vicky, you knew I was planning an early supper. You knew I had to go to a selectmen's meeting."

"I suppose you won't believe this," Vicky said, "but Jim had a flat tire."

"Why wouldn't I believe it?"

"You don't seem to believe a lot of things I tell you these days," Vicky said, and flounced out of the kitchen to go upstairs and get dressed.

Chet appeared fifteen minutes later, as Jan was finishing her coffee and stealing the chance to take a look at the morning paper.

"Mom, got some cold soft drinks on tap?" he asked her. "It's blazing hot out in the cottage. Someone should have gone out early and opened the windows."

Jan remembered closing the windows before she left the cottage with Doug the other day, because rain had been imminent. Yesterday had been quite warm, though. Yes, the cottage, closed up, probably was "blazing hot."

She said, "I'm low on the soft drinks, but I can make lemonade."

"That'd be great," Chet said, and disappeared again.

Jan dug lemonade concentrate out of the freezer, and made enough lemonade to fill a gallon thermos jug. She found some plastic glasses, left over from a party the twins had given here in the house, and a couple of packages of peanut butter and cheese crackers. She wished Vicky would hurry up and come downstairs so she could send her out to the cottage with the refreshments.

Finally she sought out Vicky—who shouldn't be taking this long to get dressed. But the upstairs bathroom door was closed, and she heard the sound of the shower. Vicky had never taken a quick shower in her life.

I guess I'm elected, Jan muttered to herself, and set forth with the lemonade, the crackers, and a package of molasses cookies she added at the last minute.

The door to the cottage stood open, and the twin beds from the second bedroom were set on the grass outside, the box springs and mattresses slightly askew. Floppy was curled up on top of one of the mattresses, and Abigail on the other.

Inside the cottage the windows had all been opened, but there wasn't much air stirring. It was hot and stuffy.

Jan found Doug, Chet and Chet's two friends in the second bedroom, setting up a fairly large bookcase, which she vaguely remembered.

"There's lemonade in the kitchen," she announced.

"Great," Doug said, mopping his brow with a large white handkerchief. "That was really nice of you, Janny."

The boys were already on their way to get a cold drink.

Doug glanced toward the bookcase and said, "I hope you don't mind."

"Mind?"

"It belongs to you," he said, "in case you didn't immediately recognize it. I asked Chet where I might find a secondhand bookcase around somewhere, and he told me there was one stored in your barn."

"I'd forgotten about that," Jan admitted.

When Jonas was alive, they'd shared the upstairs master bedroom. Chet and Vicky had each had smaller rooms of their own. The downstairs room off the living room, which she'd since converted into her own bedroom, had been used by Jonas as a study. He'd been a great reader. The bookcase shelves had been filled with a variety of books. She'd given some of them to the Ellis Falls library. Others were stored in cartons in the garage.

Doug said, "Look, if you have any objection to my using—"

"None at all," she said, cutting him off. "Don't you want some lemonade?"

"Yes," he said. But he made no move to head for the kitchen. Again, he was watching her closely, and that intense scrutiny began to make Jan feel uncomfortable.

She said, "I'd better be getting back to the house."

"How about joining me for a glass of lemonade first?"

"I just finished a cup of coffee." Jan was moving out of the room as she spoke. She had the feeling Doug was about to pose another question to her, undoubtedly one she either wouldn't want, or wouldn't be able, to answer.

She said, "By the way, Vicky plans to have lunch ready for everyone. Around twelve-thirty."

"You don't have to do that," Doug protested.

"I'm not doing it," Jan said. "Vicky is."

VICKY HAD BEEN hard at work. She'd made platters of egg salad and ham-and-cheese sandwiches, and put out bowls of pickles and potato chips, plus an assortment of cookies for dessert. She'd also made a pitcher of iced coffee and had plenty of chilled soft drinks on hand.

Doug, surveying the spread that practically filled the kitchen table, said, "This is a feast."

The kids loaded paper plates with food and went out on the back porch to eat. Doug sat down at the kitchen table and looked across at Jan who was watering a geranium in the window.

"You are going to join me, aren't you?" he asked her.

There was no graceful way to back out. She poured herself a glass of iced coffee and sat down. The kitchen was nicely shaded by the big old maples around the house. It was cool and comfortable inside the pleasant, yellow-painted room. Jan just wished she could relax and enjoy the near-perfect summer day.

Sounds of laughter floated in from the back porch, and Doug, nodding in that direction, said, "Those are great kids. They've really been helpful."

"It's good for them to do things for people," Jan said.

"You're a strict mother, aren't you, Janny?"

That certainly wasn't the kind of question she would have expected from him, and she wasn't sure how to answer it. "I don't consider myself a slave driver, if that's what you mean," she hedged. "I do believe in discipline. You have to set rules and parameters with kids. Even more for their sake than for your own."

"Vicky mentioned that she'd driven over to a neighborhood market to get some of the stuff for lunch," Doug said. "I got the impression you don't give her the use of the car too often."

"We have one car, Doug," Jan said stiffly. "As it happens, I have to use it a good bit of the time myself. My kids are never without transportation when they need it, though."

She heard the coldness in her voice but he had it coming, damn it! He hadn't even moved in yet and he was already getting into her family affairs. That was one situation she was *definitely* going to have to set some parameters to!

"Hey," he said, "I wasn't criticizing. What I wanted to tell you was that I'm going to turn in the sports car Monday and I plan to buy a station wagon. When I'm working I'll be holed in for hours at a time. I was going to suggest that the kids might use my car when I won't be needing it, if you wouldn't object."

"I don't think that would be a good idea." The response was automatic.

Jan was not about to tell him about her fears about the twins driving at all. She knew that millions of people of all ages drove regularly, all across the country—all around the world—without mishaps. That didn't alter this gut fear of hers which, she was the first to admit, did need to be exorcised. But every time she let Chet or Vicky take the car she found it impossible to relax until they were home again.

Doug didn't pursue the matter. He finished his sandwich and said, "I'd better get back out there or the kids'll call me a shirker." He paused. "I know Vicky fixed the lunch," he said, "but thanks anyway, Janny."

THAT SATURDAY NIGHT Vicky had a date to go to the movies with Jim Farrish. She suggested to Chet that he ask Cathy Ferguson to go along, so they could make up a foursome. Chet reluctantly agreed.

Jan was alone in the house, and as the evening wore on she was reminded of the title of an old song, "Saturday Night is the Loneliest Night of the Week."

She was lonely. She was very lonely. And her loneliness was only enhanced when she went to her bedroom window and saw lights glowing in the cottage out back.

Doug was sleeping there tonight, even though there was still some more furniture moving to be done. Earlier, as she was fixing some supper for the twins, she'd heard his car pull up at the far end of the side driveway. As she watched from the kitchen window, he got out of the car and made for the cottage, carrying a large brown paper bag under each arm.

He'd obviously been grocery shopping. He was settling in.

Jan was sure that if Vicky hadn't had a date she would have urged her mother to invite Doug over for Saturday night supper. So, for once, Jan was glad Vicky was going out with Jim Farrish.

She went to bed early, trying to pretend that she was enjoying this luxury of curling up with a good book, with nothing and no one to disturb her. But, after a time she admitted she was kidding herself.

Much later, she heard car doors slam, and Vicky's "Good night" was followed by Chet's, "Thanks a lot, Jim."

Still later, she heard both twins talking in low voices as they headed up the stairs to their rooms. Only then did she turn over and fall into a sound sleep.

MIKE AND AL arrived toward midmorning on Sunday, and Chet joined them to go out to the cottage again. Vicky said, "I'd better start fixing some sandwich fillings," and Jan—who'd been reading the Sunday paper—looked up with a frown.

"You're not putting on another lunch today, are you, Vicky?" she asked.

"It's no trouble, Mummy," Vicky said. "Anyway, I got enough stuff yesterday to last two days."

After a time, Vicky, too, trailed out to the cottage. "I thought maybe I could wash some windows or something," she said in parting, and Jan raised her eyebrows. Vicky, under ordinary circumstances, detested housework.

Fortunately, the cottage was far enough away from the house so that no sounds traveled over the intervening distance. If they were all having a great time out there and laughing their heads off as they worked, Jan didn't want to hear them.

She took the Sunday paper into the living room and started working on the crossword puzzle.

Shortly, Chet interrupted her. "Mom," he said, "remember that old desk that belonged to Dad?"

Jan remembered the rolltop desk Chet was speaking about very well. It had been Jonas's pride and joy.

"Yes," she said.

"It's in the barn," Chet informed her, as if she didn't already know that. "I wondered if you'd mind if Doug uses it. When he spotted it, he said he'd always wanted a rolltop. He has some office stuff coming tomorrow. He bought a computer and a printer and other things he needs over in Pittsfield. But I think he'd really like to have Dad's rolltop around."

Jan said, "I marvel there's space in that room for so many things."

"With the beds and the dresser out of there, there's more room than you'd think," Chet said enthusiastically. "The rolltop would fit right in where the dresser was."

Jan nodded. "All right."

Fifteen minutes later she heard a rap at the back door. Doug stood on the threshold, and he looked troubled.

"Jan," he began, "I didn't realize..."

Puzzled, she asked, "What didn't you realize?"

"Well, yesterday it never dawned on me that the bookcase had belonged to your husband. Or, a while ago, that the rolltop desk was his. Chet told me, and I feel ashamed of myself. Believe me, I didn't intend to be so intrusive."

Jan said slowly, "I don't feel you've been intrusive, Doug." She owed him that much honesty. "I'm sure having you take the bookcase and the desk was Chet's idea, and I'm agreeable to it. They were Jonas's, true. But I'm sure he'd much rather have someone else use them than for them to keep gathering dust in the barn."

"The rolltop's quite a beauty."

"Yes, I know. I simply didn't have anyplace to put it, once I moved into the downstairs room that had been Jonas's study," Jan confessed.

"I see."

Doug waited, and she felt he was expecting her to say more. But she was not about to volunteer that she'd moved downstairs because the master bedroom upstairs had simply become too lonely.

Finally Doug said, "I appreciate everything you and the twins and their friends are doing for me, Janny. So, I hope you'll let me show a small token of that appreciation."

Jan wished she wasn't so quick to go on the defensive with him. "There's really no need for that," she said, and immediately hated her own abruptness.

"On the contrary, I would really like to take all of you to dinner at the inn tonight."

"Doug, honestly, there's no need..."

Doug's lips tightened and, for once, he let his impatience show. "I know there's no need," he told her. "This is something I want to do. Suppose I make reservations for seven? Would that be all right with you?"

Jan nodded and said, "Yes, that would be fine." Because she would have felt like a total Scrooge if she'd said anything else.

AS THEY WALKED into the dining room at the Ellis Falls Inn, Jan had a sudden memory of her parents bringing her here for a festive dinner on her sixteenth birthday.

The decor had been changed slightly over the years. The color scheme was blue, now, instead of green. But the atmosphere hadn't altered. The inn had always prided itself on epitomizing gracious living. Somehow, even in these last frenetic years of the twentieth century, it was still managing to do exactly that.

There were six of them at the large center table Doug had reserved. Chet, Mike and Al looked as if they'd been freshly scrubbed; Jan couldn't ever recall having ever seen this trio quite so immaculate. Vicky was wearing a pale blue cotton dress, the color almost matching the wallpaper. She'd tied her hair into a ponytail with a deeper blue ribbon, and she looked very pretty.

Doug was wearing pale gray summer slacks, and a darker gray, lightweight jacket. Certainly he'd never looked more handsome, and Jan had to admit that any red-blooded female would have to respond to the sight of him. Also, he was being utterly charming. She realized that, over the years, Doug had become very polished when he wished to be. The inn staff treated him with deference, and he accepted it with a graciousness that would have made one think he'd been accustomed to this kind of treatment all his life.

He'd come a long, long way from the struggling but ambitious Doug MacKenzie of twenty years ago.

He ordered ginger ale concoctions for the kids, and suggested frozen daiquiris for Jan and himself. When the drinks were served, he lifted his glass in a toast and said, "Thanks, all of you. I can't begin to tell you how much I'm looking forward to the next six months."

His eyes met Jan's as he spoke, but surprisingly she saw a question mark in that deep blue gaze. Was she the one thing here in Ellis Falls he was still unsure about?

The band came back after a break and started playing a slow song. Doug announced, "Kids, I'm claiming the first dance with Janny."

Jan, embarrassed, tried to think up an excuse to decline. But she was acutely aware that she was the unwavering focus of four pairs of eyes. There was nothing to do but get to her feet and let Doug lead her to the dance floor.

As Doug slid his arm around Jan's waist, he murmured, "That dress you are wearing is absolutely stunning."

She was wearing a white dress banded in green that Nancy had persuaded her to buy in Boston, when they'd gone to the city together on a brief business trip a couple of months ago. She'd paid more for the dress than she usually paid for her clothes, but she had fallen in love with it. Then, tonight, she'd been more careful than usual with makeup, knowing that Vicky would say something if she didn't put on a little shadow and eyeliner. Mock emeralds, matching the shade of green in the dress, twinkled at her ears. And she'd dabbed on some of the Chanel No. 5 Chet had given her last Christmas.

"You were lovely at eighteen. You're even lovelier at thirty-eight," Doug said softly.

Jan felt her pulse begin to flutter, and she told herself she was reacting to his flattery like someone Vicky's age would. But suddenly she didn't want to summon up any more sternness in her responses to him. She just wanted to relax, and let herself be swayed by Doug and the music, and the lovely atmosphere of the old inn.

When he drew her a little closer, she didn't pull back. After a moment, she leaned her head on his shoulder, and he bent slightly so their cheeks touched. He used a subtle after-shave, and its scent was sexy. Desire stirred, and there wasn't much Jan could do about it. Even if she might have been able to achieve the mental discipline, her body was giving her away. She couldn't help responding to Doug, and she felt an inner shiver that went all the way from her throat to her toes.

After a time the music stopped, and they went back to their table. Doug didn't say anything. Neither did Jan.

As the evening passed, he danced with Vicky, and each of the boys put on his best manner and asked Jan to dance. But, in between, she danced with Doug.

They didn't speak, as they danced. They didn't need to. Their body language was speaking for them.

When they left the inn, the air was heavy with the scent of honeysuckle, and the moon was an early harvest gold. It was a night dangerously suited to romance.

They had used Jan's sedan tonight, since there was no way to get six people into the red sports car. Jan, on the spur of the moment, told Chet he could drive. He looked as if he couldn't believe his ears, but he took the car keys from her.

Mike and Al were already in the back seat. Jan slid in next to them, silently branding herself a wimp. But right now she felt like she'd fall apart if she wedged into the front seat, between Chet and Doug.

Chet dropped Mike off first, then drove over to Al's house. When Al got out of the car, so did Doug. He opened the back door and got in next to Jan. "Thought I'd give Vicky a little more breathing space," he explained.

Jan became aware of two things simultaneously: the inches separating Doug and herself, and the couple of feet, if that, between the twins in the front seat, and herself in the back. She was sure the twins' ears were wide open.

Doug reached for her hand, and she let him take it. He turned it palm up, then began to trace her lifeline and her love line and all the other lines with a feather-light touch that was incredibly erotic. Sensation followed sensation, each to become knotted deep inside her like a growing string of shimmering pearls.

Chet pulled the car into the driveway, and Doug held the door for Jan. She looked up at him, and said, "Thanks so much, Doug. It was a lovely evening."

"My pleasure," he said smoothly. But the moonlight was just bright enough so that Jan saw the knowing smile that curved his lips. And suddenly she felt more unsure of herself that she had on that long-ago night when Doug had taken her to their junior prom.

Unless Doug started backing off, how was she going to resist him?

CHAPTER SEVEN

WEDNESDAY MORNING Jan attended the selectmen's weekly public meeting, which culminated with a fairly long executive session. She was tired, she'd had a restless night's sleep, and—not for the first time—she wished Bartlett Folger would stop pontificating so they could get through with some issues that were not all that world shaking.

It was nearly twelve-thirty when she left the town office building. She stopped to pick up a sandwich and a soft drink at the deli on Main Street, then headed for Chocolate Fantasies. She needed to get some material together for the company accountant.

When she walked into the shop, Leona Martin was busy rearranging a candy display. Leona beckoned to her, then held a warning finger to her lips. Mystified, Jan joined Leona behind the counter. "What's up?" she asked, keeping her voice low.

"Nancy's back in the office," Leona said. "Frankly, Jan, she looks terrible and she's not acting like herself."

"Any idea what's wrong?"

"No. She said she had a splitting headache. I asked her if I could get her something for it, and she said she'd already taken some aspirin."

"How long has she been here?"

"About an hour."

Jan tried on a smile that she hoped looked reassuring. "I'll see what I can do," she promised.

Nancy was leaning back in her desk chair, her eyes closed. Jan had a brief opportunity to look at her before she sat bolt upright, opened her eyes and blinked. It was a revealing moment. Leona was right. Nancy did look terrible: haggard, her features drawn.

The question was inevitable. "Nancy, what is it?"

"What is what?" Nancy retorted. She opened a desk drawer and peered into it as she spoke.

"You look bushed," Jan said frankly.

Nancy didn't attempt to hide her irritation. "You're imagining things," she said crisply. She went on, "I had a letter from Filenes, in Boston, about producing some special Halloween chocolates for them. Have you seen it?"

"No," Jan said, "I haven't seen it. And I think, right now, we have some more immediate concerns than Halloween chocolates. I think we need to talk."

Nancy reached into her handbag and produced a pack of cigarettes. As Jan watched, she flicked a silver lighter. A flame flared. Nancy inhaled deeply, then exhaled a thin wisp of pale blue smoke. If Jan had needed anything further to convince her that Nancy was having problems, this was it.

When they'd first met, Nancy had been a heavy smoker. After a worrisome session with bronchitis, her doctor and her friends had finally persuaded her that she should make the attempt to quit, if she valued her health, more specifically, her lungs. At first, she'd scoffed. Then, one day, she'd stopped smoking... cold turkey. That was three years ago, and though Nancy had been frank in saying she still missed cigarettes, she'd also emphasized that she'd never go back to them, knowing the hazard they held for her.

Jan, her eyes glued to Nancy's cigarette, asked, "When did you start up again?"

"A couple of weeks ago," Nancy said. "And please don't give me a lecture, okay?"

Jan smiled wryly. "I'm not about to give you a lecture, Nancy. You're a big girl. I do think we need to talk, though. But this isn't the place. How about if we go out and get some lunch?"

Jan watched Nancy's face as she issued the invitation, and became sure she was going to get a quick refusal. She was right. Nancy said, "I'd like to, Jan, but I have a luncheon date. I just stopped by to see if I could find the letter from Filenes. It can wait, though."

She stood as she spoke, brushing a small fleck of ash from the skirt of her white cotton dress. As Jan watched, she snuffed out her cigarette, and picked up her handbag. Jan realized Nancy was avoiding looking her straight in the eye, and suddenly Nancy— usually so direct—seemed remote, like a stranger.

Nancy was at the office door when Jan said, "Wait a minute, will you?"

She thought Nancy looked like a horse at the starting gate in a race. Ready to go, annoyed at being restrained, even momentarily. But this was something that had to be aired.

"Nancy," she said, choosing her words carefully, "I just want to say one thing. We're not merely business partners. We're friends. Close friends. I'd like to think if I had a problem I could go to you with it, and you'd listen. I want you to know that same thing applies in reverse. If you ever want someone to listen, I'm here."

She saw Nancy's hesitation. Nancy's lips trembled; for a moment Jan thought maybe she'd come back and sit down at the desk again and start to talk about... whatever it was that was bothering her so terribly. But then Nancy got hold of herself.

Still, her voice wasn't all that steady as she said, "Thanks, Jan. I'll remember that."

Jan nodded.

For the next hour, Jan worked on accounts. Then, becoming aware that her stomach was growling, she reached for the sandwich and drink she'd bought earlier.

She ate as she worked, then worked on until almost four o'clock, the shop's summer closing hour. Then she left Leona Martin to lock up, and went home.

She was depressed. The books had told a story that had a further bearing on Nancy's odd attitude. Late spring orders had been down—orders in the metropolitan areas that were within Nancy's domain. Nor, despite her early summer traveling, had Nancy come back with the volume of fall and advance winter orders she usually brought in. Jan had to admit that it didn't look like Nancy had been carrying as much of her share of the load as she usually did.

That meant that her troubles—whatever they might be—weren't as recent as Jan had assumed they were.

JAN STOPPED at the supermarket on her way home to make a few purchases. She was lugging a heavy bag of groceries as she pushed open her kitchen door, Floppy and the cats at her heels.

The stillness of the house told her there was no-body home. Then, she saw a scrap of yellow paper on the kitchen table, anchored by the sugar bowl, and read the note Vicky had left for her.

"Doug had to go over to Pittsfield to pick up a few more computer supplies, and he asked me to go along for the ride," Vicky had written, in a scrawl that still had an appealingly childish quality about it. "Be home in time for supper. How about we just char-coal some hamburgers—I checked, and there are plenty made up in the freezer. I'll ask Doug to join us."

Jan crunched up the note, and tossed it into the wastebasket under the sink, annoyed. After the day she'd put in she didn't need the added stress of hav-ing Doug MacKenzie around for supper.

She went over to the fridge and poured herself a glass of chilled white wine. Glass in hand, she went out to the back porch and sat down on the old swing-for-two Jonas had put up years and years ago.

The swing creaked as she rocked back and forth. A late-afternoon breeze stirred, bringing with it the scent of phlox and honeysuckle. The sun was a huge, golden circle, suspended in a very blue sky. Jan sipped her wine and tried to work out her annoyance, her frustration, tried to force herself to relax. But noth-ing was going right either at work or at home, and the tension was like an itch she couldn't scratch.

She couldn't blame Doug if Vicky had developed an adolescent crush on him and might very well make a pest of herself unless he gently but firmly put her in her place. She couldn't blame Vicky, for that matter, for being attracted to Doug. He was handsome, world famous, interesting and fun to be around. Certainly Vicky had never met anyone like him.

She couldn't blame Vicky—or Chet—for extending invitations to Doug to brunch or lunch or supper or whatever. She'd taught her kids to be hospitable. Also—where Chet was concerned—it must be good to have a man around. She wouldn't call Doug a father figure, but he was an exciting, contemporary man, someone Chet could relate to. Further, he seemed to genuinely like the twins, to like kids, for that matter. He'd been great with all four teenagers at the inn on Sunday night.

Jan was still sitting in the swing, her glass of wine half-full, when a cream-colored station wagon swung up the driveway, raising some dust as it came to a quick stop at the edge of the path that led out to the cottage.

Jan saw Vicky climb out of the driver's side, and anger surfaced. Doug had no right to let Vicky drive an unfamiliar car over the mountain roads that stretched between here and Pittsfield.

She heard Vicky laugh, heard Doug laugh, too, as he got out of the wagon and joined her. The two of them trailed toward the house, quite oblivious to her presence. They'd not yet spotted her.

She saw Vicky sober. Vicky seemed to be talking to Doug about something serious, because he sobered, too, and was listening intently to what Vicky was saying. The sound of Vicky's voice carried as far as the porch, but Jan could not make out her words.

Then, just as Vicky came within hearing range, she looked up and saw her mother and stopped short. Doug followed her gaze, saw Jan, and said, "Well, hi, there."

"Hello," Jan said, telling herself that there was no reason why she should feel like the outsider in this trio.

"I didn't know Vicky had taken a computer course at school," Doug said as he climbed the back steps. "She was a big help."

"Come on, Doug," Vicky scoffed. "You know three times as much about computers as I'll ever know. Would you like a cold drink?"

"Love one," Doug said.

Doug sat down on an old wooden chair near the swing and his eyes met Jan's across the short intervening distance. It was obvious she wasn't pleased.

He guessed he had it coming. He supposed he should have asked her permission before inviting her daughter to go along to Pittsfield with him. But Vicky had been sunning out on the grassy space next to the small kitchen garden. She'd looked bored and lonely. He'd felt lonely.

He'd been wishing ever since Sunday that he could have had a few more minutes with Jan alone, after they got home. God, he'd wanted so much to take her in his arms, to kiss away that guard she kept throwing up between the two of them. The night, certainly, had been made for love. All that gorgeous moonlight, all those twinkling stars, all the soft fragrant breezes . . . going to waste.

They were two adults of consenting age, after all. And, whether Jan was going to let herself admit it or not, the physical attraction between them was undeniable. He wanted Jan. The need was getting stronger each time he saw her. But she'd put a wall between them. Sometimes he felt he could see through the wall, just a little bit. Sometimes he felt he couldn't see through it at all.

He said—wishing Jan didn't make him feel so uncertain about things—"I hope you didn't object to my taking Vicky over to Pittsfield with me."

"It would be a little late if I did, wouldn't it?" Jan asked.

"Okay," Doug said, her stiffness annoying him. "It won't happen again. I didn't realize I was going to need more stuff until I unpacked what I'd already gotten. Otherwise, I would have approached you this morning before you left for your meeting."

As he spoke, he wondered if Janny realized that Vicky wasn't having much of a summer, so far. Three afternoons a week she worked in her mother's store. The rest of the time, there wasn't much for her to do. Often, she was stuck here on the outskirts of town without transportation. Her boyfriend, Jim, worked full-time, summers, in Herb Flynn's hardware store down on Main Street. Vicky had mentioned that a couple of her other friends were junior counselors, this summer, at a camp over on Deep Pines Lake. She'd said, rather wistfully, that she wished she could have a job like that. But, to hold it down, you'd have to have your own car.

Janny appeared to have a hang-up where her kids and cars were concerned, and Doug doubted that her concern was a question of money. She'd been unreceptive to his suggestion that the kids could take turns using his car when he didn't need it. Maybe right now she was angry because he'd allowed Vicky to drive back from Pittsfield...and he supposed that, strictly speaking, he'd had no right to do so. But when Janny was seventeen years old she'd had her license and she'd driven all over the place. Didn't she remember that?

It was so easy and convenient to forget what you didn't want to remember.

Vicky came out with the soft drinks and handed Doug a frosty can. He felt as though he should take it and go back to the cottage. But Vicky curled up on an old leather hassock and asked, "Did you get my note about having hamburgers, Mummy?"

"Yes," Jan said.

"Doug can stay..."

"Look," Doug interrupted hastily, "I think maybe it would be better if I didn't, Vicky. I bought some TV dinners, I can stick one in the oven and eat it while I'm going through my research notes." He managed a somewhat lopsided grin. "I need to light a fire under this project and get it started," he said.

Jan suddenly felt like a heel. Doug was making her feel ashamed of herself—whether or not that's what he was trying to do.

"Don't be silly," she said rather brusquely. "You're more than welcome to stay. Unless you really need to start in on your notes tonight..."

Doug virtually forced her to make eye contact with him. "No," he said. "Actually the notes could wait till morning."

Vicky had been watching the two of them, a slight frown creasing her forehead. The frown converted into a wide smile as she said, "Great! Look, you guys, I'm going to go boil some potatoes. I'll make us a super potato salad."

Once Vicky was inside the kitchen, Doug stood up and moved over to the swing. "Mind if I join you?" he asked Jan.

She shook her head.

He eased into the seat across from hers. With one foot he set the swing rocking back and forth very gently. Then he glanced at the wine in Jan's glass and smiled.

"Hoarding that?" he asked her.

"No. It's gotten warm. I don't want the rest of it."

"Would you like me to refill your glass with some chilled stuff?"

"No. No, thanks."

"Janny," Doug said, feeling the need to get this out regardless of her reaction, "when you agreed to rent your cottage to me I told you I wouldn't get in your hair. I don't intend to. Vicky said you were going to charcoal hamburgers and, frankly, I don't know when I last had a good old American hamburger cooked on a grill. I let temptation overrule my common sense. But, I promise you, I won't say yes another time."

Jan listened and, again, felt ashamed of herself. "Doug," she protested, "you're more than welcome to share hamburgers with us. If I gave you the wrong impression it's because I was . . . somewhat preoccupied, when you and Vicky drove up. A couple of business problems."

"I see," Doug said. Then added, "Speaking of driving—is there a reason why you don't want your kids to do much driving, Janny?"

Jan stared at him. He was being too perceptive for comfort.

"I ask you that," he persisted, "because as soon as I mentioned the kids could use my car when I didn't need it I had the feeling I'd put my foot in some very deep mud."

Jan couldn't come up with an immediate answer. She'd never discussed her feelings about the twins driving with anyone. The fear was something pent-up inside her that she knew she was going to have to get over, for their sake. She didn't need to be told she couldn't protect them forever. But if only she might, for a while longer...

She said slowly, "I read the statistics about teenage driving, and they frighten me. I know about a couple of pretty terrible incidents that happened around here. In fact, you must remember that a classmate of ours was killed driving a car on that road that goes to Pine Mountain."

"Yes."

"I get scared when it comes to the twins driving," Jan admitted, the admission coming haltingly. "I don't want to be a possessive mother, I don't want to smother my kids. But sometimes it sort of overwhelms me that they're all I have. And, that's wrong, too. They need to be free to lead their own lives. But they're still so young..."

Her words trailed off. Finally she glanced directly at Doug, and was surprised at the compassion she saw etched on his face and mirrored in his eyes.

"I can appreciate how you must feel," he said. "I've never had kids of my own, but I've seen a lot of tragedies, in all parts of the world. I've seen what the loss of a child does to the parents. Suffering's a universal bond, Janny. Like love.

"Still," he went on, "there is another side to the coin, Janny. You gave them life. You do have to let them live it."

Their eyes met and held. And Jan wondered what they might have said next, if Chet hadn't arrived back home at that particular moment. The landscapers' truck careened into the driveway. Chet climbed down, looking tired and hot and dusty. But, when he saw Doug, his face creased into a grin.

"Going to be around for supper?" he immediately asked Doug.

"Looks like it," Doug replied.

"Give me a chance to shower, I'll be right back down," Chet said, and hurried into the house.

Jan wondered if the slight twinge that twisted in her chest at that moment might properly be diagnosed as jealousy.

FOR THE NEXT WEEK, Doug kept his word and his distance. Had it not been for lights in the cottage at night, Jan would have had no idea there was anyone else living on her property.

She was busy at the town hall. The selectmen held a series of meetings designed for summer residents, people who owned property in the area that they occupied only during the warm months.

She was also busy at Chocolate Fantasies. Things were not getting better with Nancy; they were getting worse. When the two of them met in the office, Nancy seemed vague, preoccupied. A couple of times Jan would have sworn Nancy had had a couple of drinks that had affected her, even though—both times—it was only early afternoon. And, she'd taken up smoking again in earnest. She'd brought in a big ashtray for her desk, and most of the time it was full of cigarette butts.

Jan was also worried about both Chet and Vicky. She'd been at them again to get going on college applications; she'd even written away for a few more college catalogs to add to the heap she'd already obtained for them. Their excuses for not getting on with this particular job were growing thin. She knew before long they were going to have to talk about it.

She went to bed early most nights, always aware of those lights burning out in the cottage at the edge of the woods. Was Doug deliberately keeping out of her way? Or were they just not crossing paths because they were going different places at different times?

On Wednesday night, as Jan was about to climb into bed, she heard a knock at the kitchen door. Since she hadn't heard a car pull up, she was sure it was Doug.

She was right. He stood on the threshold, looking tired, in need of a shave, his hair mussed. He also looked surprised to see her.

"I didn't mean to bother you, Janny," he said quickly.

Jan had put on a green silk dressing gown over her nightgown, and she was barefoot. She'd washed her face, twisted her hair into a soft bun at the back of her head. She became aware that she was about as au naturel as a person could be, and she felt she must look every one of her thirty-eight years.

Doug added, "I thought one of the kids was probably watching TV, and would come to the door."

"No," she said. "Chet and Vicky are at a barbecue." She held the door open a little wider. "You're not bothering me," she said. "Come in."

Doug seemed uncomfortable as he stepped into the kitchen. He said—as if certain he'd interrupted her in the middle of something important—"I won't keep you. The thing is, my fridge appears to have broken down. Nothing serious, probably, and I don't have much food in it. What there is will keep till tomorrow. I'll call a repairman first thing in the morning...."

"I'll call Bernie Crocker," Jan said. Bernie had gone to school with them.

"Bernie's an electrician?" Doug asked. "As I remember, he couldn't sit still more than five minutes, and everyone wondered if he'd ever settle down to anything."

"He specializes in repairing kitchen appliances," Jan said. "Fridges, stoves, dishwashers, disposals. He's very good at what he does."

"Okay, then, I'll give him a call."

"I'll call him," she reiterated. She prefaced her next statement with a smile. "Remember, I'm the landlord, you're the tenant? This is my responsibility."

Doug looked down at her, and Jan was suddenly aware of how much taller he was than she. She was barefoot, of course. Even so...

She couldn't read his expression as he said, "It's all right, Janny. I'm used to handling routine repairs."

"But..."

She still couldn't read his expression as he asked, "Doesn't it ever occur to you that you don't have to handle absolutely everything by yourself?"

Jan had no ready answer for that. For a long time, she pretty much had had to handle most things by herself. She'd had two growing children to cope with, then she'd added a growing business to that, and topped it off with her political job. Her parents were in Florida. In earlier years, they'd come back for Christmas, at least. But last year, her father's arthritis had flared up, so they'd stayed in Sarasota over the holidays and hadn't been back north since.

She had a lot of friends—and a large number of acquaintances. But none of them, not even Nancy, were people she'd feel comfortable turning to for help. So...

Doug said, "In any event, all I wanted to request was the loan of a few ice cubes."

"What?" Jan was still thinking about that last statement of his. *Did* she really behave as though she had the weight of the world on her shoulders?

"Ice cubes," Doug said, and favored her with a crooked smile.

Why was it crooked smiles seemed to have twisting, gut-spiraling effects that nice, ordinary smiles didn't have? Jan looked at Doug and felt her pulse thumping a little harder. An inner voice murmured, *"Right now, he looks like the sexiest man in the world, doesn't he? Oh, God, it would be so great to go to him, to let him take me, to let him take me over, for just a little while. To let him make love to me..."*

"Late this afternoon I dumped the ice-cube trays into that plastic container thing," Doug said, obviously oblivious to her reaction—for which Jan was grateful. "I meant to refill them but I didn't. The ones in the plastic container melted. The thing is, this is going to be a long night. I'm into something I want to get all the way through. So I wanted to fix some iced coffee."

Ice. That's what he wanted. That's why he'd come over.

Jan said, "I have a thermal ice bucket. I'll fill it for you. The cubes should keep frozen for quite awhile.

Meantime, if you want to bring over any perishables you may have and put them in my fridge..."

"No need," Doug said.

Jan kept the thermal bucket in a cabinet in her dining room. She tried to regroup as she went to get it. Tried to clutch her emotions, which seemed to be wandering in different directions, and to bring them back under control. But she felt...ragged. She saw her hands were trembling slightly as she reached for the ice bucket. Inwardly she was trembling even more.

As she loaded the bucket with ice cubes for Doug she felt as if his eyes were boring into her spine. Was she being hopelessly transparent? Did he have any idea at all of the effect he was having on her?

If he did, he kept the knowledge to himself. He accepted the ice cubes, smiled another crooked smile and thanked her.

Jan closed the kitchen door behind him, then quickly went back to her bedroom. Standing at the darkened window, she watched the moonlight silver his silhouette, then follow him all the way to the cottage, like a celestial spotlight.

CHAPTER EIGHT

THE NIGHT AFTER Doug had come to the house seeking ice cubes, Jan saw her daughter returning from the cottage shortly after midnight.

Jan had gotten up to go to the bathroom. Before getting back in bed again, she went over to the window and glanced toward the cottage—an action that was getting to be a habit with her. Lights were still glowing in the living room. Jan had excellent distance vision and, as she watched, she saw a deeper center of golden light, and realized the front door had been opened.

Then she saw the slim silhouette emerging and, despite herself, she froze.

It never occurred to her she might be watching Vicky. Rather, she assumed that Doug had invited a woman to the cottage—something, she reminded herself, he certainly had a right to do.

She and the twins had gone to bed around ten o'clock. The woman must have slipped in quietly, since then.

Well...whoever she was, she wasn't staying the night.

As she watched the slim figure coming closer, Jan began to feel uncomfortable, as if she were spying. Then something about the way the woman walked became unexpectedly familiar. And, a sudden shaft of moonlight, poking from behind a cloud, showed Vicky, still wearing the short pink dress she'd been wearing when, earlier, she'd bid her mother goodnight.

Jan lost sight of Vicky as she came closer to the back of the house. But the back porch light was on, and it cast a radiance out onto the grassy path that Jan could see from her bedroom window.

Suddenly the radiance was obliterated. Vicky, Jan thought, must have turned the porch light out. She started for her bedroom door, prepared to confront her daughter. But, midway, she paused. This was Doug whom Vicky had been visiting, and when she considered the situation rationally she doubted very much that Doug had initiated the visit.

She remembered the conversation about kids she'd had with Doug the other night. She knew that though he'd never had kids of his own he empathized with kids all over the world. Certainly he'd hit it off with the twins almost from the moment he met them. And she was sure his interest in them was genuine.

Whatever she felt about Doug herself, whatever lingering scars—and attendant pain—remained from the way he had treated her, had nothing to do with this.

She instinctively trusted today's mature Doug MacKenzie. She knew, without having to be told, that he'd never in God's world seduce her daughter.

Jan went to her bedroom door and listened. And, a moment later, heard Vicky edging her way up the stairs. The fifth step creaked. The fifth step always creaked. Vicky paused, waited. Jan could imagine her huddling in the staircase in the dark, wondering whether she was about to be found out. Then, Vicky shuffled on again, and after a few seconds Jan heard her bedroom door thud softly.

It was not easy to face Vicky the next morning without saying anything. Vicky looked tired and she was cross. She snapped at Chet when he took the last piece of raisin bread and toasted it for himself.

Jan held her tongue. It took all her willpower not to tell Vicky she'd been seen last night. And, as the day passed, she wondered why she hadn't.

Then she realized that she was actually nervous about confronting her daughter! She didn't know how to approach her. What could Vicky possibly be talking to Doug about?

Perhaps, Jan thought, it would be easier to learn the truth from Doug. Then she could decide how best to handle Vicky. Jan made up her mind that as soon as possible she would seek Doug out, and have a talk with him.

That night, though, there was a special town meeting at which all the selectmen were required to be present. Then, the weekend arrived. Jan expected she'd be seeing Doug—coming and going, anyway—unless he planned to hole up and work through Saturday and Sunday. When he didn't appear on Saturday, she decided that must be what he was doing. Then, Saturday night, when she went to her bedroom window she saw that the cottage was dark.

Sunday morning Jan made a more careful survey and noted that Doug's station wagon was not parked in the side driveway. It probably hadn't been parked there yesterday, either, and she simply hadn't noticed. Saturday had been rainy; she'd spent her time in the house, doing some of the thousand chores that were always waiting to be done whenever there was a spare moment.

The rain had slacked off Saturday night, then started in again late Sunday afternoon. As Jan, Chet and Vicky ate their supper at the kitchen table, Chet said, "Doug's going to have a rotten drive back."

"Where has he been?" Jan asked.

"In Vermont, visiting some friends who are vacationing up near Stowe. He was going to head back this evening, though."

There were still no lights in the cottage when Jan went to bed. Sleep proved to be elusive, so she heard Doug's car when he came home. She glanced at the illuminated dial on her bedside clock. It was almost two. She got up and went over to the window, but it was so dark, the rain still coming down so hard, she couldn't see anything. After a while, though, distant yellow globes became visible through the rain and darkness. The lights in the cottage were on again, and Jan was surprised that she should feel such a profound sense of relief.

NANCY CALLED at nine o'clock Monday night. Jan wasn't much of a TV watcher, but there was one weekly mystery program she liked, and it had just concluded when the phone rang.

Chet dashed out to the kitchen to answer the phone, and Jan smiled. He probably was expecting a call from Cathy Ferguson. She'd called him several times, lately. But, Chet returned to the living room to say, "It's for you, Mom. Mrs. Ellis." He looked puzzled, frowning slightly as he added, "She sounds pretty strange."

Nancy not only sounded "strange," she was almost hysterical.

"Where are you, Nancy?" Jan managed to ask, when Nancy's almost incoherent monologue stopped briefly, and there was only the sound of sobbing.

"H-home," Nancy stammered.

"I'll be right over," Jan promised.

The Ellises lived on Mansion Street, the prime residential street in town. It was about a fifteen-minute drive from Jan's house, and she worried every foot of the way. She pulled up in front of the beautiful home she'd always thought looked like a smaller replica of *Gone With the Wind*'s Tara, and wondered what she was going to find inside.

She saw Nancy's car in the driveway, which meant that either Bob wasn't home, or he'd put his Mercedes in the three-car garage at the back of the property. The twin lights by the front door spilled a pool of pale gold over the brick walk and the white front steps. And it looked as if every light in the place had been turned on. Upstairs and down, the house was blazing with a brightness that gave the impression the owners must be hosting a large party.

Jan rang the bell and heard the door chimes echo. Nothing happened, and so she rang again. This time, the door was opened a cautious slot. Then Nancy said, "It's you," and pushed the door open wide.

Without waiting for Jan to enter, Nancy turned and headed for the drawing room, weaving so slightly that only someone who knew her very well would even have noticed the unsteadiness of her gait.

Jan followed. Nancy had switched on the big central chandelier in the drawing room, and all the table lamps as well. The pillows on an ivory brocade couch were heaped in disarray. There was a half-full glass of clear liquid on the coffee table in front of the couch, and a china pitcher beside the glass, with a stirrer in it.

Nancy picked up the glass and took a long swallow. Then she said, "You didn't have to come over."

"What did you expect me to do?" Jan asked her.

"I shouldn't have called you."

"Come on, Nancy," Jan protested. "That's ridiculous, and you know it. Look, will you kindly sit down?"

"Before I fall down?"

"I didn't say that."

"You didn't have to. I can still see, and you have a very expressive face, Jan. Anyway, before I sit down, I might as well tell you."

Nancy's face was dead white, and her eyes were like glowing coals set into the pallor. Her long dark hair was disheveled. Her rose-colored dress was wrinkled. Her voice, pitched higher than usual, trembled as she said, "Bob's left me."

"What are you saying?"

"You heard me. Bob has packed his things and walked out. About two hours ago. This is it. He's gone to her."

"Gone to whom, Nancy?"

Nancy's lips twisted. "The other woman," she said bitterly. "Clarisse Chase. You must know her. She's been Bob's secretary the past two years."

"I've met her," Jan conceded. She was trying to conjure up a mental picture of Bob's secretary, but nothing was coming clear. She could vaguely picture a rather plump woman of medium height, dark haired, if she remembered rightly, but with very clear, very light blue eyes. She remembered the eyes. The color was unusual.

Clarisse Chase had come before the selectmen a year or so ago, in connection with some matter of so little significance Jan couldn't remember what it had been. As Jan thought about her, her image became clearer. There had been an insinuation that because Clarisse worked for Bob Ellis, she had some political clout. Clarisse had refuted that, and there'd been honesty in her indignation. She'd asked for no special privileges; she hadn't been granted any.

Jan remembered that she was a soft-spoken woman. Pleasant faced, but neither pretty nor beautiful. Somewhat on the dumpy side.

It was difficult to believe that Clarisse Chase was breaking up Nancy's home.

"You must be mistaken," she told Nancy, then knew she'd spoken too hastily.

Nancy's eyes narrowed, and she looked at Jan as if she were the ultimate traitor. "You know her," she accused. "You're on her side."

"Don't be ridiculous," Jan snapped. She watched Nancy reach for her glass again and asked sharply, "What are you drinking?"

"Vodka martinis. Want one?"

"No. But I'd appreciate it if you'd pour the rest of what's in that glass down the sink. And get rid of whatever's left in the pitcher at the same time. We need to talk, and we're not going to make sense out of much if you're drunk."

Nancy surveyed her. "Drunk, eh?" she said, her words slightly slurred. "What a prig you can be sometimes, Jan. Don't you ever let down? Don't you ever let yourself go?"

Nancy sat down on the couch and put the martini glass back on the coffee table again. "You don't know what it's like," she said, staring at the table. "Ever since last Christmas I've known there was something. Someone. But it never occurred to me it might be Clarisse."

Jan sat down on a straight-backed chair, inset with fine tapestry, and said, "You have to be wrong about this, Nancy."

"No, I'm not wrong about it," Nancy said. She smiled, a twisted little smile. "You know," she said, "it's like something out of a movie. I first smelled her perfume."

"What do you mean?"

"I smelled her perfume . . . on Bob. The stuff she uses smells like orange blossoms. I could smell it in his clothes, the scent lingered especially in winter, when he was wearing heavy wools and tweeds. Then I found a handkerchief with lipstick on it. Cliché, cliché, cliché," Nancy said, reaching for a pack of cigarettes on the cocktail table. She flicked the silver lighter, drew in and then exhaled before she said again, "It's like a cheap movie."

"Did Bob actually pack his belongings and take them with him when he left here tonight?" Jan asked.

"You're damned right he did. Enough of them, anyway. He walked out the door and he's not coming back, Jan. He's never coming back."

Nancy's face crumpled, and the tears started to flow again.

Jan picked up Nancy's drink, and the pitcher. "That does it," she said. "Let's go brew some coffee. Then maybe we can see where we can get with this."

Nancy's spacious kitchen looked like something out of a decorator magazine. The coffee maker was state of the art; Jan had to read the instructions before she could use it. Then, the coffee made, she and Nancy huddled at the square kitchen table that was like an oversize butcher block. Slowly, Nancy's story emerged.

It was an age-old story, which was one of the things that made it so sad, Jan reflected as she drove home. A marriage where two people had lost the spark along the way. A marriage in which the man wanted children—heirs—and the woman couldn't provide them because she'd had a hysterectomy when she was only twenty-six.

Bob had known that, Nancy said, and had insisted it didn't matter...in the beginning. He said they could adopt. But then, as the years passed, he'd begun to brood about being the last in his line.

And so, one thing had led to another, Nancy told Jan. Their sex life had gone down the tube, because that special something just wasn't there anymore. Bob became more and more distant.

"It was Chocolate Fantasies that saved me," Nancy said. "Working with you gave my life some meaning. I even tried, again, with Bob. But now I know it was a matter of too little, too late. Bob was gone from me by then. But I still can't believe he turned to Clarisse. Crazy, isn't it? She's as old as I am. She's not going to be giving him any kids, either."

Strange, how femme fatales were not always glamorous Cleopatras, Jan reflected as she pulled into her driveway and brought the car to a stop. She leaned back, a deep weariness invading her.

This session with Nancy had exhausted her. She'd offered to stay the night at the Ellis home, but by then Nancy had gotten a grip on herself. She had promised—word of honor—that she wouldn't take another drink, or load up with sleeping pills once she went to bed.

Jan believed her. Somehow, Nancy had mustered some strength. Tonight, she'd be all right. But tomorrow?

Jan sighed, slipped out of the car and started across a strip of grass to the back steps...just as Doug MacKenzie closed the porch door and started down them.

The back porch light was on. Jan and Doug were both caught within the web of its faintly golden glow. Doug, halting three steps above Jan, stared down at her. Jan stared back. Neither of them moved. It was like they'd been captured within a single frame in a soundless movie.

Then Doug broke the spell. He took the rest of the steps quickly and came to a halt at Jan's side. His eyes fixed on her face, he said, "Chet told me he suspected you might be walking into a problem tonight. I hope that didn't happen."

She hadn't expected a comment like that. She sidestepped it and came out with what was on her mind. "Why are you here?"

Doug glanced over his shoulder at the house behind him. "I walked Chet back," he said.

"Back from where?"

"The cottage? He came over a while earlier."

"Oh?"

"He had a couple of things he wanted to talk to me about."

"Oh?"

"Why do you sound like that?" Doug asked, his eyebrows drawing together. "You're acting like I've done something wrong."

"What about Vicky?"

"What about her?"

"Where is she?"

"She was in bed by the time Chet and I got over here. What is this, Janny?"

"Vicky was at your house the other night until almost midnight." She was so overtired, so on edge, she couldn't keep herself from blurting out the words.

Doug's eyes narrowed. "So that's it," he said. "You must have seen Vicky coming back here to the house. Why didn't you say something about it?"

"To her?"

"Well, yes. Why the hell not to her?"

"I wanted to speak to you first."

"I've been available, Janny," Doug said.

"You were away for the weekend."

"So, I was away for the weekend. I've been here since the weekend. Exactly what is eating you?" As he spoke, Doug took hold of her arm, urged her toward the back steps.

He sat and tugged her down beside him. Jan didn't even try to resist. She was exhausted, both physically and emotionally.

His voice gentle, Doug said, "Why don't you get it off your chest?"

"All right," Jan said. "I want to know what my daughter was doing at your place until midnight the other night. I want to know what my son was doing at your place tonight."

"In each case," Doug said, "the twins had something they wanted to talk to me about."

"What?" Jan demanded.

Doug, his voice still gentle, said, "I can't tell you that, Janny."

She faced him, her voice hostile. "Why not?" she demanded.

"Because they were confiding in me," Doug said simply. "I would not consider violating their confidences . . . even for you. If you want to ask them why they sought me out, that's your business. Maybe even your right. I personally think that you need to talk to both Chet and Vicky. They have problems that need resolving. . . ."

"And they chose you to talk to about their problems?"

Jan saw Doug wince. He said, "You act as if I'm the last person in the world anyone would turn to in time of trouble. Well . . . maybe you feel that way. I haven't yet been able to figure out how you really feel about a lot of things, Janny. But when it comes to kids—I've had experience in listening. That's what this book I'm trying to write is all about. Today's kids—tomorrow's promise. The young people I deal with in the book are in very different circumstances than Chet and Vicky, true. Most of them live in war-torn countries, or in countries where the political strife is intense. But, to tell you the truth, I've been thinking of including a chapter about teenage life and problems in America. For all of our supposedly affluent society, being a teenager in the United States today isn't all that easy. . . ."

"And I suppose you intend to use Chet and Vicky as guinea pigs?" Jan accused.

Doug's eyes grew cold. So was his voice as he said, "No, I do not intend to use Chet and Vicky as guinea pigs. Your twins and I have become friends. I feel honored that they chose me to talk to about things that concern them. If I wrote about their concerns, I assure you I would protect their identities. And, I would only write about them with their permission. Contrary to what you may or may not think, I do not sabotage my friends, Janny."

Jan was silent for a moment. Then she said, "I'm sorry, Doug. I—I've been so on edge lately myself I'm afraid I've been blind to the twins' problems. Naturally I wish they had come to me rather than to... someone who was a stranger not that long ago. I don't mean to insult you when I say that. I've seen the rapport you've achieved with Chet and Vicky in such a short space of time. I envy your ability to relate to kids. As a parent, maybe it's something I could use a lot more of. But..."

The gentleness returned to Doug's voice. "What's put you so on edge, Janny?" he asked her.

Jan wanted to confess, "You." Because his proximity, having him live on her property, never knowing when she might suddenly come face-to-face with him, was indeed taking its toll. Each time they met, his effect on her was that much greater. It was an effect she was striving not only to ignore but to erase. And she wasn't doing very well...

She chose to discuss a safer subject. "I've been having some business problems," she said.

"At the town hall?" Doug asked.

"No, no. With Chocolate Fantasies. More precisely, with my partner."

She hadn't intended to be so specific.

"Money problems?" Doug suggested.

"No," Jan said quickly. "Personal problems. My partner's personal problems, really. She's having a very bad time with her marriage and it's affecting not only her work but her health, maybe even her sanity as well."

"That's where you were tonight? With her?"

"Yes."

"Chet said you'd received a kind of emergency summons."

Jan nodded. "Nancy's husband packed up his bags and walked out tonight. She called me. She was in a terrible state. Fortunately she calmed down. Or I wouldn't have left her. But tomorrow's going to be another day. When she has to face reality, I don't know what's going to happen to her. Her nerves are frazzled. She's taken up smoking again, she's drinking too much. Looking back I can see there were signposts I never recognized these past few months. I should have. I wish I had."

The words tumbled out, and to her astonishment Jan let them come.

"I've thought all along that Nancy and I were ideal partners. Now I'm not so sure," she admitted.

"Sounds like Nancy has a lot of problems," Doug observed. "Enough to make her go off track. But based on what you've told me about her in the past, I think she's a woman who'll work them out. Right now, she needs a break, don't you think?"

"Yes, of course she does. And I've been more than willing to give it to her. I'm just wondering..."

"Yes?"

"If Nancy's really become an alcoholic, I don't know how to handle it, Doug. She's the traveling partner in our business...."

"Would you want to change roles?"

"No. She's good at what she does, I'm good at what I do. I can't risk her going off on trips, though, if...well, if she's going to drink too much when she's traveling. Needless to say, it would be terrible for our business. But I'm far more concerned about Nancy personally. It would be so dangerous..."

Doug listened as Jan talked. Occasionally he commented, and gradually Jan began to relax, to feel more at peace with herself.

Doug, she realized was a very good listener. She knew that a large part of his work must involve interviewing people under circumstances where he had to be a good listener. Nevertheless, she was struck by this dimension in him. She found that—for the first time since he'd come back to Ellis Falls—she was looking at Douglas MacKenzie, the man, without seeing shadows of Doug MacKenzie, the boy who'd left her twenty years ago.

And the man impressed her. She could see why the twins had sought out Doug to talk to, to confide in. This time, it was she who was following in her children's path.

When, finally, she had said all she needed to say, Jan felt exhausted, yet also profoundly relieved. And, suddenly, very sleepy.

She yawned, and Doug chuckled. "It's quitting time, I'd say," he told her.

He stood and held out a helping hand. Jan took it, and let him pull her to her feet. But, once she was standing next to him, he didn't let go of her hand.

Instead, he slowly, deliberately, drew her into his arms.

His fingers touched her chin, tilting her head back. He seemed to be waiting for something. Maybe he expected her to withdraw? Jan became aware that he was moving slowly, cautiously. He was not about to push himself on her.

She didn't move. But, when Doug's lips sought hers, she was ready. Their lips fused in a kiss that was like nectar dispensed by the gods. The headiness, the sweetness, seeped deeper and deeper, until Jan was clinging to Doug, forgetful of yesterday, uncaring of tomorrow, living only in this moment as passion surfaced, and she yielded to the impulses of her body, mind and soul.

Then Doug broke that intimate contact, but he didn't let her go. He held her, gently, tenderly, and she rested her head against his shoulder, and let his warmth and caring and strength transfuse her.

Finally Doug said huskily, ''Time for you to go to bed, Janny.''

She nodded, like an obedient child.

Doug released her, then bent again to kiss her, but this time his lips only brushed hers in a fleeting caress.

Jan went up the back steps and into the house as if she were in a trance, putting one foot in front of the other by habit. She stood at the kitchen window, waiting until she saw lights go on in the cottage. Then she turned, and slowly walked to her bedroom, possessed by an overwhelming truth.

It would be easy, so easy, to fall in love with Doug MacKenzie for the second time in her life.

CHAPTER NINE

DOUG PULLED the front door of the cottage closed, and leaned against it. He felt as if he had been holding his breath for hours. Now he expelled it in a great, gusty sigh.

Janny would never know the effort it had taken to break away from her tonight. It had taken his last centigram of willpower to set her on her course up the back steps, and then trod down the path to the cottage alone.

Letting her go had been sheer agony. His body was protesting violently. His emotions were raw. He was wondering if he'd been a total damned fool to let logic keep the upper hand? Yet, he had known that if he came on too fast to Janny, too strong, he'd risk losing her altogether.

He couldn't let her go out of his life again. Not if he could possibly, possibly, help it.

Unfortunately the obstacles he saw strewn in their path were not merely stones; they were giant-size boulders. Though he would swear that Janny had wanted him just now as much as he'd wanted her, things were not right between them. She was annoyed because her kids were seeking him out, which was understandable. But far more important was the issue of whatever it was she was holding deep inside her and why she refused to let it out.

Doug went out to the kitchen, took a bottle of bourbon out of a cupboard, poured out a shot and downed it. The whiskey scorched his throat; he imagined he could feel its fiery path all the way to his stomach.

There were supper dishes in the sink. He splashed detergent on them, ran hot water, then left them in the soapy suds to soak till morning.

The computer in his study was still on. He'd been working when Chet had dropped by earlier. Now the screen winked at him, and he was tempted to try to put down some words before he called it a night. But he knew he couldn't write anything worthwhile tonight. He'd merely be escaping, trying to purge Janny from his mind and his heart in the hope of getting a good night's sleep without dreaming tormented dreams about her.

Doug saved the text on the screen onto a disk, then switched off the computer and went back to the kitchen. He made himself another drink, adding a hefty measure of soda and took it into the living room. Sprawled in an armchair, his long legs stretched out in front of him, he tried to make sense out of Janny's attitude toward him.

Whatever was griping her went way back. Twenty years back. But he couldn't believe she'd held a grudge for two decades because they'd lost track of each other.

For years, he'd kept the pictures he had of her and the letters she'd written to him once he moved to California. Then, when he got his first overseas assignment, he'd stored most of his belongings in his uncle's house in Pasadena. There'd been a fire in the attic, where the things were being kept, and so he'd lost all his mementos of her. But, by then, of course, Janny had gone on with her life just as he'd gone on with his. She must have been married by then, probably expecting the twins.

Doug decided that was the crux of the matter. It wasn't as if Janny had stayed single, cherishing her high school romance deep in her heart as the years went by. Hell, she'd lived a very full life. And certainly she'd been devoted to her husband. She still wore his wedding ring.

She'd put the past behind her just as he had, Doug reasoned. She'd been his first love; God knows he'd never forgotten her. He hoped he occupied an equally special place in her heart and memory. But he wasn't too sure of anything right now with Janny.

Perhaps it was not the past that was at issue at all, but the present. Had he done something since his return to Ellis Falls that had turned her off? Was she really resentful of the friendship that was being forged between the twins and himself?

Doug vetoed those possibilities. He could see Janny had been antipathetic toward him since the beginning. That had been evident enough when she made it so plain she didn't want to rent her cottage to him.

There had been a lot of talk about his mother before she finally left town, Doug knew that. He'd seen his mother a couple of times before she died, and she'd vented her resentment at the people of Ellis Falls and the way they'd treated her.

Maybe Janny had heard gossip about his mother a long time ago—which evidently had become pretty nasty—and she'd realized that her parents had been right about her high school sweetheart. He had been all wrong for her.

Doug didn't like that idea, but he had to admit it was possible.

He polished off his drink and went to bed.

CHET STOPPED BY the cottage the next afternoon after work.

"I was wondering if you're going to be using your wagon tonight?" he asked Doug.

"No," Doug said.

"Would it be okay if I took it? Some of the kids are going to have a cookout over at Deep Pines Lake. I told Vicky if it was okay with you about the wagon I could take her and Jim, and Cathy, and maybe one other couple." Chet grinned. "I promise it won't go beyond that. I won't cram the wagon full of kids."

"Is this all right with your mother?" Doug asked.

"I haven't asked her yet," Chet said. "I thought I'd check it out with you first."

Doug frowned. "Chet," he said honestly, "I don't want to get in the middle here. Your mother knows I'm willing to let you and Vicky use the wagon when I don't need it. But I think it's fairly obvious she's not keen on the idea."

"She has this thing about Vicky and me driving," Chet admitted.

"Yes, I know. We spoke about it, in fact. The reason for her concern about you driving is that she cares so much about you kids...."

"Then why did she urge us to take driver ed so we could get our licenses early?"

"I'd say she doesn't want to hold you back," Doug said. "On the other hand, she's human like the rest of us. She has certain fears. We all have certain fears."

Chet didn't answer.

Doug surveyed Jan's tall, good-looking son. He said, "Chet, regardless of the difference in our ages I feel we're friends."

"That goes for me, too." Chet looked faintly embarrassed at the admission.

"I don't want to violate our friendship," Doug went on. "But your mom is my friend, too. She has been for a long time. Also, she's your parent. She has rights I don't have. To add to that, she's done a damned good job of bringing you and Vicky up, single-handedly. I give her a lot of credit. I think maybe the two of you should give her more credit than you do. I know you feel she's overprotective sometimes, but you can understand where that comes from, can't you, if you really stop to think about it? She's had the sole responsibility for the two of you since you were little kids."

Chet said reluctantly, "I guess I've never looked at it that way."

"Well, you and Vicky are at an age where you should begin to see and understand that your mother hasn't always had an easy time of it. You should also be able to understand her motivations for what she does, even if you don't always agree with her. She deserves to have you level with her, Chet.

"Don't misunderstand me," Doug added hastily. "Anything you want to bounce off me is fine with me. I just don't want to think that the ball is always going to stop here, that's all. What I'm saying is . . . I want you to feel free to talk to me about anything you want to talk to me about. But, when it's an important issue, I'd like to think you're going to discuss it with your mom, too."

Chet said, "You're talking about college."

Doug nodded. "That's right. I keep thinking about our conversation last night and, to be honest with you, I don't see why you can't tell your mother what you told me."

"Because she wouldn't understand," Chet said.

Doug smiled wryly. "Chet," he said, "kids all through history have taken it for granted that their parents 'wouldn't understand.' You have more sense than that. You know that when your mother pushes you about college she's thinking about you, not herself. Do you seriously believe she'd want you to be unhappy?"

"My father was a teacher," Chet said. "Maybe you know that. He had his master's degree. Evidently he was great for education, even though apparently it never bothered him that my mother hadn't gone to college. She married him when she was just a couple of years out of high school. I think, later, she wished she'd gone on to get her degree. But, by then, she had Vicky and me. Then, my father died...."

Chet said, "I think parents have this idea they should do their utmost to give their kids what they didn't have themselves. I don't think they think enough about whether that's what the kids want or not. Sometimes," he added bitterly, "I wish I'd bombed on the SATs. But I got good scores. Good enough so I'd probably be admitted to most places I might apply to. The kind of colleges Mom wants me to go to. She inherited quite a bit of insurance money from Dad. She stowed away practically all of it, and I don't know how many times she's told me there'll be plenty if I want to be a doctor or a lawyer or maybe President of the United States."

"There's nothing wrong with what you actually want to do," Doug said.

Chet smiled grimly. "Mom wouldn't agree with that," he said. "Mom loves flowers, trees, shrubs, nature...but she takes all those things pretty much for granted. If I went into landscaping as a career, she'd feel I wasn't doing much more than pushing a lot of dirt around. Grady Brett, for instance, who owns the landscaping firm I work for, has never moved in the same social circle with Mom and her family."

Neither did I, Doug thought silently.

"I'm not saying Mom's a snob," Chet went on. "I know what she wants is the best for Vicky and me. But I've been working for Grady since I was eleven years old...and like I told you last night, I love it. I love working with the soil, making things grow, making places more beautiful. Grady says I have a real talent for it. Grady figures in maybe eight or ten more years he's going to want to retire. He says he'd like to see me take over his business at that point. I don't need a law degree, or anything like it, to run Grady's business, Doug."

"No," Doug agreed. "But that doesn't mean you should rule out post-high school education. As I pointed out to you last night, if you go to a horticultural school you'll learn techniques and methods that can be of great value to both Grady Brett and yourself. You can learn the scientific aspects of what you're doing now, and that's a kind of knowledge that will pay off for you. As I understand it, the University of Massachusetts has an excellent school in Stockbridge, which isn't that far away. There are others. Yale, I think, for one. Seems to me that's the line you should explore, Chet.''

Chet shook his head. ''Mom would never go for it,'' he said. ''She wants me in a career in a major city, in an office where I'll have to wear a three-piece suit to work every day. Or else teaching in a university.''

Doug said, ''Why not talk to her about it, Chet. You may be wrong.''

''I guess before the summer's out I'm going to have to talk to her about it,'' Chet admitted, ''or I'll be trapped. She keeps piling up the college catalogs. Keeps pressuring me to fill out application forms. So far, I've hedged. But, before school starts again I know she's going to pin me down.''

Chet looked at Doug, his smile rueful. ''My big problem is that I love her,'' he said, ''and I hate to disappoint her.''

JAN YIELDED, that night, to the idea of Chet's borrowing Doug's station wagon to go to the lake with his friends. She asked him to be back by eleven. Chet tried briefly to stretch the hour till midnight, then let it go. As it was, Jan didn't relax until she heard the station wagon pull into the side yard just as the grandfather clock in the living room struck eleven. Then she scurried to her room, because she didn't want her kids to know she'd been waiting up for them. At the moment, that implied a lack of trust.

The late July weather turned scorchingly hot. Jan saw very little of Doug; they literally met in passing, usually when he'd been out shopping for something, and she was on her way home from Chocolate Fantasies, Nancy's, or the town hall.

Sometimes, she wished she could stretch out the hours. It was difficult to give Nancy as much time as she wanted to, these days, and to keep up with everything else, too. Also, she knew Nancy was becoming too dependent on her, which wasn't good. It was one thing to be there when a friend needed you. It was another thing to be in danger of becoming that friend's personal crutch.

But Nancy was getting thinner, still smoking and maybe going back to the vodka bottle when she was alone. At least she didn't drink when they were together.

Jan had to applaud Nancy for making the effort to come into Chocolate Fantasies each day, regardless of the summer schedule they'd set for themselves, so she could get the fall orders together and the winter orders lined up. But she couldn't help but wonder whether Nancy was capable, right now, of attending to business as it should be attended to. She kept having the feeling that she should recheck Nancy's work herself, but she couldn't do that with Nancy present. And, she hated the thought of sneaking back into the office after hours to go over what Nancy had done.

At least whatever had been bothering Vicky seemed to be on hold. Vicky was her usual exuberant self. So, maybe Doug had solved her problem for her, whatever it was.

Chet, though, was still preoccupied. Jan tried to find a right moment in which to come out and ask him what was bothering him, but there never seemed to be one.

Most of all…when she did run into Doug, she felt uncomfortable around him. The memory of his kiss haunted her. He'd demonstrated so graphically how much she was missing in her life. But he was the last person in the world she should become involved with, no matter how greatly he tempted her, no matter how much he attracted her. Come the first of the year, he'd be moving on.

Did she want to be his leftover girl twice?

August tenth would mark the twins' seventeenth birthday. Jan wanted to have a surprise party for them, but she knew she couldn't manage it all by herself. Someone had to get the twins out of the way to give the invited guests time to arrive. Preparations had to be done while Chet and Vicky weren't around. Phone calls made to classmates whom she knew were close friends. They, in turn, could extend invitations to those who should be included.

At first, August tenth seemed reasonably far away. But one day Jan admitted that time was going to run out on her if she didn't swing into action. And, she had to admit to herself that the logical person to ask for help was Doug.

Her opportunity came on a Wednesday when the selectmen had a short morning meeting, for once. Jan stopped briefly at Chocolate Fantasies. The day was hot, sultry, promising thunderstorms. Leona reported that business was slow. Also, Vicky had called to say that she had a ride in to work, so her mother didn't need to bother to drive home to get her.

Jim's decrepit old car was parked at the curb as Jan turned into her driveway, and Vicky was crossing the lawn to meet him.

Jan strolled toward her and couldn't refrain from asking, "Does Jim have the day off?"

"No," Vicky said. "He's on his lunch hour, so we'd better get going."

Vicky looked as if she might say something more, but she didn't. On an impulse, Jan reached out and gave her daughter a hug. Vicky looked startled and, surprisingly, tears welled in her eyes. But before Jan could ask her what the matter was, she hurried off.

They were going to have to have their long over-due talk, Jan decided as she climbed the back steps. She'd been avoiding confrontation with Vicky. Now, she knew she needed to come out and tell her daughter she'd seen her coming back from Doug's that night. She needed to ask Vicky what had prompted her to seek Doug's advice. She had to make Vicky realize that she, also, was here for her, ready to lend a listening ear or a helping hand.

JAN TOOK TIME out to drink a glass of ice water before approaching Doug about the birthday party. Then she deliberated about whether she should go to the cottage, or ask Doug to come over to the house. His station wagon was parked at the edge of the path. She knew he was home.

She decided the least she could do was go to him.

Doug opened the door to her a few minutes later, and he could not possibly have looked more astonished.

He was wearing a pair of dark-rimmed glasses, which he evidently used for close-up work, and he ripped them off. Then he peered at Jan again as if to make sure it really was her he was seeing.

"Come in," he invited.

She stepped into the living room. It was the first time she'd been in the cottage since the weekend when she'd brought lemonade over at Chet's request. She saw that Doug had rearranged the furniture, and she liked what he'd done with it. His arrangement made the room look larger. He'd bought a TV. There'd never been one in the cottage. When her parents were living here they'd come over to the house to watch television.

There was a VCR next to the TV, and a stack of videocassettes on a side table. Doug had bought a new rug that splashed color into the pine-paneled room, and accurately picked up the tones in the drapes and slipcovers. He had a big bunch of zinnias on the coffee table that emphasized summer's bright sun colors. There were a few books and newspapers strewn around, plus a couple of magazines. The room looked comfortable and well lived-in. Doug had converted the cottage into a home, Jan thought. This was something she'd not expected. She had thought he'd be a person who, like a nomadic Arab, folded up his tent when he wanted to move on and disappeared into the night. But Doug even had a small assortment of bric-a-brac strewn around. Carved animal figures, she noted, among them.

He followed her gaze and said, "My collection, such as it is. I've picked up the animals in different places I've been. They make small, easily portable souvenirs."

There was a real animal, curled up in an armchair. Abigail looked as if she'd always belonged exactly where she was.

Jan frowned. "I hope the cats—and Floppy, too— aren't pestering you," she said.

"Not at all," Doug said. "I like having them stop by. I admit, I usually have a tidbit or two on hand for them. I hope you don't object to that?"

"No...though feeding them does encourage them."

"Well, I rather like to encourage them," Doug said. He gestured toward the couch. "Sit down, won't you?" he suggested politely. "I just made a pitcher of iced tea. Care for a glass?"

"Thank you." She nodded.

They sounded like two strangers . . . but it was better that way, Jan thought as she settled down on the couch and noticed he'd also bought a couple of new toss pillows. Again, she lauded his good eye for color.

Doug brought back two glasses of iced tea, and took a chair opposite the couch. He flashed Jan that lopsided grin of his and asked, "To what do I owe the honor of this visit?"

"I've come to ask a favor of you," Jan admitted.

"Oh?" he queried, the grin still lingering.

"The twins will be seventeen on the tenth, and I feel like the tenth's right on top of me. I want to give them a surprise party but . . ."

Before she elaborated on the "but," Jan took a couple of sips of tea. Doug had flavored it with lemon, sugared it slightly. It was delicious . . . and very refreshing on this hot day.

Maybe the tea fortified her. Whatever, she found it easier to outline her party plans to him than she'd expected it would be.

When she finished, she asked, "Would you have time to help out a bit on this?"

It was also occurring to her that she'd barged in here in the middle of the day, and undoubtedly had interrupted his work. Being on his turf—temporary turf, but very definitely his now—somehow made her freshly aware of the fact that this was Douglas MacKenzie she was dealing with. An internationally famous celebrity, though he surely never called attention to that fact, never stressed his own fame or even touched on it, for that matter.

She sensed, rather than saw, his annoyance. And heard the very slight edge to his voice as he said, "Of course I'd have time to help with a party for the twins. I can think of few things I'd rather do."

"That's really great," Jan murmured.

Doug's smile returned. "I'll warn you, Janny, this isn't going to be easy." When she looked at him questioningly, he added, "It's going to be a challenge to try to pull the wool over the twins' eyes, so they don't get wind of what's going on. You have two sharp kids there. We're going to have to keep our wits about us and be sure we don't make any slips."

Jan gave him a return smile. "You're right," she said. "I hadn't really thought about that. I just hope their friends know how to keep a secret."

"Kids can be amazingly good at keeping secrets if they're motivated," Doug said. "Why don't I call Al and Mike this evening and get the ball rolling? And, Cathy. And, Jim."

"That would be great of you," Jan said.

"Then consider it done. Since it may not be too easy for us to get together and talk about this without one of the other of the twins showing up, how about if he have our discussions over a couple of dinners? Maybe at the inn?"

"That's not necessary, Doug."

Again...Jan was aware of his impatience with her, even though the pleasant expression on his face remained as if it had been engraved there. And there was only the very slightest telltale edge to his voice as he said, "Maybe it's not necessary, Janny, but personally I'd enjoy it. It'll be fun to map things out together. Also, we can figure out a motif for the party. Maybe I can pick up some supplies and favors in Pittsfield. I have to go over there at some point the next few days to get some more computer paper.''

Doug paused. ''Maybe you'd like to trek over with me when I go, and then you can help pick out the party stuff.''

''Maybe,'' Jan hedged.

Doug felt as if he had won a victory. A very slight victory, but nevertheless a victory. He intended to translate Janny's ''maybe'' into a commitment to at least go as far as Pittsfield with him. And, to go out to dinner a couple of times.

He blessed the twins for having a birthday coming up.

This was the first chance he'd had to do something together with Janny. Alone together, since secrecy was imperative.

Doug intended to make the most of it.

CHAPTER TEN

"HOW ABOUT TAKING OFF for Pittsfield in about an hour? We can have a late lunch on the way back."

It was nine-thirty Thursday morning. Jan had answered the phone on the second ring, expecting Nancy to be the caller. Four out of five calls she'd been getting lately were from Nancy.

When she heard Doug's voice, she felt a sudden weakness in her knees.

He sounded as cheerful as the morning sunshine.

"You don't have to go into Chocolate Fantasies today, do you?" he persisted.

"Well..."

"And you don't have to go into the town hall, do you?"

She didn't.

"Meet you in an hour," Doug said, and hung up before Jan could come up with an excuse to decline.

This was crazy, she thought as she washed up the breakfast dishes and then went to her room to dress. She yearned to go to Pittsfield with Doug. The idea of taking even such a short and innocuous trip with him made her feel like a girl going out on a special date. On the other hand, she was afraid of being alone with him. She reacted too intensely to him.

But this was daytime, bright daytime, golden first-of-August sunshine splashing over everything.

Grow up, Jan advised herself.

Chet had left for work ages ago. Vicky and a friend, Patty Mulligan, had set off for town to do some exploratory browsing for school clothes. Jan left a note on the kitchen table, in case one of the twins should come home unexpectedly.

"Gone out for a while," she wrote. "Be back by midafternoon."

As she went out to meet Doug, she wondered why she hadn't leveled and simply written, "I'm driving over to Pittsfield with Doug, and we're going to stop somewhere for lunch."

Doug was leaning against the station wagon. He'd picked a daisy in the field and was twirling it between his fingers. He straightened when he saw Jan, smiling a slow and easy smile.

"You look terrific," he said.

She was wearing a pretty yellow cotton dress. She'd twisted her dark red hair into a coil on the top of her head, mainly because she liked to keep it off her neck in hot weather. Nevertheless, the hairstyle suited her. She couldn't deny that she liked the look of appreciation in Doug's eyes. It was a look that made her feel like she was someone special. After all, she rationalized, now and then everyone needed to be made to feel they were special.

Doug opened the door of the wagon, then handed her the daisy. "I should have picked you a whole bunch of these," he said. "Daisies go well with your dress."

She had a sudden memory of Doug, years ago, on a weekend day when they'd gone off on a picnic together. They'd spread a blanket in a field where daisies grew. Doug had picked one of the flowers and plucked its petals, grinning as he singsonged, "She loves me, she loves me not..."

"What's the verdict?" Jan had teased.

"She loves me," Doug had reported. He'd tickled her lips with the shorn daisy then leaned forward, bringing his face close to hers, his eyes even bluer than the vivid summer sky. She'd been overpowered by the nearness of him, the warmth of him, the clean, masculine scent of him. She'd reached out to him, and he'd clasped her in his strong, young arms. Their feelings for each other, their responses, had been as natural as the air they breathed....

Now she watched him walk around to his side of the wagon. He was wearing pale gray summer slacks and a gray-and-white-striped shirt. His hair had been a shade longer back then, but it still had that deep velvet texture and was almost as dark as night, without even a smattering of silver at the temples, so far. He had kept that trim, well-toned physique; except now she was looking at a man, not a boy. A controlled, extremely well-developed man, who carried himself with an air of confidence the Doug MacKenzie she'd known had strived for, but never quite achieved.

From the distance of even a few feet, Doug gave the illusion of looking as young—almost as young—as he had back in high school. Up close, she could see that time had left a few ineradicable marks on his face. Little lines that fanned out from his eyes—from laughing, or maybe from years of squinting into the bright sunlight of remote and exotic places. Tighter lines, fanning from his nostrils to his lips, that might have been defined as tension lines except that when he smiled they seemed to fade away. Some frown lines crossed his forehead; not deep ones, but they were there. But these small evidences of the years that had passed stamped his face with character that hadn't been there twenty years ago.

The boy she had known had changed, even as she had changed. He had become a man, just as she had become a woman, Jan thought, with a twinge of sadness.

Those years they had spent apart could not be negated. They could not erase them, no matter how much either of them might want to. They could not go back . . .

Jan felt as if a cloud suddenly had been cast over the day's perfection. She watched Doug put on a pair of sunglasses, then smile across at her as he turned the key in the ignition switch. And it struck her that she didn't even know Douglas MacKenzie, the man. Ever since he'd come back to Ellis Falls, she'd unconsciously been acting toward him as if he were Doug MacKenzie, the boy. . . .

Doug chattered casually as they started out, then fell silent. Jan did not pick up the conversation. They traveled the back roads over to Route 7, then headed north, crossing under the Mass Pike. The scenery was gorgeous. The Berkshires were dressed in dazzling shades of summer green, and now and then they came upon a deep blue jewel of a lake that was like an unexpected gift from nature. Once on Route 7, they drove through one picturesque New England town after another. Lovely old homes lined tree-bordered streets. Classic white churches lifted their spires to the sky. "Progress" had infiltrated in the form of shopping centers and condominiums, but there was still plenty of charm.

Doug, observing the scenery, said, "This is a beautiful part of the country. A beautiful part of the world."

Jan nodded. "I agree. Though I don't have much grounds for comparison."

"Never done any traveling, Janny?"

"Not much. Jonas and I went to Quebec on our honeymoon. I've been to New York three or four times, but never long enough to get a real feel for the city. The size and scope and pace of Manhattan dazzles me. But that's about it."

"I love to travel," Doug commented. "And I've surely done my share of it. There are few places I haven't been. But . . . there's something to be said for roots."

"Is that why you came back to Ellis Falls?" she asked, half teasing. "To reestablish your roots?"

His smile was wry. "I'm afraid my roots here never went very deep," he admitted. "I was born in western New York State—Utica. My parents came here when I was about four. But...my Ellis Falls roots are the only ones I've ever had. I just wanted to find a quiet, familiar place off the beaten track where I could work. But I guess maybe my subconscious was sending me messages."

He slanted a glance in Jan's direction, and he said, "Regardless, I'm glad I came back." And then he threw her an unexpected curve. "Are you?" he asked her.

She didn't know what to say.

Was she glad he'd come back? How did one define "glad," in this instance? Doug's return had stirred up so much. Until his reappearance, she'd been content with her life. Now she wondered if she'd be content with it again, once he went away. When he'd kissed her, the other night, she'd realized that she'd built a dam inside herself at some point way back in time, and the dam was in danger of crumbling. The resulting flood, should it happen, would be disastrous for her.

She wasn't sure she could pull herself together twice, where Doug MacKenzie was concerned.

She glanced at him, and saw that he was staring straight ahead, a set look on his face. She knew her hesitation had given her away. If she'd been glad he'd come back, she would have said so immediately. Instead, she'd held back the words... and she still couldn't speak them because she still didn't know.

"Doug..." she began.

"It was a stupid question, Janny," Doug said evenly. "Forget it. Listen... about the twins' party. Have you thought up a theme for it?"

He was offering a diversion. Jan latched on to it gratefully. "When I think about planning a birthday party for the twins I mainly concentrate on having tons of food and two birthday cakes," she confessed.

"Two birthday cakes?"

"Yes. The twins weren't very old before they decided they were being shortchanged in having only one cake. Every other person, they pointed out, had his or her own birthday cake. They were two people, it just wasn't right they couldn't have two cakes. Anyway, Chet likes chocolate frosting on his cake and Vicky likes white frosting on hers. So... for years we've had twin cakes."

Doug chuckled. Then he said, "Well, twin cakes won't interfere with the theme I have in mind. If you go for it, that is. How about putting on a Hawaiian luau for the twins?''

Jan smiled. ''In the food department, I don't think I could handle anything more complicated than hamburgers and hot dogs with lots of potato chips and pickles,'' she admitted.

''We don't have to deviate too much from that menu,'' Doug said. ''We might add a few extra touches—maybe chunks of fresh pineapple, a few things like that. I was thinking more of the atmosphere. We could string up paper lanterns outside, and put out some extension speakers from your stereo so we could play Hawaiian music. We could have paper leis and maybe a hula contest . . .''

''You are ambitious,'' Jan said.

''I've never had a hand in planning a birthday party for teenagers,'' Doug said. ''Or, for kids of any age, for that matter. I think it would be fun to have a luau of sorts . . . unless you'd rather we do something else.''

Jan laughed. ''If we can achieve a luau in Ellis Falls,'' she said, ''I think it would be great.''

The party store they went to in Pittsfield didn't have much in the way of material for a luau, however. Jan bought some bright colored paper napkins and crepe paper streamers and candles for the cake.

Out on the street again, Doug suddenly said, ''I don't know why I didn't think of it sooner. There's a place in New York that specializes in Hawaiian stuff for parties. I can get the leis there and everything else we'll want.''

''Doug,'' Jan said quickly, ''you're not thinking of making a special trip to New York for this, are you?''

He shook his head. ''I can handle it on the phone,'' he told her. ''Think no more about it, Janny. Let me take over the theme stuff. You handle the two birthday cakes. We can join forces in working out a menu. Okay?''

His enthusiasm was contagious. "Okay," she said. Then added cautiously, "Don't go overboard, though, Doug."

She was thinking that party decorations could be outrageously expensive, and although she wanted to give the twins the best party possible there were limits to her budget.

"I'll keep things in line," Doug promised rather cryptically, and she let it go at that.

Doug mentioned a charming old inn in Lenox for lunch. Jan—knowing that lunch in such a place would be a leisurely affair—was tempted to suggest they just stop for a sandwich somewhere. But she couldn't quite resist the idea of relaxing for a time in such lovely surroundings.

They ate in a glass-enclosed room that looked out over a garden where summer flowers bloomed in an eye-catching profusion of color. Doug kept the conversation light. They didn't touch upon the twins, or Ellis Falls, or their past relationship. Rather, Doug asked her questions about herself, as if they'd met just a short time ago and this was one of their first dates together.

Doug led her into telling him about the kind of music she liked, the kind of art she liked, the kind of books she liked to read.

"I've been going back to the classics," she admitted. "Reading Jane Austin and Henry James, and some of the Russian writers. The sort of literature most of us groaned over in high school."

Doug smiled at her. "Very impressive," he said.

"Wait, I also go in for occult stuff now and then," Jan confessed. "There's nothing like a good ghost story on a rainy October night."

He laughed. "What do you put on the stereo for background?"

"Mood music, like echoes of the sea." She grinned. "Would you believe?"

"Yes, because I've done the same thing, or close to it."

"You asked me about art. I love the French Impressionists. Maybe someday I'll get rich, rich, rich—and if I do, I'm going to buy an original Monet!"

"I think I'd buy an original Rodin if I were that rich," Doug confessed. "And maybe a small château in the Loire Valley. Vineyards with it, of course. I'd put out a choice selection of wine under my own label."

"You like France best of the places you've lived in?"

"I haven't really lived in many places, Janny," he said. "Long visits—recurring visits, sometimes. Yes, I like France. The French countryside, that's to say. Paris is Paris—it can be one of the most exciting cities in the world, but it's still a big, noisy city. When it comes to cities—maybe it's crazy, but one of the cities I spent some time in I like almost best of all is Las Palmas, in the Canary Islands. I was there for Carnival time—it was like a month-long fiesta." He drew a deep breath and said—and meant it—"I wish you'd been there with me."

Jan didn't respond to that, and Doug didn't pursue it. He switched the subject and told her about other places he'd been, things that he'd done. He'd visited most of the world's great museums, been to the famous opera houses, heard the masterpiece symphonies played by the finest orchestras. Truly, Jan thought, the range of his experience was extraordinary.

Later, driving back to Ellis Falls, Jan couldn't remember when she'd ever discussed so many diverse subjects with anyone in the course of a single luncheon. She certainly liked what she was learning about this "new" Douglas MacKenzie, who was an astonishingly attractive and fascinating man.

That evening, though, nostalgia claimed Jan again, and she yielded to it. The twins were watching a movie about a rock star on TV. Jan escaped to her room, settled down with her book, but she couldn't confine her attention to the printed page.

She wandered to the window and looked out…and saw lights in the cottage. Doug had mentioned that he planned to work tonight. She could picture him going over notes, or putting down new material on his word processor. And, even while she thought about the lovely time the two of them had shared today, sweet, long-ago memories swirled.

She'd not intended to get down the blue cardboard box again. But, she did. She sat on her bed, surveying the faded gardenia corsages and the prom dance programs and the other miscellany that were the only tangible remains of her long-ago romance with Doug.

She picked up the yearbook and carried it over to her armchair and, settling down again, started to turn the pages.

She'd forgotten that Doug had been in the debating society in high school. He'd also been on the football team, and he'd participated in a number of one-time events so he appeared in quite a few of the photos scattered throughout the album. And then there was, of course, his formal, senior-class portrait.

Jan studied the portrait, and the youthful features looked so soft, compared to the Doug MacKenzie of today. He'd been almost startlingly handsome as a boy, but maturity had improved him.

She was thinking about that when the door opened and Vicky walked in.

Vicky evidently had been arguing with Chet. Her eyes were snapping, her cheeks were flushed, and she began angrily, "Mummy, I wish you'd tell Chet..."

Then her eyes fell on the yearbook her mother was holding and her gaze swept on to the bed, and the open, blue cardboard box.

Jan snapped the yearbook closed, and wished it weren't so large. She clutched it, wishing she could thrust it under a chair, and make it disappear.

Vicky said, "Is that your high school yearbook?"

"Yes," Jan said, and stood up, determined to reach the blue cardboard box before Vicky did. But Vicky was closer. She peered into the box curiously, and picked up the faded gardenia corsage.

"Mummy," she said, "these things must go back to when you were dating Doug MacKenzie...."

Jan plucked the corsage out of Vicky's fingers, returned it and the yearbook to the box, and replaced the box's cover. "Just a lot of old things I shouldn't have bothered saving," she said, then added hastily, "Doug and I were talking about a couple of our classmates today. I remembered a few things about them when we were in school together, and I wanted to check."

The excuse sounded as lame as it was. Jan was aware Vicky was looking at her curiously, and she couldn't blame her. She said quickly, "What's the problem with you and Chet?"

"Nothing important," Vicky said. "Mummy... when you were in high school with Doug..."

"Vicky, I don't want to get into a discussion about what it was like when I was in high school," Jan said bluntly. "Maybe some other time. I was about to head for bed when you came in."

"Why do you dislike him so?" Vicky asked.

Jan stared at her. "What?"

"I asked you why you dislike Doug so much, Mummy," Vicky said. "On the surface you're usually nice enough to him, but it shows through."

"What do you think shows through, Vicky?"

"Sometimes I think you hate him," Vicky said.

"That's ridiculous."

"No. Sometimes I think something must have happened between the two of you when you were back in school that made you hate him. Doug doesn't say much about you..."

"I don't like the thought the two of you have said anything about me," Jan stated hotly. "It's enough that you've been out to the cottage pouring your heart out to him about yourself."

The words came out, and she couldn't take them back. Vicky stood very still, Jan felt she could actually see the color draining from her face.

"Is that what Doug called it?" Vicky asked.

"No," Jan said quickly. She sighed; it felt as though the sigh went all the way to her toes. "I should have brought this up with you sooner," she said. "I saw you come back from the cottage one night. It was almost midnight. I told Doug I'd seen you."

"What did he say?" Vicky looked even whiter.

"He said you'd come out to talk to him about something. He said it was in confidence and he wouldn't betray your trust." She couldn't help herself, she flung the accusation out at Vicky. "How do you think that makes me feel?" she demanded. "If you had something to confide, why didn't you come to me instead of going to a—a stranger?"

"By the time I went and talked to Doug I felt he was my friend," Vicky said, her voice wavering slightly. "I feel he's the best friend I've ever had—the best grown-up friend, that is. Chet feels the same way about him. He's a person you can talk to, a person who understands."

"And I don't?"

"No, you don't."

Stung, Jan stared at her daughter. "How can you say that?" she asked. "You haven't even tried me."

"I've tried you," Vicky said. "Maybe I should say I've tried to try you. But you haven't listened. You've been busy, or you just haven't wanted to listen. Sometimes it's hard enough to say something in the first place, Mummy. But when the person you're trying to talk to can't bother to even try to understand . . ."

"That's what you think about me?"

"How can I help it?"

"All right, then, suppose you try me? Suppose you tell me what was so important you had to go out to the cottage and talk to Doug about it in the middle of the night."

Vicky stared at one of the pale pink roses that bordered Jan's bedroom rug. "I thought I was pregnant," she said.

Jan sat down abruptly on the side of her bed. Shock rippled through her in an icy wave that made her feel nauseated. Things like this happened to other people and their children. But not to her, not to Vicky, not to Chet.

Vicky said, "Mummy, nothing happened."

Jan raised her eyes. "What do you mean, nothing happened?"

"My period was late. I panicked. I didn't know what to do. So I . . . I went to Doug."

"I see."

"No, you don't see. Doug calmed me down. But what he told me was that if I didn't get my period within the next couple of days I had to go to you. He said he wouldn't tell you what I'd told him. But . . . I had to go to you."

"I can imagine he didn't want the responsibility," Jan said dryly.

"No," Vicky protested. "No, that's not what it was at all. Doug's the last person in the world who'd sidestep taking responsibility. But, you're my mother. That's what he made me see. You're my mother and somehow I—" Vicky broke off helplessly.

Jan said, "So, you got your period."

"Yes."

"And you decided not to say anything to me."

"There wasn't anything to say to you then," Vicky said. Then she said slowly, again staring at the faded rosebud, "That's not so. Yes, there was. The same thing I've been trying to say to you for a long time."

Jan frowned. "What are you talking about, Vicky?"

"For a long time I... I've tried to talk to you," Vicky said. "Each time...you've been busy or Chet's come in or something's come up so I...I just haven't been able to say what I need to say."

"What have you needed to say?"

"It's not that simple," Vicky said. As she spoke, she looked so young and fragile and vulnerable it made Jan ache, deep inside, to watch her.

Vicky had feared she was pregnant, which meant Vicky and Jim had been having sex. For how long? And where had she been all this time? Hadn't she seen that her daughter was growing up? Had she forgotten what *she'd* been doing when she was Vicky's age? How she'd felt? How in love she'd been with Doug? How impossible it had become for the two of them to resist each other?

Jan said, "You're talking about protection. That's it, isn't it?"

Vicky nodded.

"I know you're saying I wasn't hearing you," Jan went on, "but you should have made me listen."

"I couldn't," Vicky said. "It's hard enough..."

She didn't have to finish. Jan knew what she meant. She could imagine herself going to her own mother, when she was in high school, and trying to initiate a conversation about birth control. The idea was unthinkable. Instead, she and Doug had taken chances.

Jan folded her hands in her lap, and began to feel more in control. "You and I," she said to Vicky, "should have talked about a lot of things a long time ago. I've tried—I've always tried—to instill a high

moral standard in you and Chet. About everything . . . including the way you deal with other people in your life, and the way you handle yourselves. I
think—I hope—I've also taught you that your body
is a very precious part of you. So is your mind. So is
your soul. None should be given lightly, Vicky."

"Mummy . . . I haven't given anything lightly."

"You're so young," Jan said, almost as if she were
speaking to herself. "You're still so very young. . . ."

"To you," Vicky said with a sweet-sad little smile.
"But not to me, Mummy. Jim and I . . . yes, we're
young. But we're also growing up. Do you know what
I mean? We've *been* growing up, and I don't think
that people, once they're older, ever remember how
hard that is."

"I remember," Jan said softly. "But . . . things
change, Vicky. Love changes. You change. Nothing's an absolute in life. The way you are. The way
you feel. It all changes as time goes by. One day you
may not feel about Jim the way you do now—though
I know that's hard, perhaps impossible, for you to
believe.

"I suppose," Jan said, "mostly . . . mostly . . . I don't
want you to be hurt."

"Jim would never hurt me," Vicky said, and hearing that, Jan wanted to cry.

Twenty years ago she would have said that Doug
MacKenzie would never have hurt her. Nothing—no
one—could have made her believe that Doug would
discard their love as casually as if it were a faded
flower. She'd even kept the faded flower, she thought
wryly. Two of them. The gardenias, brown and
wilted, yet still with that faint scent that could evoke
memories of an early summer evening and dancing in

Doug's arms, and being so sure that the moon and the stars were where they should be, and all was right with her world.

Jan said gently, "Someday, when you're a mother yourself, you'll better understand the way I feel right now. Sort of mixed up, Vicky," she confessed. "Because I have to accept the fact that you're not a little girl anymore. I have to accept the fact that you're a young woman, and you and I need to relate to each other in a different way."

She managed a shaky smile. "I'll call Dr. Anderson in the morning," she promised, "and we'll make an appointment."

CHAPTER ELEVEN

DOUG LOOKED PLEASED with himself. "The situation's under control," he announced. "I contacted the place in New York. We'll have everything in the way of Hawaiian atmosphere except a smoldering volcano."

"Doug," Jan protested. She wished she wasn't so conditioned to automatically consider costs, but she'd felt she had to be that way ever since Jonas died. She'd kept most of his insurance money intact, securely invested for the twins' education, except for a relatively small "starter" she'd permitted herself to get Chocolate Fantasies launched. Before becoming involved in Chocolate Fantasies, she'd worked as secretary to the high school principal, a job she'd detested. But it had paid better than most jobs in Ellis Falls.

Now, thanks to the success of the chocolate business and the added stipend from her part-time selectman's job, she had a little more financial latitude. But not that much, she warned herself.

Doug, to her chagrin, got her message. He said, "Janny... I hope you'll let the Hawaiian touches be a birthday gift to the twins from me. It's not that much."

Embarrassed, she said, "I wouldn't think of it, Doug. After all, it's up to me to put on the twins' party. It's more than enough that you're helping with the organizing, and—''

''Still can't let anyone into your act, can you, Janny?'' Doug asked, the smile that had been so exuberant a moment before fading fast.

''It isn't that.''

''What is it, then?''

''Just that I...''

''I'm going to ask one more time,'' Doug said. ''Otherwise, I'll cancel the order for the Hawaiian stuff. May I please provide the background material for the twins' party?''

Why was it he had this ability to make her feel ashamed of herself? Jan felt as though she'd been backed into a corner.

''That would be very kind of you,'' she said a little less than graciously.

''I wasn't intending to be kind,'' Doug said. ''It's something I want to do, that's all.''

It was early afternoon. Jan had spent the morning at Chocolate Fantasies and then at the town hall, then had come home and fixed herself iced tea and a sandwich for lunch. When Doug appeared unexpectedly, she'd offered him a glass of iced tea and he'd accepted. Now they were sitting opposite each other at the kitchen table.

The day was hot and sultry. Jan said, ''I wish we'd have a thunderstorm—a good one. Maybe it'd cool things off.''

''Well, I noticed some big black clouds in the sky on my way over here,'' Doug said. ''Incidentally, I had calls from both Mike and Al last night. They have the guest list well in hand. We're going to have a lot of kids around, Janny.''

"How many?"

"I don't have an accurate head count yet. But I will have, in plenty of time to get the food.

"By the way," he added, "I met your friend Nancy's husband yesterday."

"Bob Ellis?"

"Yes. He's heading a committee for a fund drive to benefit the hospital and I guess your fellow Selectman Bartlett Folger put him in touch with me," Doug said. "They're thinking in terms of a holiday ball during the Christmas season. I was asked to serve on the committee for the ball. Matter of fact, they're wondering if maybe I'd be master of ceremonies." He grinned. "I agreed to be on the committee," he said, "but I intend to sidestep the MC bit."

"Why? You should make a very good MC."

"Are you saying I've developed into an extrovert?"

His tone was light, Jan tried to match it. "Well," she allowed, "you'd have to be something of an extrovert to hold the kind of job you have, wouldn't you?" She saw his expression change, and added carefully, "All I'm saying is, you're used to meeting the public, accustomed to appearing on national TV..."

Doug frowned. "Maybe our definition of extrovert differs," he said. "I don't picture myself as that kind of outgoing personality. Anyway...to get back to Bob Ellis, he seemed like a nice guy. He said he was in college when we were in high school, which is why I don't remember him from back in the early days."

"Bob wasn't around much when we were in high school," Jan agreed. "Summers, he traveled a lot. Went to Europe, mountain climbing out in Colorado and the California Sierras. He wasn't an athletic, physical type, big as he is. Nancy says she doesn't think he was ever meant to be a lawyer. Not that lawyers can't be athletic and physical. She thinks Bob was pressured into his profession by his parents. There's a background of attorneys and judges in his branch of the Ellis family.''

Doug shrugged. "In any event, he seems like a nice enough guy."

"He's not on my favorite-person list right now," Jan admitted. "So I shouldn't be the one to comment on that."

"How's your friend Nancy doing?"

"She's hanging in. She seems to be a bit more stable. At least, she's buckled down to work and she's getting our fall and winter orders lined up. She has upcoming trips to Boston and New York and a couple of other places scheduled, and I think it'll do her good to get out of town. What worries me is that she's working on her nerves, and that's risky."

"Yes," Doug agreed, "it is. Look…I didn't mean to imply I'm taking sides in their marital dispute. I know nothing about Bob Ellis's personal situation, and I still haven't met Nancy."

"She'll be coming to the twins' party. At least, she always has. I think in some ways she looks upon them as surrogate children."

Doug didn't comment on that. Instead he started to stir the remnants of his tea with a long-handled spoon. Jan, watching him, suspected he had something further on his mind, something he was hesitant about coming out with.

"Speaking of old times…" he said.

They hadn't really been speaking of old times. Jan could feel herself tensing. She didn't want to get into a discussion of "old times" with Doug.

"Vicky told me you and she had a talk," Doug said.

Jan stared at him, puzzled. She couldn't see what her talk with Vicky could have to do with "old times."

"I'm glad," he went on. "And I'm glad you've taken Vicky to a doctor. That's quite a load off her mind. Too many teenagers become pregnant when a little parental help would prevent it."

Jan didn't comment.

"I didn't intend to get into that," Doug said, looking up at her and meeting her eyes with that steady blue gaze of his. "What brought it to my mind was that when Vicky told me about your conversation she also happened to mention you've kept a box of mementos, harking back to our high school days. Including our school yearbook.

"That," he said, "touched me. Vicky said there were a couple of faded gardenia corsages, among other things? The flowers I gave you when I took you to our proms, Janny?"

He didn't wait for her to answer, but went on, "I'd love to take a look at that yearbook. I'll bet the pictures in it are a riot. I never bought one—money was pretty tight for me back then."

Jan was so taken aback she couldn't hide her feelings. Incredulity, resentment, then a slow, seething anger that soon grew into outrage played across her face, like changing images viewed through a kaleidoscope. She felt that her emotions were as fragmented as kaleidoscopic images. For a moment, she came very close to hating him.

Doug stared at Jan in astonishment. The last thing he'd have expected was the burning anger he saw on her face. Watching her, he honestly couldn't understand why his wanting to see their high school yearbook should have this effect on her. He imagined the pictures in it would be pretty funny, viewed from their present perspective. He would have thought Janny might find them funny, too. Now it slowly dawned on him he should have known better.

Looking at Janny, he felt like the biggest fool God had ever put on earth. He could see it all, as if a curtain suddenly had parted. He knew—with a sickening certainty—that the box of mementos Vicky had spoken about weren't merely a few souvenirs of her adolescence to Janny. They were considerably more. She'd hoarded the corsages he'd given her all those years ago even after her marriage to someone else. And the yearbook—there was nothing funny to Janny about that yearbook. It was part of a past the two of them had shared. A past, he could see now, that had a very different significance to her than it did to him.

"I should have thrown that book out years ago. And everything else that went with it," she muttered between gritted teeth, then glared at Doug. "Don't you have any idea what you did to me?"

She stood up, facing him, her fists clenched. Her cheeks were flushed, her breath coming fast. "Damn you," she said, "all those years you never gave me so much as a second thought, did you? You walked out of here and never looked back. You left me. Did you ever leave me! If you'd kept contact with anyone here in town you'd know that for a long time I had a nickname, Doug MacKenzie's 'leftover girl.' That's what people—what our classmates—said about me behind my back. Naturally, I heard the echoes. In a small town like Ellis Falls you always hear the echoes of the things being said about you."

Stunned, Doug stood without even being aware of what he was doing. The table separated them. As if she were striking out at him, Jan pounded her fist down on the wooden surface.

"Didn't you know that by coming back here you'd stir things up all over again?" she asked him. The color faded from her face as suddenly as it had risen. Now she was pale, and her brown eyes—glittered. "Why do you think I didn't want you in my cottage?" She threw the question at him. "Because it would cause gossip, still more gossip, that's why. God, after you went away I was the subject of more gossip than I want to hear for the rest of my life. Then, after a while, Jonas came to town, thank God, and I met him and that was the beginning of a whole new life." She added, vehemently, "He had more integrity in his little finger than you have in your whole body."

Doug clutched the edge of the table, his knuckles whitening. "Oh, my God," he said, "I had no idea." His voice was so husky he could barely speak as he went on, "I was a fool. As complete a damned fool as anyone could be. A blind, arrogant kid...even though that's certainly not the way I saw myself then and it's difficult even now to realize how...how callous I must have been.

"I thought life was moving on for you, just as it was for me. Time moves fast for kids, Janny. And that's what we were. We were kids, Janny, only a year older than Chet and Vicky are right now.''

She still didn't answer.

"When I left,'' Doug said, "when I took the bus to Hartford and got on that plane to California, all I could think about was how soon I could come back to you. I meant to write you every day, but I was so busy. I meant to call you...but, frankly, I didn't have the money, and my uncle didn't allow me to make long-distance calls on his phone.''

Doug ran an agitated hand through his hair. "God, Janny, what can I say to you?'' he demanded helplessly.

"Nothing,'' she said. "It's too late. It was too late a long time ago.''

She was still pale, but her anger was subsiding. "I was so stupid,'' she murmured softly.

"No,'' Doug protested. He felt more chagrined over this, more ashamed, than he'd ever felt over anything in his entire life. Could he make her believe that? Could he make her see that the last thing in God's world he ever would have wanted was to make her suffer in any way, for even a minute? He'd loved her, damn it!

His smile was sad. "Even though I surely was as thick as any eighteen-year-old kid ever could be, there's another side to the story,'' he said slowly. "As time passed on, you became less and less real to me, but in a beautiful way, if you can understand that. You were like the silk from which the most wonderful and impossible dreams were spun. Time went on, and you became such a beautiful memory.

"I loved you, you know," he told her. "Not that my saying that matters much, after all this time. But . . . I did love you, Janny."

He laughed shortly. "I think, unwittingly, I've compared you to every girl—and then to every woman—I've ever met. If it's any consolation to you, none measured up. Obviously, you didn't have the same problem. You found someone who more than measured up."

He heard again what she'd said. *He had more integrity in his little finger than you have in your whole body.* Doug felt as though he would hear the echo of those words for the rest of his life. . . .

Doug looked at her and knew that his love for her was more alive than it had ever been. He loved her for the girl she'd been twenty years ago, and for the woman she had become. Janny Phelps was a success in a way he'd never be a success, Doug thought grimly. She'd rounded out her life. She'd made her mark as a wife, as a mother, as a career woman, even as a politician, he thought with a small, wry smile. In comparison, his life had been—was—one-dimensional.

He envied her.

THE PHONE RANG. It was a welcome diversion. Jan answered it, then turned to Doug. "It's Mike," she said. "He wondered if you might be over here. Something to do with the party."

She turned away as Doug spoke into the receiver. She heard his voice as background, but she didn't bother to try to distinguish the words he was speaking. She felt exhausted, as if the energy had been

drained from her. Even more than that, she felt like
such a fool.

Why had she let herself unleash all that latent resentment and anger on Doug? As she'd said it was too
late. Much too late. You couldn't undo the past.

Tonight, she promised herself, once the twins were
asleep, she'd take the blue box and put it, and its
contents, exactly where they belonged: in the gar-
bage can.

She wandered over to the window, her back to
Doug who was still talking on the phone. Looking
out, she saw the cottage and berated herself for ever
having rented it to him. She'd let the twins—and
Doug himself—pressure her into it. She'd felt at the
time that to refuse would give the impression of at-
taching undue importance to having Doug around.
Six months, she'd thought, and then he'd be gone.

Now...less than five months, and he'd be gone.

It can't come soon enough, Jan told herself...and
knew she was lying through her teeth.

She started when Doug spoke. He'd come up quietly and was standing close behind her. "Look," he
said, "I'm sorry. Until now I didn't realize my presence was such a thorn to you. Oh...I knew you
weren't all that crazy about having me around, most
of the time. But, there've been moments..."

Jan thought of the night when she'd spilled out all
her feelings and frustrations about Nancy. And the
kiss, the subsequent kiss, that somehow had managed to simultaneously fill her with desire, yet soothe
her soul.

Yes, there had been moments.

She said carefully, "Doug...just now you touched
an open wound. It's a wound that should have healed

long before now. So maybe it's as well this came out in the open. That's the one way to exorcise old ghosts, isn't it?''

He smiled ruefully. "I don't exactly like to picture myself as an old ghost."

"You know what I'm saying. Sometimes we cling to things we shouldn't cling to. Memories...well, memories can turn into cobwebs, and I'm not all that crazy about cobwebs."

"Now," Doug said, "I have the feeling you're relegating me to the farthest recesses in the attic of your mind."

"The attic of my mind?" she repeated. "I rather like that. Do you write like that, Doug?"

"No," he said, "I don't write like that. That's not a style that would suit my subject matter."

"Look," Jan said. "I overreacted just now. I want you to know I know I overreacted. I let out a lot that's been held in—and building up—ever since I heard you were coming back to Ellis Falls. Now I think I've given you the impression I've been suffering in silence for the past twenty years, and that's not true. Yes, I was hurt. But I got over it. I met someone else and fell deeply in love with him and married him.''

Doug said slowly, "You don't need to tell me that, Janny. I'm well aware. After all, you're still wearing the wedding ring he gave you."

Jan glanced down at the plain gold band on her finger. She was so accustomed to it, she'd worn it so long, it was like a part of herself. She'd thought, now and then, of taking it off, but she'd never done so. Somehow she'd felt protected, with Jonas's ring still on her finger.

When Jan said nothing, Doug went on, "I'll leave Ellis Falls if you want me to, Janny. I think I owe you that much. I had no idea I was going to cause you grief by coming back here. Matter of fact, I didn't expect you to be here. I imagined you'd married someone from somewhere else and moved away. That's sort of the norm, wouldn't you say? It was probably more of a shock for me to see you on the reviewing stand, the Fourth of July, than it was for you to see me. You knew I was coming. I didn't know you'd be here.

"But . . . it was so damned wonderful to see you," Doug added simply. "Then, when the twins told me about your cottage, I felt like I was stumbling into six months of . . . perfection. You should have told me to get lost, Janny."

"I think I tried to," she said, her smile softening the words. "But it's much too late for you to get lost, Doug. You've become very important to the twins. They'd never forgive me if you suddenly moved away. So, unless you want to move away, I'd say that our agreement is still in effect."

Doug nodded, without comment. "I'd better get back to work," he said after a moment. "Mike wanted to let me know that some of the kids are working out a plan to get Vicky and Chet away from here while we set up for the party, so it'll be a real surprise to them. As soon as he gets back to me with the logistics of his diversion plan I'll fill you in."

DOUG TRUDGED across the field to the cottage, his footsteps lagging. There was a lot more he'd wanted to say to Janny . . . but his common sense had warned him that enough had already been said, for the time being.

He sat down at his computer and tried to get to work. But the dull green screen stared at him blankly. He tried to take himself—mentally and emotionally—back to a spring afternoon in Beijing when all hell was breaking loose. He couldn't. China was not merely thousands but millions of miles away from him right now. His concentration was focused on a woman who'd just told him she'd finally managed to exorcise his ghost. And she was discovering memories were like cobwebs. In other words, they could be dusted away, eradicated.

Doug switched the computer off, and watched the screen fade into darkness. His body needed action. He had to move, stir up his circulation by doing some hard, physical exercise.

He put on a pair of sweatpants and a loose-fitting T-shirt. It was miserably hot and humid out; the dark thunderclouds still hovered but, so far, they were hoarding their burden. Doug struck out, running at an even pace down Jan's driveway and then into Sandisfield Street. He kept an even pace through the streets at the edge of town until he came to open countryside. Then he ran along dirt trails that plunged into woods so thick he felt as if he'd stumbled into a tropical jungle.

He heard thunder rumble, but he couldn't see the lightning for the trees. Common sense made him turn and start back, out of the woods. By the time he reached the first of the paved streets the rain was coming straight down, an enormous celestial shower set loose, and he was soaked through within seconds. Lightning jagged across the sky, brighter than the brightest city lights. Thunder growled, low and ominous, like a giant, irate animal. Doug kept running, concentrating on the body movement, falling into a rhythm—after the first bout with exhaustion—that was a kind of euphoric high.

Finally he turned into Jan's driveway. As he passed her house, he saw a figure silhouetted in the side window and he suspected it was Janny. He could imagine that she must think he was a damned fool, out running in the middle of a thunderstorm. But then, she pretty much thought that about him anyway. Didn't she?

CHAPTER TWELVE

JAN'S BACKYARD had been transformed into a Pacific island paradise. Colored lanterns were strung all the way out to the path that led to the cottage. Soft Hawaiian music lulled the senses—thanks to Mike's genius with the stereo system. The aroma of roasting pork ribs, basted with a ginger and pineapple syrup mixture, tantalized appetites. Floppy was keeping guard over the barbecue grill, while sniffing ecstatically. The cats were not far behind her.

The guests—girls and boys alike—were each presented with a colorful paper lei on arrival. The kids had gotten into the spirit of the occasion, and were wearing the most colorful clothes they'd been able to uncover. Several of the girls had muumuus, and a few had improvised South Sea island sarongs. A number of the boys were wearing brightly patterned tropical shirts, some of which, Jan suspected, they'd borrowed from their fathers.

Doug was wearing a bright blue shirt with a vivid Hawaiian print. It had a certain authentic look about it and, when she asked him, he told Jan he'd bought it in Hilo a couple of years earlier. With it he wore white chinos, and sandals. He looked very handsome.

Jan had remembered an old summer cotton dress—long, and close fitting—that she'd stored away because she liked it so much she couldn't bear to part with it, though at the time it had gone out of style. She dug it out, hoping it still fit, and it did. The cloth blended turquoise and rose and amethyst in a swirling pattern, and Doug told her she looked like a Hawaiian sunset. Which, he added hastily, was meant to be a compliment.

He'd smiled as he said that, then had plunged into his role of masterminding the "luau." He was genuinely busy, still Jan had the feeling he was avoiding her. She couldn't blame him, when she thought of the things she'd said to him the last time they'd been alone together. Doug had pretty much kept his distance since that afternoon when she'd finally given vent to all the resentment she'd harbored for so long. He'd even phoned her when there was something to discuss about the party, rather than simply coming over.

Again, he was making her feel ashamed of herself—though Jan doubted that was really his intention. Probably, he simply didn't want any more hassles. He hadn't come back to Ellis Falls for hassles; he'd come back to find the peace and serenity in which to write an important book.

Had she spoiled that for him with her outburst? She wondered about that as she filled some bowls with chunks of fresh pineapple, and others with popcorn over which she sprinkled macadamia nuts, per Doug's instructions.

Eager volunteers conveyed the food to the tables that had been set up outdoors, as fast as Jan could put things together. Each time one of the girls came in to help, she noticed the bright colored lei swinging around her neck. Jan was the only female present upon whom Doug had not bestowed a lei. It was childish to even think about anything like that. But even so...

Al came to the kitchen door to report, "They're coming, Mrs. Grayson. Come on outside."

Jan went out to the back porch and hurried down the steps. Everyone was gathering to one side of the driveway. As she watched, she saw Peter Bennett's old Ford slide to a smooth stop. Peter, and some of the others, had invited the twins to go to the carnival, as a birthday present—and diversionary tactic. The twins, in turn, had asked Jan if it would be okay to bring their friends back later for ice cream and cake.

Jan had teased, "How are you so sure there's going to be any cake?"

"Come on, Mom," Chet had protested. To him, birthday cake was one of life's constants, like a Christmas tree or a pumpkin on Halloween.

Now Al whispered in Jan's ears, "The guy's have blindfolded Vicky and Chet. They have no idea where they're being taken."

As Jan watched, the twins were led out of the car and they stood uncertainly at the edge of their own driveway. The lanterns cast myriad colors over everything, including faces; the effect was both eerie, and strangely beautiful.

Suddenly the volume of the music went up, and the beat of the Hawaiian War Chant filled the air. Then Doug gave a signal, the twins were unmasked, and for a moment they stood still, dazed and blinking.

Jan noticed that Doug was holding a very large plastic bag. He turned and said, "Janny...will you come here please?"

When she hesitated, Al gave her a very slight shove and said, "Go on, Mrs. Grayson."

Jan slowly crossed the distance between the bottom of the back steps and the edge of the driveway. Doug said, "Here, right next to Vicky, if you please." Then he reached into the plastic bag and withdrew a magnificent lei fashioned out of dozens of miniature orchids. With a bow, he encircled Vicky's neck with the lei, then said solemnly, "Aloha," and leaned forward and kissed her on both cheeks.

Before Vicky could recover, Doug reached into the bag again and brought forth another orchid lei, even more elaborate than the first one. He approached Jan, held it out and carefully dropped it over her head. He said softly, "Aloha," and kissed her on the cheeks just as he kissed Vicky. But in that moment before he did so, Jan looked directly into his eyes and she was shocked at the expression of raw pain she saw in them.

Doug was—outwardly—being the perfect master of ceremonies. But inwardly he was hurting. And she knew she was the cause of that hurt.

Jan's instincts took over. Without even stopping to think about what she was doing, she reached out and clasped a hand on either side of his face. Then—almost standing on tiptoe to do it—she kissed him lightly on the lips. "Thank you," she said, and became aware that all of the kids were either cheering or applauding or both.

Vicky followed suit and kissed Doug, too, and he quipped, "Boy, we're going to have to go through this lei ceremony more often." But, as he spoke, his eyes again searched Jan's face, and this time he looked puzzled.

Then the evening got into full swing, and the exchange was temporarily set aside, if not forgotten.

The young guests feasted. Then Doug set up a series of contests for them to participate in, including a hula contest in which he insisted both girls and boys take part. The results ranged from the sublime to the ridiculous, and Jan found herself laughing more freely than she had in ages.

Doug produced imported-from-Hawaii prizes for the winners of each event, including pikake perfume for the girls, cans of poi for the boys and some genuine grass skirts as well.

The evening was well under way before Jan realized that Nancy, to whom she'd issued a special invitation, had not shown up. She thought about calling her but then decided to let it go. Nancy would have come if she wanted to. There'd be time enough to talk with her tomorrow.

A flat, grassy area had been set aside for dancing. It wasn't the most perfect dance floor in the world, but no one complained. Doug kept the music menu to island music, and no one complained about that, either. The kids swayed together, caught up in the atmosphere Doug had created for them.

Mike and Al each claimed Jan for a dance. Then, she was about to go back to the house to get another bowl of pineapple chunks when Doug loomed in front of her.

"May I?" he asked, extending an arm.

He led Jan into the improvised dance area, and she slid willingly into his arms. They swayed together to the sensual, exotic tempo of "Song of the Islands." Jan was aware that some of the young guests were watching them—trying to be surreptitious about it, which made the covert glances funny. She could imagine that by now some of these friends of Vicky's and Chet's had heard about that long-ago romance between Doug and herself.

And suddenly she didn't give a damn.

The feeling of being held close in Doug's arms was wonderful. His nearness was wonderful. His touch on her bare back was in itself an aphrodisiac. Not that she needed an aphrodisiac. Being around Doug, even when he wasn't within three feet of her, wasn't touching her at all, was enough in itself to arouse her... when she was honest enough to admit it.

And she was being honest with herself now. She wanted Doug. She wanted to go to bed with him. She wanted him to make love to her. She wanted to respond, without inhibitions and—especially—with no echoes of the past. Because they were two different people, the Janet Grayson and Douglas MacKenzie of today, and thus essentially new to each other. All she had to do was look around her, at the faces of these kids also swaying to the tempo of "Song of the Islands" and she could see the difference between attraction at eighteen and attraction at thirty-eight. And she had no doubts about which was the more potent.

Doug, as if he'd read her mind—or, more accurately, had translated her body language—drew her a little closer.

Jan laughed shakily. "You're crushing my lei," she said.

He chuckled. "There are lots more where that came from."

"Doug, this has all been so terrific of you. I want to thank—"

"Don't talk," Doug ordered softly.

He was right. This was not a moment for talk, for thanks, for words of any kind. It was a small space in time designed to be devoted solely to the senses. And Jan let herself go. She swayed in Doug's arms and gave herself up to the music of the night...and to him.

Since most of the guests were under eighteen—and so couldn't drive after 1:00 a.m. according to Massachusetts law—the party broke up shortly after midnight. The young people, departing, called out, "Aloha," instead of good-night. And when the last guest had gone, Vicky turned to Doug and threw her arms around him, hugging him so tightly he protested, "Ouch, you're squeezing the breath out of me."

Vicky giggled. Then she said, "Doug, that was so marvelous. So absolutely marvelous."

"Hey," Doug said, "give your mother some of the credit."

Jan shook her head. "The credit's all yours," she said. "You thought up the idea of having a luau and you masterminded the whole production."

"It was great," Chet said. "But Doug's right. You deserve some of the credit, too, Mom. The food was super!"

"Oh, Mummy," Vicky said. She came over to Jan and hugged her. "It was terrific. You were terrific. I think it's the happiest birthday I've ever had."

There was still some punch left, and Doug suggested, "How about a nightcap, then we'll call it quits?"

"How about another piece of cake to go with the nightcap?" Chet suggested, and the others groaned.

Vicky said, "I've been gorging all night. I won't be able to get into my cheerleader's uniform. Guys, frankly, I'm bushed. Do you mind if I skip the punch and trail off to bed?''

Chet, after demolishing some more of his birthday cake, followed his sister's example. And Jan said slowly, reluctant, herself, to bring the night to an end, ''I guess I'd better think about the cleanup.''

''Most of the mess is paper or plastic,'' Doug said. ''It won't be too much of a job.''

''There are quite a few pots and pans.''

''True,'' Doug agreed. ''Look, I'll make a bargain with you.''

''Oh?''

''Fruit punch is fine,'' Doug said, ''but after a while you get satiated with it. I think you and I could use one real drink to celebrate our success, and I'd like to make you a genuine Mai-Tai. How about walking over to the cottage with me, and we can relax a while? I promise I'll come back and help you with the cleanup first thing in the morning.''

Jan laughed. ''That's an offer I can't resist.''

They walked, hand in hand, along the path to the cottage. The closer they got to the woods, the more aware Jan became of the scent of pine. A pale gold moon rode low in the sky, and the stars were brilliant. Suddenly she thought of the quote from Pippa Passes: ''God's in his heaven, all's right with the world.'' The words described this moment.

Doug switched on a light in the cottage, but he chose a dim light. He said, ''Make yourself comfortable while I fix our drinks. I'll put some music on.''

He chose Mozart, but he kept the volume low so that the music became beautiful background. A gentle breeze stirred the curtains, bringing with it that scent of pine. Jan slipped off her shoes and curled up

on the couch, and let herself experience peace—
something that was too much of a rarity to her.

As Doug handed her the drink he'd concocted he
glanced down at her hand, and he stiffened. "You've
taken off your wedding ring," he said, an odd note in
his voice.

"Yes," Jan said. She'd taken the ring off tonight,
as she dressed for the party...because it suddenly had
seemed to her that it was time to put the past behind
her. She imagined that even Jonas, could he see her,
would have approved of this small action.

Doug didn't comment further. He sat down on the
couch next to her, and for a time they sipped their
drinks and listened to the music and didn't say anything. Jan discovered silence could be a perfect means
of communication between two people when everything was right. And, just now, everything was right.
There was no past, no future, only a moonlit present.

The timing was right when Doug put his glass down
on the cocktail table, and reached for her. Jan went
into his arms, and he held her gently as she rested her
head on his shoulder. He wanted to let her yield to
him at her own tempo. This, he warned himself, was
not something he was about to rush—no matter how
desperately he wanted Janny. And he wanted her very
desperately indeed.

He slowly spread his fingers across the nape of her
neck, letting them begin to work their way across her
skin in a gentle massage. His lips brushed her temples, nuzzled her earlobe, then touched her cheeks in
passing until they centered upon her mouth. Jan,
who'd been acting like a person in a trance these past

few minutes, came to life. And she began to give as much as she was receiving.

Their tongues probed, touched, and Doug felt as if he'd been given a sudden charge of electricity. Jan moved in his arms with a sensuousness that began to drive him crazy, and he knew that all his repeated cautions to himself about going slowly were going to be worthless if she kept pressing against him like that.

They clutched, then began to gyrate against each other as their kisses intensified. And passion nudged logic aside, taking over. Doug felt as if he'd been set free, and he knew, intuitively, that he didn't need to be so careful with Janny. He didn't need to coax her because she was here, as ready for him as he was for her.

They clung to each other as they spanned the distance from the living room to the bedroom. Doug was gentle as he lowered Jan onto the bed, gentle as he unzipped her dress. But then he saw how little she had on under the dress: a blue satin bra, blue satin-and-lace panties. And he couldn't keep his hands away from her.

He caressed every inch of her body as he removed the bra, then the panties, his hands playing with her flesh as if she were an exquisite instrument, and he a musician. He felt her fingers on his shirt, she fumbled as she tugged at the buttons, and finally he helped her. For one last moment they lay inches apart, staring at each other as the moonlight splashed over them. Then they came together, and now it was a mutual symphony they were orchestrating. They touched, they felt, they gave to each other, until Doug claimed Jan, and she took him into herself until they shattered together.

They lay for a long time in each other's arms, quiet, gradually coming back to earth. But even earth seemed like a different place now. And, as Doug held her, Jan knew she'd never experienced anything like this before.

She didn't try to make comparisons. There were no comparisons to be made. She'd loved Jonas, and he'd been a tender and wonderful lover, but that was in the past. She was living in the present.

Nor was there any comparison to be made to the Doug MacKenzie and Janny Phelps who, so long ago, had made love. That had been a beautiful, adolescent kind of love, but the time was long since gone when its memory should have been put to rest. The girl in the fluffy pink dress, the boy in the white pants and navy-blue jacket he'd worn to their prom, faded into oblivion. Which is where they belonged.

Jan reached for Doug, and there was enough moonlight so she could see his lazy grin.

"Are you saying 'again'?" he asked her.

"I'm saying 'again,'" she murmured.

JAN DIDN'T WANT to go back to her house that night. She wanted to stay with Doug, to wake in his bed with him by her side.

Only the thought of the twins waking in the morning and finding her absent motivated her enough to leave him.

He walked with her down the path and around to her back steps. They stood at the foot of the stairs, and he brushed back a straying lock of her hair. "You smell like pikake," he said.

"I won a bottle of perfume for pronouncing all those royal Hawaiian names right, remember?" she teased.

"I remember," he said. "You also smell like you. That's even better."

He kissed her, and then he groaned. "Go on inside," he said, "or I won't be responsible for what happens."

She laughed. "You're not that much out of control."

"No? Want to tempt me?"

"Yes," she said. "But, no."

Doug reached for her, and held her, but only for a moment. "I'm not kidding," he said huskily. "I'm beginning to think there's no end to my wanting you. Go to bed, beautiful. But dream of me, will you?"

Jan shook her head. "Nope."

"Please," Doug urged, with a mock frown.

"Nope," Jan said, "I'm going to dream of heaven. That's where I've been tonight."

AS IT HAPPENED, Jan didn't dream of anything. She was so at peace with herself, so physically and emotionally satisfied, that she simply slept.

When she woke in the morning, it was with a special zest, and eagerness to face the day. First on her list, she thought with a smile, was a party cleanup with Doug to help her.

He arrived at eight o'clock, quietly slipping in through the kitchen door and looking slightly startled when he saw her at the table, drinking her first cup of coffee.

"I didn't mean to sneak in," he said, "but I thought maybe you might still be asleep, and I could get started."

He looked around. "Hey...you've got half the job done."

"Not really," Jan said. "I got up about an hour ago—the twins are still asleep, incidentally. The kids had brought in just about all of the outdoor stuff last night. Except for the lanterns. And I hate to take them down."

"Then leave them up," Doug suggested.

"No. First time it rains they'd be ruined. I'd rather salvage them for another occasion." She hesitated. "What did you do with my lei, Doug?"

He grinned. "It's reposing in a plastic bag in my fridge. I'll get it for you, after a while. You can wear it to your next selectmen's meeting."

"Can't you just picture that?" She smiled at him, her brown eyes clear and sparkling. "Want coffee?" she asked.

"No, thanks. I already had a cup. What did you do with all the paper stuff?"

"Put it in trash bags. It's out on the back porch. You walked right past it."

"My one objective this morning," Doug said, "is the kitchen."

He spoke lightly, but his eyes told her something the words weren't saying. He had another objective. Her. Somewhere deep inside, Jan felt a warm, warm glow that threatened to become a heat wave.

"I'll take the trash over to the dump later," she said, trying to force her mind—herself—back to the business at hand.

"I can do that. There's more room in the wagon,"
Doug said. He'd moved over to the sink and turned
on the hot water tap. "Suppose I wash and you dry?"
he suggested. "We can get rid of the pots and pans,
then appraise the situation and see what else needs to
be done."

They worked companionably, side by side. Jan
wouldn't have believed that she could derive so much
pleasure from drying pots and pans. As Doug handed
things over to her, his warm, wet fingers touched hers,
and the small contact was incredibly sexy. *He* was incredibly sexy. He'd shaved this morning, splashed on
a little after-shave. He looked good; he smelled good.

Whoa! Jan warned herself. This is apt to get out of
hand.

Vicky appeared as they were finishing the last of the
pots and pans. She yawned as she stood in the kitchen
doorway, surveying them. "You two guys working
already?" she asked them.

"Lazybones," Doug chided her. "The sun's already high in the sky."

"Not in my sky," Vicky retorted. She glanced at
the kitchen clock. "It isn't even nine, yet. Maybe I
should go back to bed. Chet's still asleep, the bum."

Vicky went over to the fridge as she spoke and got
out a carton of orange juice. She poured herself a
glass and sat down at the kitchen table. "If you guys
would wait a while, I'd help," she said.

"There's not that much more to do," Jan said.
"Your friends were a big help last night. They
brought just about everything indoors before they
left."

"It was the greatest party," Vicky said dreamily.
"The absolute greatest. How can we ever possibly top

it next year, when we're eighteen? Or even more importantly, when we turn twenty-one?''

''We'll think of a way,'' Doug promised.

The easy statement, casual though it was, had a startling effect on Jan. Where would Doug be a year from now, when the kids turned eighteen? To say nothing of when they turned twenty-one? Long gone from Ellis Falls, that was for sure.

Chet appeared in the doorway, blinking sleepily. ''What's going on?'' he demanded. He glanced at the kitchen clock. ''Whew! I'm late for work.''

''You have the day off,'' Jan advised him. ''A birthday present from Grady Brett.''

''You're sure?'' Chet asked.

''Absolutely. We let him in on the party secret, and he was the first to say he didn't think you'd want to come into work today.''

''Wow,'' Chet said. ''That's perfect. Got any of the hot dogs left from last night, Mom?''

''No,'' Jan said. ''Why?''

''I thought maybe I could organize a trek over to Deep Pines Lake, and a cookout. Just hot dogs,'' Chet said.

''Party animal,'' Vicky accused. ''Anyway, most of the other kids are probably working.''

''Not all of them,'' Chet said. ''Some of the guys have part-time jobs.''

''Great,'' Vicky informed him. ''But Jim's working.''

''Can't you go anywhere without Jim?'' Chet complained. ''Even to a daytime cookout?''

''It's not a question of what I can or can't do,'' Vicky began, and Doug interceded.

"Guys," he protested, "if you start bickering it'll take all the joy out of whatever you decide to do."

"How about coming along with us, Doug?" Chet suggested. "You can keep the peace. You, too, Mom," he added.

"Sorry, but I've got to do some work today," Doug said.

"So do I," Jan echoed.

"Er," Chet began, "do you suppose maybe we could use the wagon?"

"I'll make a deal with you if it's okay with your mother," Doug said. "Take the trash over to the dump, and the wagon is yours." He turned toward Jan, his gaze questioning.

"It's okay with me," she said. And she knew it had to be. She needed to get over her deep-seated apprehension about the twins' driving. In a way it was like being afraid of flying—and you couldn't get many places in the jet age unless you tabled your fears and got on a plane.

Doug went outside to dismantle the lanterns. Chet made a few phone calls and finally so did Vicky. She even checked with Jim at the hardware store, but Jim said dourly that his boss was not about to give him the afternoon off.

"See you tonight," Vicky said then, softly, and hung up.

Jan had been putting away some of the silverware they'd used for the party. She hadn't intended to eavesdrop on Vicky, but she couldn't help hearing her, and she had a sudden vision of the way Vicky and Jim had looked when they were dancing last night.

Much like she and Doug must have looked twenty years ago, she thought wryly. But they were so young.

She couldn't get used to the idea of Vicky using birth control. Yet she knew she ought to be relieved that her daughter was acting responsibly. When she was Vicky's age, she and Doug had been such innocents. They'd been incredibly lucky.

The twins got their act together. Jan gave them some money for hot dogs and rolls and other fixings, and Doug gave them the keys to the wagon.

Doug and Jan stood together at the edge of the driveway as the twins drove off. Then Doug turned, and their eyes met.

Jan had been having the funny feeling that Doug was as much one of the twins' parents as she was. But when he looked at her, his expression wasn't at all fatherly.

"I should go to work," he said.

It was an oblique invitation, but she got the message.

She countered, "I should get down to the shop."

Doug said softly, "It isn't every day we have the chance to be alone."

"I know," Jan answered, her voice equally soft.

"Janny..."

Jan held out her hand, and they walked up the back steps together.

CHAPTER THIRTEEN

NANCY WAS HYSTERICAL. "The sheriff just came by and served papers on me," she sobbed into the phone.

"What kind of papers?" Jan asked.

"Divorce papers," Nancy moaned. "Bob actually wants a divorce."

Jan tried to put herself in Nancy's position. She tried to appreciate how much of a shock it would be to be served divorce papers—even if, in your heart of hearts, you'd known what was coming.

Maybe Nancy really hadn't known what was coming. Maybe all this time she'd been hoping Bob would come back to her, even though she'd said repeatedly that she wouldn't have him if he came crawling.

Jan had run into Bob a few times at the town hall over the past couple of weeks. As always, he'd been pleasant and courteous. He'd even inquired after the twins. If she'd been asked to sum up her impressions of him, Jan would have said he seemed comfortable with himself. If there was any adjusting to do he'd done it.

She couldn't say the same about Nancy. Nancy was a bundle of nerves. The only positive note was that she'd cut down on her drinking.

Now, Jan wondered what this latest development was going to do to Nancy.

She sighed. It was noon on the Friday after the twins' birthday party. Bartlett Folger had called a special selectmen's meeting for two o'clock, and she had a dozen things she needed to get done before she took off for town.

"Nancy," she said, "I wish I could come over right now, but I'm due at the town hall shortly. I don't know how long I'll be, but hang in, will you? I'll get to your place as soon as I can."

"How could he do this?" Nancy wailed, as if she hadn't even heard Jan. "I can't believe that after all the years we've had together—"

"We'll talk about it," Jan said. "Now... hang in, will you?"

Nancy mumbled something, and Jan felt frustrated and helpless as she hung up the phone.

She heard a knock at the back door and answered it to find Doug on the threshold.

"I'm making a pot of my world-famous beef stew," he announced. "How about you and the twins coming over for supper tonight?"

"I don't know," Jan said, still thinking about Nancy and wondering how she was going to handle her.

Doug peered at her. "Something wrong?" he asked.

She nodded. "Nancy."

"Again?"

"Yes. The sheriff came around this morning and served her with divorce papers."

Doug came into the kitchen, closed the door behind him and said, "Do you realize, I still haven't met this woman? But I can't help but wonder—why is she always leaning on you, Janny?"

"I guess because she doesn't have anyone else," Jan said. "Not in this part of the country, anyway. She's from California, originally. She still has some family out there."

"So why doesn't she retreat to California for a while?"

"We're in business together, Doug," Jan reminded him. "Nancy is conscientious about the business. She's been doing her utmost lately, under very difficult circumstances."

"Lots of people separate, get divorced and still have to tend to business."

"Yes, I know. But I'm discovering Nancy is...very vulnerable. She seems a lot more sure of herself than she is."

"Maybe she needs to stiffen her spine."

Doug went over to the kitchen table, pulled out a chair and sat down. "You don't need her problems," he said.

"Most of us have problems we don't need," Jan reminded him. "Anyway...Nancy's a good friend. The least I can do is be there for her when she's going through a bad time."

"I do realize that," Doug admitted with a wry grin. "I suppose it's selfish of me, but I wish I could get a cut of the time you give to Nancy."

"She needs me, Doug."

"Could be I need you, too," Doug said, but he said it lightly. He pushed himself to his feet. "How about supper?" he asked again.

"I have a selectmen's meeting at two," Jan said reluctantly. "We have to deal with a couple of dull things that'll probably take ages to get through. I promised Nancy I'd go to her place, once I'm out of the town hall . . ."

"You still have to eat at some point."

"Yes, but I don't know when I'll be back. Also, the twins said something about going for chili dogs with some friends, and then over to the drive-in movie in South Eddington."

"Then that'd make just the two of us," Doug said. "For that matter, there are just the two of us right now."

He was staring at her intently. Jan had to meet that steady, blue gaze, and she felt as if she were melting. It was a warm and sensual feeling, and she yearned to yield to it. But she couldn't. Time was rushing by, and she was caught up in its momentum.

"Doug," she said, "I honestly have to get ready to go to the town hall."

Doug came close, and put firm hands on her shoulders. "Well, at least you look somewhat disappointed," he observed. He smiled down at her. "A rain check?" he suggested.

"A rain check," Jan agreed.

Doug bent, and kissed her lightly. Then he said huskily, "I'd better get the hell out of here, or I'll be blocking the path of civic progress."

At the door, he turned and added, "I'll keep the stew warm, just in case you're hungry when you get home."

THE MEETING was as long and dull as Jan had expected it would be. The one bright spot was that she saw Tom Prentice and Rose Ladue conferring in a way that suggested private rather than town business. Maybe Rose's "pursuit" was beginning to pay off.

When she arrived at Nancy's, Jan found that Nancy had been drinking again. White wine, this time, which was perhaps a better choice than vodka. But not that much of a better choice, under the circumstances.

Nancy offered her a glass of wine. Jan declined. Shared wine denoted sociability, and this wasn't a social visit. Though she wanted to help Nancy, she was tired, and she didn't want to linger any longer than she had to.

Nancy produced a long, official-looking envelope and held it out. "Read it," she urged Jan.

"Nancy, there's no need," Jan protested.

"Bob's suing for irreconcilable differences," Nancy said. "I guess that's sort of the 'in' thing these days, where grounds for divorce are concerned. If he wants to get rid of me so badly, I wonder why he doesn't go down to the Virgin Islands, or someplace else where he could get a quickie decree. Instead, he's filing in Massachusetts. The whole damn case will probably be heard right here in Berkshire County. Everyone will know all the gory details...."

"Why do there have to be any gory details?" Jan asked quietly.

"He has to give the judge some sort of explanation, doesn't he?"

"Not if you don't contest the divorce. Then it becomes a no-fault sort of thing."

"I'm going to contest the hell out of the divorce," Nancy announced bitterly.

Jan faced the issue. "Do you think you and Bob could pick up the pieces of your marriage at this point and go on together?" she asked.

"No," Nancy admitted. "No. I could never forgive him for what he's done to me. But that doesn't mean I'm about to hand him over to another woman without a fight."

Jan sighed. "You're not thinking, Nancy," she said gently. "What would be the point of putting yourself through all the agony of a contested divorce if you already know your marriage is beyond saving?"

"Because Bob needs to learn a little about agony."

"Don't you imagine he already has? Do you think it was easy for him to leave you?" Jan was surprised at herself for taking Bob Ellis's part, if only momentarily.

"He left, and that's what counts," Nancy snapped.

"Have you tried to contact him? Do you think it might help if the two of you talked?"

"He's called here a few times," Nancy confessed. "I hung up on him."

Jan stared at her partner. "You never told me that."

"There didn't seem any point in telling you. I had no intention of talking to him."

"If you won't communicate with a person you can't hope to resolve anything, Nancy."

"I suppose you're right," Nancy admitted, looking small and sad as she spoke. "But the truth is, I couldn't talk to him, Jan. I couldn't have said five words to him without breaking down. Things haven't been going well between Bob and me for a long time, but I still care about him."

Nancy said morosely, "Maybe if I'd been able to have children..."

"Children are great," Jan said, "but they don't necessarily solve the problems that come up between spouses."

"I suppose you're right," Nancy said, and poured herself another glass of wine.

IT WAS AFTER EIGHT when Jan pulled into the driveway. She dragged herself wearily up the back steps, got as far as the swing on the porch and collapsed into it.

She'd managed to get Nancy to eat some soup and toast, and she'd listened to Nancy talk for what seemed like twice as many hours as actually had passed. Now she was drained.

Across the field, at the edge of the woods, the lights in the cottage glowed through the warm August night. Closer, Jan saw fireflies, their lights flickering quick and bright, like small, fast-moving stars. She thought the fireflies gave a lovely light that, unfortunately, was as ephemeral as happiness.

She heard the kitchen phone ringing, and she was sure it was Doug even before she answered and heard his voice.

"The flavors in the stew have blended magnificently," he told her. "I have an excellent bottle of red wine, which I uncapped as soon as I saw your headlights, so now it's breathing. By the time you get over here, it should be just right to drink."

"That sounds very tempting," Jan said wearily, "but, frankly, I'd be lousy company tonight. I'm wiped out."

"Then what you need is recharging," Doug told her. "Look, if you like, I can bring the food and wine over there."

"I should take a bath, flop into bed and go to sleep," Jan said. "I don't even need to eat."

"You need soft lights and sweet music and a person who has a shoulder you can use for a pillow," Doug said. "I can offer all three."

She laughed, despite herself. "You're not going to take no for an answer?"

"No, I'm not going to take no for an answer."

"Fifteen minutes," Jan said.

DOUG PUT ON A TAPE of music from the forties. World War II romantic songs like "People Will Say We're In Love," and "All Or Nothing At All," and "A Nightingale Sang In Berkeley Square." He kept the volume low, and the soft, sweet strains created a soothing background. Jan felt herself begin to relax.

He brought forth the wine, two glasses and a plate of cheese and crackers. He plumped up the pillows on the couch and smiled at this picture of himself in the role of housekeeper. But, in such a short space of time, the cottage had become home.

Jan had changed from the summer suit she'd worn to the selectmen's meeting into a pink cotton dress with a scooped neckline. She'd put her hair back in a ponytail and tied it with a pink ribbon. As Doug opened the door for her, she reminded him, almost painfully, of the girl he'd loved so much twenty years ago.

Then he saw the fatigue stamped on her face, the small lines etched around her mouth and at the corner of her eyes. He felt an overwhelming desire to comfort her, and at the same time, a full awareness of a fact that had become incontrovertible.

He loved this woman standing before him far more deeply than he could ever have loved the girl she'd been at eighteen. Twenty years ago he hadn't had the capacity for this kind of love.

Jan was attracted to him. He knew that. The chemistry between them was irresistible. But Doug wondered, could that be all that was drawing her to him? Love and sexual attraction were two different things. The sensual response could exist by itself alone. It was human to want, to desire, to seek physical satisfaction with someone who excited you.

He wanted so much more than that with Janny.

Doug settled Jan on the couch, gave her wine, passed the cheese and crackers, then went to reverse the tape on the stereo. He turned to see her leaning back against the cushions, her eyes closed, the wine still untouched.

Tenderness welled in him, evoking a tidal wave of emotion. He wanted to care for her, to protect her, to cherish her. His impulses toward her were age-old. He could have been the guardian at the door of their cave, he thought whimsically, ready to brandish his club against all intruders.

He sat down on the couch beside her, and took the wineglass out of her hand. He put an arm around her, gently tugging her closer. She put her head on his shoulder, and neither of them said anything. Doug held her, listening to the music, feeling her warmth, inhaling her perfume, and experienced a rare kind of peace and contentment.

This, in its way, was fulfillment...if it could go on forever.

Doug heard the tenor of Jan's breathing change, and he knew she'd fallen asleep. After a while the music ran out, but the silence was like soft velvet. Doug, willing himself not to move a muscle, held Jan, as time ticked by.

JAN WAS DREAMING, and the dream became so vivid she suddenly awakened. She sat up straight, baffled, because for a few seconds she didn't know where she was. The contents of the dream were forgotten with the return to consciousness. She knew only that the dream had been intensely real, and it had involved Doug.

She turned and saw him leaning back against the couch pillows, smiling a lazy smile as he watched her.

Embarrassment came quickly. "I'm sorry," she said, stumbling over the apology. "I've never done anything like that before. Fallen asleep in someone else's living room." Chagrined, she repeated, "I'm sorry."

"I'm flattered," Doug said.

"Flattered?"

"Yes, I'd say falling asleep in someone's arms is a sign of trust. At least, I hope it's a sign of trust."

Before Jan could comment on that, Doug continued, "Stop apologizing, Janny. You were exhausted. Is the problem business, politics . . . or Nancy?"

"A combination, I guess," Jan admitted ruefully. "The meeting was every bit as boring as I thought it would be. This morning I spent a couple of hours at Chocolate Fantasies and, unfortunately, I discovered that Nancy hasn't been coping as well as I'd thought."

"What do you mean?"

"Nancy started out fine, once she pulled herself together and got on with her work," Jan said. "She made a lot of appointments, I think I told you she'll be doing some traveling. At least, that's what I expected. But I found out this morning that there are a number of our very good customers she hasn't even contacted yet. A couple of them called while I was at the office. I got our fall-winter catalog and our updated price list out to them before I left. But there are still a lot of bases to be covered."

"And Nancy's in no shape to cover the bases?"

"Not unless a miracle happens," Jan said soberly.

"Will she make the trips she needs to make?"

"I wouldn't want to see her start out in the condition she's in, even if she wanted to."

"Does that mean you're going to try to do what she should be doing?"

"I don't know if I can," Jan admitted. "For one thing, I'm not a good front man."

Doug chuckled. "I can't buy that."

"I'm not. I'm just not a salesperson. It takes a certain personality, a certain kind of confidence, to walk into the head office of a major hotel chain and sell them on your product, for example, to tell them you want to reproduce their logo in chocolate, so they can put a copy of the logo on every guest's pillow, instead of giving out a fancy mint or bonbon.

"Nancy's great at that. She's stunning when she's dressed up. She looks the part, she acts the part. Time and again I've seen her go out and come back with orders I couldn't believe. For me, however, the home base is my forte. I handle the production, see that the orders go out when they should go out, take care of the books so the figures make sense when they're turned over to our accountant. I troubleshoot, when troubleshooting's needed. My work complements Nancy's, her work complements mine, which is why we've done so well as partners. Until now."

"Nancy's going through a very painful experience," Doug reminded Jan. "Maybe this divorce comes at an especially bad time for her."

"What do you mean?"

"How old is she?"

"Early forties."

"Her basic problem may not be the divorce alone, but a combination of things. She's at a stage in her life when maybe she's questioning a lot of things about herself: her own attractiveness, her own femininity. She may have looked in the mirror and seen some wrinkles that weren't there before. Maybe a few gray hairs creeping in . . ."

"Oh, come on, Doug," Jan protested. "That happens to all of us."

"People react to things differently, Janny. You've said you don't think Nancy is as self-assured as she seems. Maybe a lot of the front she presents to the world is just that, a front. I can relate to that."

"Are you telling me you're insecure, you lack confidence, you're shy at heart?"

"You might be surprised," Doug said.

He grinned as he spoke, then got to his feet in one lithe movement. "Hey," he said, "time for the stew and a little more music to go with it. Sit tight, while I get things together."

The grin, Jan supposed, as she watched him head for the kitchen, could mean that he hadn't been serious in what he'd just indicated about himself. But . . . she wondered. And she began to realize she didn't know Doug nearly as well as she thought she did. It was easy, very easy, to be taken in by his public image and not to look beyond it to the private person.

Doug didn't give her time to brood about the varying facets of his personality. He plied her with food and wine and then he made love to her. His lovemaking was unhurried, almost tentative, at first, as if he were conveying to her—without actually saying the words—that he wanted to do to her only what she wanted him to do.

She answered that message without speaking any words, either. She let her body act out her feelings. They lost themselves in closeness. When the first, shattering climax took possession of Jan, Doug reached his crescendo at the same time. For a wonderful, transcendent moment they were joined together in soul as well as body; as united as two people could ever possibly hope to be.

DOUG HAD A SMALL mantel clock that chimed. When it struck midnight, Jan said, "It can't be that late."

They had been sipping cappuccino and talking quietly.

Doug said, "If you have to leave, I'll walk you home. Did you leave a note for the twins, incidentally?"

"No," she said. "I expected to be back ages before they were."

"Well . . . maybe you still will be."

But, as they struck out on the path, Jan saw a light glowing in Vicky's window. "They're home," she whispered.

Doug laughed. "Janny, you'd think you were the teenager and the twins were your strict parents," he teased.

She didn't know what to say to that.

"Nothing wrong with having supper with a neighbor, is there?" he asked lightly.

"No," she said. "No, of course there isn't."

Doug left her at the bottom of the back steps, giving her only a brief good-night kiss.

"This," he whispered, glancing toward Vicky's lighted window, "is making me feel younger than I have in years."

CHET WAS UP before Jan the next morning. He was in the kitchen, polishing off a stack of English muffins accompanied by a tall glass of milk, when she arrived to make coffee.

"Have a good time last night?" he asked her.

"Why...yes," Jan said.

"Vicky and I figured you must have gone over to Doug's," Chet said casually. "Both your cars were in the driveway."

"Maybe you two should be detectives," Jan said. Then, deciding the moment was as right as it would ever be, added, "Speaking of which..."

"I know what you're going to say, Mom."

"Am I that transparent?"

"About this you are. You're about to get on my case about college applications. Right?"

"Chet, you don't have all the time in the world. If you expect to be accepted by a good school you have to at least expend enough effort to submit an application."

"I guess you know you have to send a fairly stiff fee with each application," Chet pointed out.

"Yes, I know that."

"It would be a waste of money, Mom."

Jan pulled out a chair and sat down abruptly. "What are you saying?" she asked.

"I don't want to go to college, Mom. Not the kind of college you want me to go to."

Jan shook her head. "I can't believe what I'm hearing."

"I didn't mean to spring it on you like this," Chet said unhappily. He leaned against the sink. "Doug told me way back I should have a talk with you," he said.

"After you had a talk with him, I presume?"

"Well . . . yes."

"That was the night he walked back here to the house with you?"

"Yes. That was one of the times."

"I guess you've done a fair bit of talking to Doug."

"He understands where I'm coming from," Chet said somewhat desperately.

"And you think I don't?"

"I didn't say that. But . . . I know you've always wanted me to follow in Dad's footsteps. You've wanted me to be a teacher. Or to get into law, or banking, or something like that. I can't do it, Mom. I'm not an academic type."

"What kind of type are you, Chet?"

"I like to work with my hands. I like to grow things. I like to deal with earth, trees, plants, flowers. And, I'm good at it, Mom. I've been working for Grady Brett since I was eleven years old, and he's always said I have a super green thumb. Grady says about ten years from now he's going to be thinking of retirement. He doesn't have any kids to take over his business. So he's as much as told me he wants me to take it over, when the time comes. You know what a solid, well-established business he has."

"That's what you really want to do with your life?"

"Is there anything wrong with wanting to do something like that with my life?"

"There's nothing wrong with doing anything to make a good, honest living," Jan said. "But, different people have different potentials. You've always been an A student in most subjects, Chet. You're college material, all your teachers have said that. It would be such a waste, your giving up a chance at a real future to... to dig in the dirt."

Chet looked at her as if she'd stung him. "I didn't expect you to understand," he admitted. "Not right off, anyway. But I wish you wouldn't take that kind of attitude. If no one wanted to grow things, where would we all be? You love flowers. What would happen if people stopped growing them?"

Chet drew a deep breath. "What Doug suggested..." he began, and then broke off.

"Yes?" Jan persisted. "What did Doug suggest?"

"I wish I hadn't brought this up." Chet looked miserable. "All it'll do is make you angry with him. But... what Doug pointed out is that I'd be of special value in a landscaping business if I got some formal education in horticulture. That's why I said I didn't want to go to the kind of college you want me to go to. It doesn't mean I don't want to get any more education after high school. Doug says..."

"Yes?" Jan queried patiently.

"Well, Doug says the University of Massachusetts has a top-notch agricultural school that deals with horticulture right in Stockbridge. The University of New Hampshire has the Thompson School of Applied Science in Durham. Then, the University of Connecticut has the Radcliffe Hicks School of Agriculture in Storrs. And there's the Essex Agricultural and Technical Institute here in Massachusetts, in Hawthorne."

"Doug rattled all of that off the top of his head?"

"Not exactly," Chet admitted uncomfortably. "He looked the schools up for me."

"I see."

They simultaneously heard the sounds of wheels crunching the stones in the driveway. Chet, sounding relieved, said, "That'll be Grady's truck."

Jan nodded and watched Chet go out the back door. Actually she felt as relieved as she was sure he did.

But, at the same time, a new resentment toward Doug began to brew. She couldn't blame him because both twins had gone to him with their problems. That wasn't his fault. But his subsequent actions were.

True, he hadn't interfered in Vicky's case. In fact, he'd counseled Vicky to talk to her mother about her problem, as Vicky had.

In Chet's case, though, Doug's advice was wrong. Chet was a brilliant, talented boy. Doug seemed to have completely overlooked that fact.

"He had no right," Jan muttered to herself as she set about making her morning coffee. "He had no right, damn it!"

CHAPTER FOURTEEN

LEONA MARTIN stood in the doorway of Jan's office, her arms akimbo. "Don't you think it's time you packed up and went home?" she asked. "What time did you come in this morning?"

"Early," Jan admitted. She brushed a strand of hair back from her forehead. "I suppose I look like hell," she sighed.

"I wouldn't exactly say that, but I've seen you look a heap better," Leona said. "Didn't anyone ever tell you a person can't burn her candle at both ends and keep the flame going?"

"Yes. But—"

"Someone should go have a good talk with Nancy Ellis and let her know what she's doing to you while she stays home and enjoys a nervous breakdown, or whatever she's having."

"Leona!"

"Sorry, but it's true. She's not the first woman to have a man walk out on her."

Jan sighed again. "I suppose at this point everyone in town knows about Bob Ellis leaving Nancy, and petitioning for divorce."

"A lot of people saw it coming before it happened," Leona said. "But more to the point..." She turned. "My!" she exclaimed. "You startled me, Mr. MacKenzie."

Doug peered over Leona's shoulder. "Sorry about that," he said. "I suddenly got a sweet tooth and decided to come down to the shop. Then I heard voices..."

"Want me to pack you up a box of dark chocolate creams?" Leona suggested.

"Since they're the best chocolate creams I've ever had, yes," Doug said. "You might throw in a couple of other varieties, too."

Leona nodded and went back into the shop.

Doug sat down in the chair Nancy usually occupied. The moment she'd spied him Jan had experienced the same surge of elation she always felt when she saw Doug unexpectedly. But as she remembered his unwelcome interference with Chet's college plans her initial pleasure evaporated and she asked suspiciously, "Did you really drive all the way into town to get a box of candy? You could have called and I would have brought some chocolates home with me."

"I had a few other errands to do," Doug said.

Several times lately, when he had "a few errands to do" Doug had included a stop at Chocolate Fantasies since Jan was going into the office on a daily basis. He'd even met Nancy a couple of times, on occasions when she happened to stop by the office. But it was Leona who still got an obvious thrill out of her encounters with him. She couldn't get over the fact that she was seeing, in the flesh, the celebrity she'd watched on television so many times.

Now Doug added cautiously, "I overheard some of what Leona was saying to you."

"They say eavesdropping's dangerous," Jan told him. "People are apt to find themselves the subject of the conversation, and they may hear things they'd as soon not know about."

"Ouch," Doug muttered. Then he said, "I wasn't eavesdropping, Jan. The shop was empty, I heard voices, I followed the sound. I wanted to see you, anyway. I wanted to ask you to have dinner with me tonight. Not at home, out somewhere. It seems to me it's a while since you sallied forth into the world, except on business."

"Why are you keeping such close tabs on me, Doug?" Jan asked, and knew she was being nasty—but, damn it, sometimes he did irk her. There were moments when he made her business, especially her family business, too much his business.

She saw irritation etch his face. He said stiffly, "I don't keep tabs on you, Janny. I'm concerned about you, that's all. Leona's right. You can't get away with burning your candle at both ends for very long. You've been working too hard, and it's telling on you. You look pooped."

"Thanks a lot."

"I'm only being honest," Doug said. "You were exhausted the night you came over and had supper with me. I've scarcely seen you since. Even Chet mentioned that you were working harder than you should."

"You and Chet do share confidences, don't you?" Jan murmured.

"Okay," Doug said, his mouth tightening. "Out with it. What's the grudge, Janny?"

"Does there have to be a grudge?"

"There is one, isn't there?"

"I don't want to get into it right now."

"Then I'll get into it for you. Chet told me he mentioned going to horticultural school to you, and I gather you were less than pleased."

"I was less than pleased."

"And you blame me for making the suggestion?"

"I suppose I blame you for putting the idea into his head, yes."

"Because you have plans of your own for Chet?"

"I'm not going to get into that," Jan warned. "Look, Doug, if you'll excuse me I'd like to get out of here sometime tonight and I still have a lot of paperwork to do."

"Okay," Doug said rising. "I take it the answer to my dinner invitation is no?"

"I can't, Doug. I simply can't take the time tonight."

"Somehow, I feel we're back to square one," Doug said and shrugged. "So," he said, "I'll pick up my candy and be on my way."

A moment later Jan heard him chatting with Leona out in the shop. She was tempted to go after him, to tell him she'd changed her mind about having dinner with him. But she resisted the temptation.

Her concentration had been shot, though. She gave up going over accounts after a few minutes, knowing she'd only start making mistakes if she persisted.

Leona looked up as she walked into the shop. "So, you're actually quitting." She applauded.

"Yes, and you might as well close up," Jan said. "I doubt there'll be any more customers today."

"I'll give it fifteen minutes more," Leona decided. "By then the movie matinee will be out and there may be people who'll want to pick up some candy to take home with them."

JAN STOPPED at the neighborhood market for a carton of milk on her way home. Chet had an insatiable appetite for milk. She pulled into the driveway expecting to see Doug's car parked at the edge of the cottage path, but she'd gotten back ahead of him.

Vicky was spending the night with Cathy Ferguson. Chet had said he and Mike were going to browse around the stores after work so they could check out clothes for school. Mike would drive him home later.

As she walked up the back steps Jan noticed the days were beginning to get shorter. Another month and it would be almost dark this time of the late afternoon.

She went to her room, kicked off her shoes and stretched out on the bed. She was tired enough for a long nap and there was no reason why she shouldn't take one, but sleep wouldn't come. After a time she heard a car door thud closed. Probably Doug coming home. She got up and went over to the window and saw him walking slowly down the path to the cottage.

He was moving as if he, too, were tired. Maybe he was. Often, when she got up in the night she saw lights burning in the cottage. She suspected sometimes he worked into the small hours, but he was noncommittal when, occasionally, she asked him how the book was coming.

"Okay," he'd say and turn the subject to something else.

She didn't sense the enthusiasm she would have expected him to show about the book. Maybe the transition from the active life he was used to leading to the relative quiet and solitude of being a writer was proving more difficult than he'd thought it would be.

It occurred to her that other people unburdened their problems to Doug. At least, she and the twins certainly had. Maybe Doug needed a confidante, too. Someone to talk to about his work and whether it was—or wasn't—going well.

Promising herself that she wouldn't mention their disagreement over Chet, she dialed Doug's number. He answered on the second ring.

"I have the makings for tuna salad in the fridge," she said. "How about I fix enough for two?"

"You gave up on the idea of working tonight?" He sounded surprised.

"Yes."

"The dinner invitation's still open, Janny."

"Frankly, I'd rather slip into something old and comfortable and relax right here," she admitted.

"Then give me half an hour, and I'll be over."

Doug appeared approximately twenty-five minutes later, carrying a bottle of chilled white wine. Jan had cleared off the old wooden table on the back porch, lugged out two kitchen chairs, was in the process of setting the table with a pretty cloth and cutlery when he walked up the steps.

"I thought it would be cooler out here," she said. "There's a good breeze."

"It's perfect," Doug said, a husky note in his voice.

Jan caught the note and looked up at him. He was staring at her as if he couldn't quite believe what he was seeing. The "something old and comfortable" she'd put on was a green-and-white cotton jumpsuit that had seen better days. She'd pinned her hair up in a coil and, so she'd look a little bit festive, had put on some dangly, green-and-white earrings. There hadn't been time for a careful makeup job. She'd settled for a little lip gloss and a dusting of eye shadow. She couldn't imagine that she looked in the least glamorous. But Doug was staring at her as if she were the most beautiful woman in the world.

Flustered, Jan searched around for a big, chunky candle to put in the middle of the table. Dusk was deepening into darkness and the fireflies were beginning to pinprick the evening with their sporadic brilliance. The porch setting, the candlelight, the summer night just beyond the screens, gave an atmosphere of intimacy Jan hadn't intended to create. On the other hand, she was not about to destroy it.

"Want to put some music on the stereo?" she invited Doug. "I'll pour us some wine."

Doug chose a Linda Ronstadt album. Jan heard the strains of "What's New?" and her throat constricted. The song was about a woman who encounters an old lover—to find he's as handsome as ever and she loves him as much as she ever did.

As I love you, Jan said silently to Doug. Only, not just as much as ever. But so much more so.

They didn't say much as they ate. They let the night and the music wash over them. Doug insisted on clearing the table, instructing Jan to stay right where she was. He'd put the wine back in the fridge. He brought it out again and refilled their glasses. It was cold and tart on Jan's lips. It tasted just right.

Doug said suddenly, "I wish I could preserve this moment. Capture it in crystal maybe. Something small I could keep in my pocket with me and take out and look at whenever I needed—"

"Needed?" Jan prompted when he broke off his words.

"You," he said simply after only a moment's hesitation.

He saw the expression on her face, a rather enigmatic smile, and he knew she thought he was talking about sex. Well—there was that too, of course. But what he was really thinking about was this kind of sharing. It was an experience he'd never had before.

They didn't have to make conversation to be in tune with each other. The silence between them could sometimes be almost more meaningful than the words they spoke. When Janny relaxed she was warm and wonderful and so easy to be with. Doug wished they could go on forever just as they were right now. But he knew the folly of such a wish. Nothing lasted. Everything, every relationship had its time, its place, its boundaries. There was no such thing as forever. Even if there were he couldn't expect Janny to want him in her life forever. As it was, he was deeply aware that he'd disrupted the order of that life. He'd caused Janny more bad moments than good ones, so far. There was still that resentment that flared in her every now and then. But right now...

Right now was perfection, and Doug decided to settle for right now.

Jan had intended to get into a discussion of his book with him but it didn't work that way. They were both too caught up in the magic of each other. After a time they wandered to her bedroom. But once Doug started making love to her Jan couldn't relax, much as she wanted him. She couldn't yield to the passion that was always there, ready to surge from the instant when he first caressed her.

After a while Doug asked gently, "What is it, Janny?"

"I keep thinking Chet will come home," she admitted.

He released her and sat up. "I suppose you're right," he said reluctantly. "We should have gone to my place."

Jan sat up too. "That wouldn't be much better," she said. "I mean ... if I start wandering back from the cottage at all hours of the night they're going to put two and two together and . . ."

"Janny," Doug said softly, "you do have a life of your own to lead."

"I know," she said, "but . . ."

"No 'buts.' You do have a life of your own to lead. You're a wonderful mother, Janny. But you're young and beautiful and there's a world out there."

"I guess I've made my world here," Jan said, her voice small.

She was sitting on the side of the bed pinning her hair back up as she spoke.

Watching her Doug said, "What are you going to do when your kids leave the nest?"

"What?"

"It isn't going to be that much longer," he warned. "They'll go away to school. They may or may not come back to live in Ellis Falls. There's a world out there for them too, after all."

She turned to him. "Don't you think I know that?"

"I think you know it on an intellectual level but not on the gut level, Janny. I'm not saying you're going to try to hang on to your kids. I don't think you'd do that. What I am saying is that it's going to be pretty damned lonely for you once they're gone unless you start leading a life of your own in the meantime."

When she didn't answer him he smiled a very lop-sided smile. "Free advice from Doug MacKenzie," he said trying to keep it light, but a small edge of bitterness filtered through. "And we all know how valuable free advice is."

CHET WANDERED IN fifteen minutes later bringing Mike with him. They foraged in the fridge for soft drinks then came into the living room and joined Jan and Doug.

Jan gave Doug a knowing look, when the opportunity arose, silently conveying, "You see. If we hadn't stopped when we did..."

Doug's return glance was noncommittal. He got into an easy conversation with the two boys, mostly about sports. Then he stood and stretched and said, "I have to be getting along. Need to put in a couple of hours of work before I turn in. Thanks for the supper, Janny."

She walked out on the back porch with him. "I'm sorry," she said softly.

"Sorry for what? There's nothing for you to be sorry about, Janny."

"Sometimes I must seem like such a wimp to you."

"No. Never that. A lot of the time I don't think you think enough about yourself, that's all. You're a very giving, caring person. You overextend yourself—"

He broke off. "There," he said, "I'm doing it again."

"Doing what again?"

"Butting in. I've butted into your life too much and I know it. Butted in where your kids are concerned, where your business is concerned, now where you are concerned."

"People seek you out, Doug," Jan said. "I've been guilty of that myself." She smiled. "I guess it's just that you're a very giving, caring person."

"Copycat," he mocked. He drew her into his arms. "Frankly, I don't give a damn who sees us," he said. And when she didn't answer, he kissed her, and tried to put everything into the kiss he didn't seem to be able to say to her.

She rocked back on her heels when he released her, looking dazed. Doug felt a little bit dazed himself. He couldn't believe the power she had over him, the scope of his love and longing for her.

He reached for her hand. "Janny," he said, "there are things we need to talk about."

She still looked dazed. "Not tonight, Doug," she said.

"I didn't mean tonight. But soon. Soon, we have to find a slot of time, okay?"

She nodded. "Soon," she promised.

"Soon," didn't come to pass. With school starting the day after Labor Day there were a thousand and one last-minute details to take care of for the twins.

There was also the matter of the college applications to be resolved.

Where Chet was concerned, Jan capitulated. "If you want to apply to the various horticultural schools you spoke about, go ahead," she told him.

She couldn't convey any enthusiasm in her tone but Chet didn't seem to notice. "Doug said if I'd just talk to you everything would turn out all right," he said. "But I never thought you'd give in."

Doug again.

Oracle Douglas MacKenzie.

How could she love him so much and still be so annoyed with him?

Jan found more evidence of Doug's influence when she approached Vicky about her college applications. It was Saturday morning. Vicky was sitting at the kitchen table carefully applying pale peach polish to her fingernails.

"Vicky," Jan said, "when you finish with that let's get down to your college applications, shall we?"

Vicky looked up. "Today, Mummy?" she protested.

"Time's not standing still," Jan said. "We should have done this weeks ago."

"Mummy..."

"Yes?"

"I need to talk to you about this."

Jan's heart began to sink. Was Vicky about to tell her she didn't want to go to college, just as Chet had?

"Mummy... what I want to say is, I'd rather not apply to four-year colleges."

"What do you mean?"

"Just that. I'd like to go to a junior college, maybe a community college here in the Berkshires region. I'd like the chance to keep up dancing lessons on the side. Just for the fun of it. Then after I get an associate degree we can... reevaluate. Take it from there. Would that be okay with you?"

Jan was so relieved that she smiled and said, "Yes. I'd say that sounds like a good compromise, Vicky."

Vicky's relief was equally obvious. "Agreed," she said. She jumped up, threw her arms around her mother and hugged her tight. "Doug said you'd see it my way if I gave you a chance," she told Jan.

JAN ALMOST literally ran into Bob Ellis in the hall outside the selectmen's office two days after Labor Day.

Bob was coming out of the town accountant's office and he stopped short when he saw Jan.

"Look," he said, "is there a chance we could talk for a few minutes?"

Jan was sure the talk would concern Nancy and she instinctively backed off. But the note of urgency in Bob's voice when he said, "Please" gave her second thoughts. She relented.

"That small meeting room down at the other end of the hall should be empty," she said. "Why don't we go there?"

The room was empty... and stuffy. Jan tried to open one of the big windows to let some air in, but it stuck. Bob did the job for her easily; he'd been an athlete before he'd become a lawyer. He pushed the window open with a minimum amount of effort.

They sat facing each other across a narrow oak table. Bob, smiling slightly, said, "This place gives me the feeling I'm at a pretrial hearing."

"Yes, there is a certain official air about it," Jan agreed.

"Well, what I'm about to say is exceedingly unofficial, Jan," Bob told her. "Just between the two of us. I hope I can rely on you to keep it that way. I know you and Nancy are close friends."

Jan made a quick decision. "I'll keep your confidence, Bob."

"Good." He leaned back, and watching him, Jan thought he looked older. Though Bob put up a good front, she could see that the divorce was taking a toll on him too.

Bob said, "I went over to see Nancy last night."

"I didn't know that. But then I haven't talked to Nancy so far today."

"I gather she's been leaning on you pretty heavily these past couple of months."

"Well..."

There was a bleakness to Bob's smile. He said, "You don't have to hedge, Jan. I'm quoting Nancy. Not verbatim, maybe, but that's approximately what she said.

"I dropped in on her unexpectedly last night," he continued. "She'd been drinking—but not enough, fortunately, so that we couldn't talk. Matter of fact, she made a pot of strong coffee and she sobered up fast. Maybe partly because having me walk in was a shock.

"I should have gone to see her long before now," Bob admitted. "I kept putting it off because I knew I'd be in for a hell of a scene."

"Were you?"

"We had quite a session...but it didn't turn out as I'd expected it would. Jan, this situation between Nancy and myself didn't happen overnight. It had been brewing a long time. There was nothing left between Nancy and me long before Clarisse ever entered the picture. I know people are blaming Clarisse, and that's so wrong."

He sighed deeply, then continued, "Nancy's had the idea that our marriage failed because she couldn't have children. That's not so. If we'd been right for each other we could have adopted, or we could have lived a happy and full life, just the two of us. But the trouble is we clung to something that wasn't there— for much too long.

"Finally, it reached the point where I felt I had to leave. so I packed up and moved out. That was the hardest decision I've ever made. But it was also the best thing I could have done, for both of us."

"You're convinced of that, aren't you Bob?"

"Yes," Bob said. "I'm more convinced of it every day. After a few days, though, I called Nancy. I knew we needed to talk. She hung up on me. I can't tell you how many times she's hung up on me. So, last night I barged in on her. And I think it cleared the air."

Bob's smile was wry. "Right now," he said, "I think she hates me. And that hurts. No matter what's happened between us I could never hate her. I hope, in time, she'll see that it's the best thing for both of us. And I hope in time she'll find someone who'll mean to her what Clarisse has come to mean to me. Meantime, it's vital that she continue her work with you ... unless you're so fed up with her you want her out. Right now, that's what she's afraid of. And I wouldn't blame you if you did want to dissolve the partnership. From what she's told me, she's let you down badly, just when your big fall-winter season is coming on ..."

"There's time to recoup those losses," Jan said. "But only if Nancy really can pull herself together and come back to work."

"I think she can," Bob said. "I think she desperately wants to. I think Nancy needs to prove herself more than she ever has."

He added, his voice husky, "Last night I told her I love her. I don't think she believed me, but I think she'll realize in time that I meant what I said. I do love her. I always will. We just couldn't live happily together."

Bob shook his head. "Life's complicated as hell, isn't it?" he asked Jan.

She could only nod in agreement.

CHAPTER FIFTEEN

IT WAS THE MIDDLE of September. Doug went to New York for a conference with his publishers. Until she saw the cottage in darkness each night when she went to bed, Jan hadn't fully realized what a deep niche he'd made in her life.

This was only a temporary absence, but she became increasingly aware of what it was going to be like once he left for good. There were only three and a half months left till the first of the year. Each day assumed a new value, and she wanted Doug back so she could make the most of every hour she might spend with him.

A couple of days after Jan's talk with Bob, Nancy had walked into the office, her eyes clear and her head held high. She'd taken over with even more than her usual vigor. At about the same time Doug left town, Nancy went off on a trip that would take her to Boston, Albany, Hartford and New York. She expected to be gone at least ten days. "And I'm coming back with some of the best orders we've ever had," she promised Jan.

Whatever Bob had said to motivate Nancy had worked. Somehow he had made Nancy see reason. Nancy didn't talk about him and didn't talk about the impending divorce; she was her own person again.

With Nancy back, Jan was able to give her full time and attention to her end of the business. And Chocolate Fantasies, which had been edging toward the red for a while, slowly swung back into the black.

The twins had slipped back easily into their school routine. Chet was busy with the basketball team. Vicky was into her cheerleading, ready to perform at the upcoming football games. Extracurricular activities often kept both twins at school after hours, so they'd come home on the late bus. Often, Jan got home before they did.

Town business was relatively quiet, for the time being. There was to be a special town meeting in November at which a number of important issues would be presented to the voters. Then, over the balance of the fall and winter, there would be sessions devoted to budgeting for the forthcoming fiscal year. The drudge part of the job, Jan called the financial end of things. The selectmen were required to approve the submitted budgets of each of the town departments, a task that always involved a lot of night meetings.

But even with two jobs and a house to run she had too much time in which to think. Also, though she'd been lonely before, this was a new kind of loneliness. The gap she was feeling in her life was like an itch she couldn't scratch.

Then Doug came home.

Jan heard Floppy's excited barking one afternoon and somehow she knew Doug was back. She went to the kitchen window and confirmed her intuition. Doug was lugging a suitcase and a briefcase out of the trunk of the station wagon and heading for the path to the cottage.

A moment later, she was out on the back porch, standing at the top of the steps.

"Hi," she called.

Doug turned, put down the suitcase, balanced the briefcase on top of it, then hurried toward her, smiling.

"Good trip?" she asked him as they hugged each other tightly.

"Not especially," he said, his expression clouding.

"Come in," she invited. "I made some iced coffee a while ago. You look like you could use a cool drink."

"I could." He glanced toward the luggage. "Why don't I stash those in the cottage?" he suggested. "I'll be right back."

Jan nodded. She felt slightly worried about him as she went back into the house. She had the coffee ready when Doug came back and she asked him, "Here, or on the porch?"

"How about on the porch? There's a good breeze."

They sat down at the oak table. Doug, eyeing her, said, "You look more rested."

"You don't," she told him frankly.

"No reason why I should," he said with a short laugh. "New York was a zoo. Then the drive back was just about bumper-to-bumper till I got past Bridgeport. I never saw so much traffic." His eyes met hers. "Things going better?" he asked her.

"Yes. Nancy's doing very well. The twins have settled into school. Everything's quiet at the town hall. That's my story. Now, why don't you tell me yours?"

He smiled reluctantly. "I don't want to burden you with my problems Janny," he said. "You've had more than your share."

"I want to hear what's wrong, Doug."

"It's not that world shaking. The book—well, the book's stalled, that's all. That's why I went to New York. I thought maybe if I talked to Hank Crowley—he's my editor—he could help me get the kinks out of my mental processes, but I feel just as blocked as ever."

Jan frowned. "How long has this been going on?"

"Since I started trying to write about Beijing," Doug said.

"When was that?"

"About the second day after I got the computer."

"You're saying the book hasn't been going well for you since the very beginning?"

He nodded. "Yeah, I guess that's what I'm saying. I wanted to get my thoughts about Beijing down first because the scene over there made more of an impression on me than any in-the-field experience I've ever had. The China section wasn't supposed to be the first in the book. I intended to lead up to it. I wanted to get it down first, that's all."

"What happened?"

"The words just wouldn't come," Doug confessed. "I kept trying. I switched back to an introduction. I tried for a segment about Afghanistan. I switched to Nicaragua. But it was like I'd never been anywhere. Everything I wanted to say was . . . bottled up."

Jan felt guilty, and said, "Maybe you were dealing with too many other things at the same time."

"Such as?"

"The twins, unloading their problems on you. Me, too, for that matter."

Doug surveyed her soberly. "You and the twins are the best things that have ever happened to me," he said.

It was a simple statement, spoken simply. Jan felt tears sting her eyes, because he so obviously meant it. But she suppressed personal feelings to say honestly, "It could be the atmosphere here."

"The atmosphere?"

"Well, yes. You're not used to this kind of a...a semirural setting."

"I happen to have become very fond of this particular semirural setting."

"Even so, it may not be the best place for you to write in. Too many diversions, perhaps."

Doug smiled. "Yes," he said, some of the soberness fading. "I admit you can be a pretty powerful diversion, Janny."

"That's not what I meant." A quick rush of warmth stung her cheeks. "What I'm saying is, I've often heard that writers do better some places than they do others. You're more used to cities, actually..."

"So what do you want me to do? Go rent a loft in Soho and see if I get inspired?"

"No," she said. "No. I just want what's best for you."

Doug slowly raised his eyes, scanned Jan's face. Then he said softly, "You mean that, don't you?"

"Yes, of course I mean it."

"Someday maybe we'll talk about what may be best for me," he said. "Meantime...the cottage, the atmosphere around here, is just fine, Janny. The problem is with me. I have a lot penned up inside me. I expected it would all spill out once I sat down and started pressing some computer keys. But it hasn't worked that way. Hank tells me it's not unusual. He advises to stop trying so hard, to let the flow come naturally. I hope he's right. That's to say, I hope the flow will at least start coming."

"You've written things before, Doug."

"Oh, sure. Articles, essays, editorials. Never anything as ambitious as a book. That's quite a different kind of undertaking."

"Is it Beijing, specifically, that's bothering you so much?"

"Yes, I guess so," he said slowly. "A lot of kids got killed in Beijing, Janny. A lot of very brave kids."

"That," she said slowly, "must have been very hard to watch."

"I thought I was conditioned," Doug said. "I'd been a lot of places, seen a lot of things. But my hide wasn't as hard as I'd thought it would be."

"You were right there, in the center of Beijing?"

"As much 'right there' as anyone could be. I was in Tiananmen Square on that early morning of June 4, 1989, when the government troops moved in against the students who'd been demonstrating for seven weeks. It's amazing, when I look back, to think that the students had been allowed their sit-in protest for the better part of two months. Then, early on that Sunday morning, everything erupted.

"It was unbelievable. All of a sudden, there were soldiers everywhere, pouring out of the Forbidden City, standing on the rooftops of Mao Zedong's mausoleum and the Great Hall of the People. Ten thousand soldiers moved into the square in a triple-fanged movement. They came from three directions. And the bloodshed began.

"I stayed on the scene for as long as I could. I reported as much as I could. By the middle of the next week I was one of a trio of American correspondents who were rounded up, charged with violating martial-law restrictions, and given seventy-two hours to get out of China. The other two were men from the Associated Press and the Voice of America.

"We had no choice in the matter," Doug continued. "We had to leave, even though the administration in Washington protested our expulsion. Anyway, I'd seen enough, in one sense. I went on to other places, other assignments. But I kept thinking about the youth of the world and the united front they can present when they take a stand. And the idea for the book began to grow."

Jan looked at Doug's troubled face, and compassion mixed with the love she felt for him. "The way you talk about it, I know it's all there," she said. "You just have to let it out."

He grimaced. "That's easier said than done."

"Maybe if you talked it out," she suggested. "Told someone, like you just told me, and at the same time recorded what you were saying. Then you could have someone type up your tapes."

"Who could I find to talk it out to?" Doug asked her. "I couldn't confide in just anyone, Janny."

"How about me?" Jan asked him.

He studied her face. "You're serious, aren't you?" he asked finally, and she nodded. "My God," he said shaking his head, "don't you already have enough to do?"

"This would be different from anything I do, or ever have done," Jan told him. "It would be fascinating, as far as I'm concerned. I'd give you as much time as I could . . . some days more than others. Most afternoons, if I get home early enough, we could work for an hour or two. That's to say, you could talk and I could listen."

Doug was so touched he didn't know what to say to her. He'd become increasingly depressed on the drive back from New York. The heat, the traffic, had gotten to him. And the more he thought about it—despite Hank Crowley's encouragement—the more he doubted he could pull the story he wanted to tell from the inner depths in which it was stored, and commit it to paper.

Now Jan was offering him what looked like a perfect solution. But how could he accept her offer? Regardless of what she was saying, he, more than anyone else, knew how full her plate was. On the other hand . . . if Nancy kept going in a straight line, if the twins kept their heads on their shoulders, and if no unexpected issues arrive in connection with Ellis Falls' town government, maybe Janny really would have some hours she could spare him.

He was rationalizing. He was trying to convince himself to take her up on her offer because it would mean a daily contact with her, a different kind of closeness. But such a welcome closeness. Maybe if he could talk about his book with Janny, a lot of other things would come clear too. Maybe some of the issues that he still felt lay between them would be resolved. Maybe the last echoes of the resentment he was certain she still felt toward him would fade away, and she'd put their romance of twenty years ago in proper perspective so they could get on with their lives.

He said, "I shouldn't say yes."

Jan smiled. "But you're going to?"

"Yes," Doug said. "Yes, I'm going to."

JAN ADDED an extra "job" to her activity list, but she quickly discovered that listening to Doug was anything but a chore. She made time each day to go over to the cottage and spend as long as she could with him as he talked his story out to her.

He talked at random, at first, not attempting to follow any specific path but going into different experiences he'd had in various parts of the world. But with each session he visibly relaxed that much more. Before long, he started adhering to his book outline, and by the time he reached the part where the story of Beijing belonged, he had no difficulty in recounting to her the seven weeks he'd spent in the vicinity of Tiananmen Square.

Jan had never before felt so close to him. She only wished she had more time to give him. But Chocolate Fantasies was coming into its busiest months and Nancy was really bringing in the orders. The big kitchen at the back of the shop was in full production and that was an area Jan supervised, though she had enough help so she no longer needed to mold the chocolates herself.

The kitchen became a wonderland, first, of orange chocolate pumpkins, black chocolate cats and white chocolate ghosts for Halloween. Then, among the novelties for which Chocolate Fantasies was becoming famous, were the chocolate Thanksgiving turkeys, pilgrims and horns of plenty. Next would come Christmas. Then Valentine's Day, then St. Patrick's Day, then Easter, then special chocolates for graduations—pink chocolate roses were an ideal gift for girl graduates. And there were special assortments to be made for baby showers, and anniversaries, and birthdays and weddings.

Doug asked one afternoon, "Do you ever eat chocolate? I can remember you used to be a regular chocoholic."

Jan wrinkled her nose. "Frankly," she said, "even a bite of chocolate candy completely turns me off these days."

"How many molds do you have, Janny?" he asked curiously.

"Hundreds," she said. "When Nancy and I first started in business we ran into an astonishing piece of luck. Nancy met up with a woman who'd run a chocolate business in New York for years, which catered to the very best places. She had retired. She had at least three hundred molds, and she didn't want them any longer. She *gave* them to Nancy, can you believe that? Till then, we'd pretty much relied on my grandmother's recipe for Chocolate Fantasies, plus chocolate creams and fudge for local consumption. But those molds gave us the chance for instant expansion. They offered us endless possibilities."

"And that's when you started making colored chocolates?"

Jan laughed. "Our 'colored' chocolates are tinted white chocolate. Actually, white chocolate isn't really chocolate, as you think of it. It has a cocoa butter base. Without it," she admitted, "making our prettiest confections, like the Christmas poinsettias, would be out of the question."

They were sitting in the living room at the cottage. Doug had complained that he'd been talking so long his throat was getting hoarse. It was late afternoon, and he'd insisted on fetching a glass of wine for both of them. Then he'd started quizzing Jan about some of the details in her business they'd never really discussed before.

Doug looked relaxed and comfortable and he said, "The weather's starting to get cooler. Pretty soon, I'll be building a fire when we have these afternoon sessions."

"I know," Jan said. "On my way back from the shop today I noticed the leaves have started to turn."

"One of the things I've missed the most about New England is the autumn foliage. Nothing anywhere else quite equals it, at least for me." Doug sat back and stretched out his legs. "Think maybe," he asked her, "we could play hooky this weekend and drive up into Vermont and maybe over to New Hampshire? I heard a foliage report. Up north the leaves should be about at peak color this Saturday and Sunday."

"I doubt the twins could get away this weekend," Jan said. "I'm not sure about Chet, but I know Vicky has a football game, and she's a dedicated cheerleader."

"I wasn't talking about the twins, Janny," Doug said. "I was talking about us."

"You mean—stay over someplace?" she asked.

He smiled. "Janny, we're well beyond the age of consent," he reminded her. "In fact, you and I will be pushing forty before long. Do you think it would be so shocking for us to go away for a weekend together?"

"No," she said, "that's not what I meant. It's just that . . ."

"It's just that you're wondering what the twins would think, right?"

"Yes," Jan admitted reluctantly.

"You can't let Chet and Vicky direct the course of your life," Doug said bluntly. "Whether it's with me or someone else, you can't go it alone forever, Janny. I've told you that before, though maybe not in these exact words.

"Loving and respecting one's mother is fine," he added. "Fine, and right. But do you think Chet and Vicky put you on such a pedestal?"

"What do you mean?"

"Do you think they view you as a saint, rather than a human being? A woman who has blood in her veins and needs a man?"

"I don't know," Jan said. And added, "I don't want to get into this."

"You don't want to get into anything that touches you too personally," Doug accused. Then he sat up straight and said, "I'm out of line again. I apologize. But . . ."

She waited.

"I'm still asking you to go away for the weekend with me."

"I . . . can't," Jan said after a moment in which her brain whirled around, emotion and logic at war with each other. "It isn't just Chet and Vicky," she went on. "If we ran into someone from town, wherever we went . . ."

Doug's eyes looked like glittering blue sapphires. "You're thinking back twenty years, aren't you?" he challenged. "You still haven't gotten over your anger at me for what I did when we were eighteen years old. I've already thoroughly apologized for that. What else do you want me to do?''

"Doug, it isn't that.''

"The hell it isn't that.''

Jan shook her head. "Ellis Falls is a small town,'' she said. "There was enough talk about us when you came back here. There are a lot of people around who remember twenty years ago, Doug. I . . . well, I just don't want to stir up any more gossip. I'm the one who'll have to go on living with it after you're gone.''

He stared at her. "After I'm gone,'' he repeated softly. "What do you think I'm going to do, Janny? Walk out of your life again?''

"Well, aren't you?''

That was a question she'd never intended to put to him, in a large part because she didn't want to hear the answer.

Doug's eyes met hers, but she couldn't read his expression. His voice, though, was so heavy with sadness that she was staggered. He said, "I have the feeling that no matter what I might say in answer to that question of yours you wouldn't believe me. Your suspicions would rule both your head and your heart.''

Before she could pull herself together enough to make a coherent reply, he said, "Now . . . I think I'd better get started transcribing today's tapes onto the computer.''

He was dismissing her.

JAN'S FOOTSTEPS lagged on her way back to her house. She was baffled, confused because she knew she had just really hurt Doug—and it hadn't occurred to her she had it in her power to hurt him to that extent.

She discovered it was a power she didn't want. Once, maybe, but no longer. The past had been exorcised. What she wanted with Doug was the present . . . and, yes, the future.

Doug was annoyed with her, that much was obvious. He'd made her feel that she was impossibly old-fashioned and narrow-minded. And he was right, damn it! Probably the twins would heartily endorse the idea of her going away with Doug for the weekend. They'd both been delighted when they learned she'd be working with him on his book.

Jan paused at the edge of the path more than half tempted to turn around and go back to the cottage and tell Doug she'd go away with him. But her pride wouldn't let her do it.

Maybe tomorrow. Maybe Doug would bring the matter up again tomorrow, when they were together, or maybe she could edge into it. And this time, she'd say yes.

She could imagine roaming with Doug through New England's autumn countryside. The burnished beauty of the leaves would be a feast for the soul. Fall was her favorite time of year. She loved the rich colors, the golds and the bronzes, the scarlets and the oranges, the clear vivid yellows and the deep green of the pines. She loved to buy apples at outdoor fruit stands, and to pick out a big pumpkin and bring it home for carving at Halloween.

Tomorrow, Jan promised herself. Tomorrow I'll tell Doug I want to go with him.

She waited for her chance the next afternoon when she arrived at Doug's for their daily session.

They were having a cup of coffee during a short break when she said, "About this weekend. The weather forecast sounds ideal." She smiled at him. "Could I have a second chance for that outing?" she asked.

Doug shook his head slightly as if he couldn't believe what he was hearing. But then the shake became decidedly negative as he said, "I'm sorry, Janny. But Chet came over last night and invited me to go to the basketball game he's playing in Saturday. He said he really wants me to see him play."

So much for a romantic weekend in the country!

CHAPTER SIXTEEN

"IF I HAD MY WAY, Halloween would be outlawed,"
Bartlett Folger said.

"Aw, come on Bart," Herb Flynn teased. "Didn't
you ever act up when you were a kid?"

Jan, amused, waited for the chairman of the selectmen to answer that question. Bartlett sidestepped
it by delving into a discussion of the activities the
town was providing for youngsters on Halloween. "I
hope these programs will keep at least a portion of
Ellis Falls' youthful population off the streets," he
finished, his "hope" sounding like a dire prediction.

The selectmen were meeting on a Thursday afternoon to prepare for a Friday night session in which a
couple of fairly serious civic issues were certain to
come under fire. Herb Flynn had brought up the
subject of Halloween activities, to see if there was
anything the board could do that might be helpful to
the other civic agencies involved in Halloween preparations. But it seemed that the Chamber of Com-
merce, the police department and both the elementary
and the high school had the situation well in hand.
There would be a daytime parade for youngsters, a
dance at the high school for teenagers, and a number
of other activities aimed toward preventing as much
"serious" mischief as possible.

Jan had always loved Halloween, and in earlier years her house had been the place where the kids could gather after they finished trick-or-treating. But now the "kids" were young adults, and this year Cathy Ferguson was going to have a predance supper at her house Halloween night. Both twins were going, and Doug had volunteered his station wagon for their use—after asking Jan, rather stiffly, if that would be okay with her.

She'd said yes. She was making a real effort to conquer her fear about the twins' driving.

The twins set forth in costume Halloween night. Chet was dressed as a monster from outer space; Vicky was a black cat. She had made her own costume, fashioning it out of a fabric that looked like black fur. The costume fit her as well as a cat's fur fit a cat and left little to the imagination. Doug, surveying her, was glad she'd have both Chet and Jim Farrish with her tonight. It wouldn't do for Vicky to be out on her own in that outfit.

Doug had sauntered over from the cottage to give Chet the car keys. Also, he'd promised the twins he'd come take a look at them in their costumes. Now, as they drove off, he turned to Jan and said, "If there are any prizes to be given out, they should both win firsts."

"They don't lack for imagination," Jan agreed. Privately, she wished Vicky had settled for something a little less revealing.

"Got any big Halloween plans yourself?" Doug asked.

"No. I like to stick around home on Halloween."

"For trick or treaters? That's why I'm staying around myself," he said. "I've bought enough candy to feed half the town."

"You may have to eat most of it yourself," Jan warned. "We don't get many trick or treaters this far out of town. When the twins were younger, their friends' parents used to drive them around. That was fun. Little kids are so cute dressed up like witches, or Cinderella, or Batman. But by the time the twins and their friends were into junior high, being chauffeured for trick-or-treating became a thing of the past. There are more activities in town now anyway, like the dance."

"I'm surprised you're not acting as chaperon," Doug said somewhat dryly.

"Thanks, but no thanks," Jan retorted, not knowing just how to interpret the remark.

She wasn't sure how to take Doug, lately, for that matter. He'd not reissued any weekend invitation. Also, their "talk-out" sessions had come to a temporary halt. As Doug explained it, he'd gotten so much down on tape in his discourses with Jan that he needed time out to transcribe the tapes onto disks. Once that was done, he would print out the disks and read his own words so he could see how his story line was working.

"Couldn't you hire someone to do the transcribing for you?" Jan had asked.

"Yes, I guess so," he'd allowed, "but I'd rather do it myself. Working with the tapes myself will give me a real feel for what I'm doing."

Jan could see the point of that. But she wondered if part of the reason why Doug wanted to do his own typing was to give them some time apart from each other.

Regardless of his motivation, she missed those daily sessions with him.

Now, she watched Doug head for the cottage, and she walked around to the front of the house. The big pumpkin the twins and some friends of theirs had carved into a jack-o'-lantern was sitting by the front door. Jan lit the chunky candle inside the pumpkin and watched the candle's yellow glow illuminate the zigzagging features. After dark, the jack-o'-lantern would be very effective.

Chet had hung a long skeleton on the front door, which was made of plastic coated with a paint that glowed in the dark. He'd fixed a small spotlight in the maple tree by the front walk that would illuminate the skeleton, and Jan turned that on, too.

After that, there wasn't much to do. She wandered back into the house thinking about those earlier years when she'd played a much bigger role in the twins' Halloweens. She'd created costumes for them to wear in the parade down Main Street, and more than once one or the other, or both, had won prizes. She'd engineered apple-dunking contests for Chet and Vicky and their friends. The standard Halloween supper fare had been goblin burgers—hamburgers on one half of a bun, the top of the hamburger topped with a slice of cheese that had been cut into a jack-o'-lantern shape and then placed under the broiler for just a couple of seconds, so the jack-o'-lantern would begin to melt.

She should have invited Doug over and made goblin burgers for the two of them, she thought whimsically. But it was too late in the day, and she didn't have the fixings anyway.

Jan poured herself a glass of cider, then turned on the TV, tuning in to a ghost story that was perfect for Halloween. No trick or treaters came to knock at her door as the evening passed, and she imagined at this point Doug must be wondering what to do with all the Halloween candy he'd purchased.

As it grew later, Jan kept the volume of the TV a shade louder than she usually did, as if that might help dispel the silence that crouched around the edges of her living room.

Holidays were bad times to be alone.

Finally she fell asleep, and when she woke, a late-night talk show had taken over on the TV screen.

It wasn't the talk show that had awakened her, though. Someone was pounding on the back door. Pounding and pounding and pounding...

Jan glanced at the mantel clock, saw it was after midnight, and knew a moment of sharp, piercing terror.

Something had happened to the twins! Her pulse was hammering against her chest as she ran to the kitchen door.

When she saw Doug on the threshold she was so irritated she glared at him. It was after midnight; this was hardly the time for him to be barging in.

Then she saw the expression on his face.

"Janny..." Doug said.

Jan knew without being told that she'd been right in the first place about the twins, and fear clutched at her heart.

"Take it easy," Doug cautioned. "Look, Janny, everything's okay. The twins have been in an accident but they're all right. Just shaken up a bit."

"Where are they?" Jan's throat was parched, her words escaped through dry lips.

"At the hospital. In the emergency room. Looks like they'll be admitting Jim."

"Oh, my God!"

"He's not hurt seriously," Doug said quickly. "Not critically, that's to say. Looks like he has a laceration on his forehead and maybe a broken leg. He was in the passenger seat."

"Who was driving?"

"Vicky."

Jan stared at him. "How do you know all this?"

"Chet called me."

"Chet called you?" She'd fallen asleep, but she hadn't been deeply asleep. The first peal of the phone and she'd have been on her feet . . .

"Janny," Doug said gently, "don't get upset because Chet called me instead of you. He was thinking of *you*, try to realize that. He thought it would be better for me to come over and tell you this, rather than to have you hear it over the phone. I agree."

Jan didn't want to listen to him. "I'm going to the hospital," she announced.

"We're going to the hospital," Doug corrected.

She wasn't about to bicker with him.

They were silent on the drive to the hospital. Doug parked as close to the emergency room entrance as he could get. He took Jan's arm as they started across the lot, and she couldn't deny that his strong grip felt good.

He said softly, "Janny, I know what this is doing to you. Just remember the kids are okay. That's the main thing."

Chet and Vicky didn't look all that "okay" to Jan when she glimpsed them huddled in a corner of the hospital waiting room. To make matters worse, there was a police officer with them, and he was getting a statement from Vicky. Jan was in such a state of shock it took her a minute to realize the police officer was Ron Evans, whom she'd known for years.

Vicky saw Doug, and she immediately flung herself into his arms and started to cry.

Chet was pale, but in control. "Mom," he said, "right off I want you to know this wasn't Vicky's fault. We'd just dropped Cathy off at her house and were going by that stretch of woods on Upper Falls Street. Some kids threw this weird thing in front of the car..."

"Kids stuff clothing until they have something that looks like a human figure," Ron Evans said. "This has become a rotten form of a Halloween prank. It's not the first time one of these effigies—or whatever you want to call them—has caused an accident."

"Vicky was driving, Jim was in the front seat with her, I was in back," Chet put in. "All of a sudden this figure came out of the dark, right in front of the headlights. I honest to God thought it was a person. Vicky slammed on her brakes but the wagon swerved. We sideswiped a tree. Doug, I'm afraid your car was totaled."

"To hell with the car," Doug said roughly.

He was still holding Vicky, but she'd stopped crying. Tears stained her cheeks, though, and she looked so young and vulnerable it was all Jan could do to hold back her own tears.

Nevertheless, Vicky's voice was remarkably firm as she tugged away from Doug and said, "I want to see Jim."

Doug nodded. "Let me check on that for you."

As Doug walked over to the emergency room reception desk he was aware that once again he was antagonizing Janny. He could empathize with the way she felt, but he also resented it. Damn it, he hadn't asked Chet to phone him first. Not only that, but he'd spoken the truth when he'd said Chet had been motivated by consideration for his mother.

Chet had said, "This is really going to upset Mom. She's scared to death of our driving as it is. Break it to her as easy as you can, will you, Doug?"

There hadn't been any "easy" way to break the news to Janny, unfortunately. He'd seen the fear in her eyes even before he started to speak. Then the resentment toward him.

Damn her resentment!

Doug got updated information on Jim and went back to Jan and the twins. Jan had her arm around Vicky. Chet was standing close to the two of them looking as if his carefully controlled composure was about to give way at any minute. Ron Evans was gone.

"Can I see Jim?" Vicky demanded as soon as Doug was within earshot.

"Not tonight," Doug said. "He's doing fine, though. His parents are with him right now, but the nurse said he's pretty groggy. I'll bring you over here tomorrow the minute visiting hours start, Vicky."

He expected Vicky to protest, but she didn't. Instead, she looked at her mother and her lips quivered as she said, "Mummy, I want to go home."

When they got back to Jan's house, Doug went inside with Jan and the twins without waiting for an invitation. He was damned if he was going to leave Jan alone tonight until he made sure she calmed down a little. It didn't take much imagination to realize how much this whole episode had affected her.

Once they were in the kitchen, Doug asked, "Do you have any brandy, Janny?"

"Yes," she said. "I keep it to flame up the plum pudding at Christmas."

He couldn't resist a smile at that. But he sought out the brandy and poured out small measures for the twins and larger ones for Jan and himself. "Just don't get the idea it would be bright of the two of you to guzzle hard liquor all the time," he told the twins.

Chet had to smile at that. But it wasn't a very long-lasting smile. The twins downed the brandy cautiously, then Jan looked at Vicky and said, "Let's get you to bed."

Vicky didn't protest.

Once his mother and sister had left the room Chet turned to Doug. "Was it bad with Mom?" he asked.

"Bad enough," Doug said honestly. "Also, I think she felt you should have called her, not me."

"I knew she would, but I still thought it would be better if you told her," Chet said.

"I thought so, too."

"Women are strange," Chet said.

Doug grinned. "I know."

"I'm glad we dropped Cathy off before this happened. Honest to God, Doug, it wasn't Vicky's fault.

This—this form, it looked like a human, just sailed out of thin air.''

"I believe you, Chet."

"Yeah, but do you think Mom does?"

"Yes," Doug said. "I think she does."

"Even so, it'll be a long time before she lets either of us get behind a wheel again," Chet predicted.

Doug thought about that a few minutes later after Chet had straggled off to bed himself. He wasn't a psychologist but he knew that if the twins, Vicky especially, didn't get back behind the wheel again soon, they could possibly develop a lifelong fear of driving. He hoped that Janny would realize this and not forbid them to drive.

He supposed he should have the good sense not to bring that issue up with Jan. On the other hand...for the twins' sake, he couldn't afford to let it go.

Jan had kindling and logs in her fireplace, ready to be lit. Probably the last thing in the world she was in the mood for right now was a fireside chat, Doug conceded. Nevertheless, he opened the damper, got the fire going and the flames were crackling on the hearth when Jan came downstairs.

She wrinkled her nose and said, "I thought I smelled smoke." She glanced at the mantel clock. "Doug, it's nearly three o'clock. Don't you think that's a bit late to make a fire?"

"No," Doug said. "There's something I have to say to you, Janny."

"Tonight?"

"Yes. Once again, I want to emphasize to you that the kids are okay. Even Jim is basically okay. He's going to be hurting for a while, but a few months from now you won't know anything ever happened to him. That's what matters.''

She faced him, her eyes still widened from shock. ''It could have been different,'' she said.

''You're saying it could have been a helluva lot worse. Yes, it could have been. But it wasn't.''

''If Vicky had been driving faster...''

''Vicky wasn't driving faster. When it comes to driving, both Chet and Vicky have considerable common sense. I know, I've driven with them. Janny, I know teenagers get bad press for being wild and irresponsible. Obviously there are those who are. But people shouldn't be condemned because of their age-group. The twins—''

Jan cut him off. ''I don't need a lecture tonight, Doug,'' she told him.

After a moment Doug said, ''Yeah, I guess you're right. So I'll get off my soapbox. But there's still something I have to say to you.''

''I'm awfully tired, Doug. Can't it wait?''

''I'm tired, too,'' Doug said. ''But no, it can't wait. You need to let those two kids drive a car tomorrow.''

''What?''

''You can't live in 'ifs,''' Doug said. ''When you're reporting in a war zone, for instance, if a bullet whizzes by your head you know that if its trajectory had been even a fraction of an inch different, you could be dead. But the thing is, you're not dead. Do you see what I'm saying?''

''No.''

He sighed. ''What I'm trying to get across to you, Janny, is that you can't live on borrowed trouble, on

what might have been. You have to live in the here
and now. That's all you've got."

Jan didn't try to hide her impatience. "Couldn't we
save this philosophy for another time?" she suggested.

"No. Because it's imperative both Chet and Vicky
get behind the wheel of a car tomorrow, or they're apt
to be nervous about driving for the rest of their lives.

"I'm pointing out some pretty well-known psy-
chological facts to you," Doug went on, telling himself he was not going to be deterred by the icy
expression on Janny's face. "If a kid falls off a bi-
cycle, the best thing he can do is get up and ride it
again. That same principle applies to a great many
things. If we put off doing something we fear, we only
come to fear it all the more."

"Doug . . . please . . ."

"Janny, please believe me," Doug said. "The more
time that passes the harder it is going to be for Chet
and Vicky to drive again."

Doug added, "It's a bit difficult to get around on
foot in today's world, Janny."

"What am I supposed to say to that?"

"You don't have to say anything," Doug said.
"Just keep on listening to me for a couple more minutes. Tomorrow morning, I'll have to see about getting a rental car for the time being. What I'm asking
is that you let Chet borrow your car and drive me over
to the rental agency. Then he can bring your car directly back here, and I'll follow.

"Then," he went on before she could speak, "I'm
going to ask you to let me allow Vicky to drive on the
way back from the hospital tomorrow. I think she'll

be too anxious going over, but once she sees Jim's going to be all right, she'll settle down.''

Jan said tautly, ''You do have it all figured out, don't you? By any chance, have you picked up your master's in psychology somewhere along the way?''

''Janny, I don't blame you for being—''

''For being what?'' she cut in. ''I don't think you have any idea how I'm feeling right now. As for tomorrow—what can I say to you? No, I don't want Vicky and Chet driving a car tomorrow. But my common sense tells me you're right.''

Jan stood up. ''I'd appreciate it if you'd douse the fire. Now if you'll excuse me, I'm going to bed.''

DOUG MADE SURE the fire was extinguished, then let himself out of Jan's house. As he walked back to the cottage he was torn between wanting to invade her bedroom to throttle her and wanting to invade her bedroom to make love to her.

He'd had to force himself to be rough with her, but he'd needed to make his point for Chet and Vicky's sake. He was surprised Janny had conceded as easily as she had. It proved that as traumatic as tonight's experience had been, she was not immune to logic.

He supposed his story about a near-miss with a bullet had been a poor analogy. But it was something that had actually happened to him.

That, and a number of other experiences, had taught him how fragile life was, and how precious. That was part of what he'd been trying to get across to Janny.

He'd also been trying to make her see that she had to let the twins go, regardless of the risks. They deserved the chance to live their own lives.

Doug didn't bother to turn on any lights in the cottage. He went into the bedroom, took off his shoes and stretched out on the bed. He felt lonely, depressed, and the stress of the twins' accident was taking its toll on him as well.

He loved those kids, damn it. He loved them, though not half as much as he loved their mother. Could he ever make her see that?

CHAPTER SEVENTEEN

JAN SLEPT the sleep of exhaustion, but it wasn't a restful sleep. She woke feeling groggy and slightly disoriented. It took a moment to bring things into focus, to remember what had happened last night.

She slipped on a dressing robe and headed toward the kitchen. Along the way, she smelled coffee. She halted and nearly went back to her own room.

Had Doug come over to check on them and brewed a pot of coffee? She wasn't sure she could face him right now.

It wasn't Doug in the kitchen, though; it was Chet. He was sitting at the table eating a bowl of cereal.

"Thought you could do with some caffeine," he said when he saw her. "Hope I made it right."

"Thanks, Chet, I'm sure it's fine." Jan's eyes were on Chet as she filled a mug with coffee. He looked tired, but the only visible evidence of last night's ordeal was a bruise on his forehead.

"How do you feel?" she asked him.

"Okay, pretty much," he said. "I'm kind of bushed. My shoulder's sort of achy."

"Vicky's still asleep?"

"Yeah, she's really wiped out. Mom . . ."

"Yes?"

"I feel rotten about Doug's wagon. What happened wasn't Vicky's fault. I absolutely swear that—"

"I believe you, Chet."

"I'm glad you do," Chet said. "Mom, the wagon's pretty smashed up. The front end's had it. My bet is the insurance company will say it's a total loss."

"Maybe that's just as well if there's been that much damage," Jan said. "Better than trying to fix it and drive it again."

"I guess so. The thing is, this leaves Doug without transportation."

"He spoke of renting a car. For now, anyway."

Chet nodded. "That's what I figured he'd do. Look, Mom, I think Vicky and I should pay for his car rental."

Jan was touched. "I don't think he'd expect that of you, Chet."

"That doesn't matter. He trusted us with his car. Even though what happened wasn't Vicky's fault, we did wreck it."

Sometimes it struck Jan that her son and daughter—even though they didn't look in the least alike—really were twins in the true sense of the word. There was a deep, unassailable loyalty between the two of them when the chips were down.

She said, "I think you should make the offer to Doug. I think he'd appreciate it very much. But don't be surprised if he won't let you pay for a rental car. He's...a very fair person, Chet. He knows what happened wasn't Vicky's fault, and he doesn't blame her. He was only thankful it wasn't worse. One thing..."

"What?"

Jan couldn't believe what she was saying. "Doug will need a ride to the car rental agency," she told Chet. "He mentioned that last night. He wondered if you'd go along with him in my car and then drive my car back."

Chet inhaled, then slowly let the air out. "Whew!" he said. "I don't know."

"What do you mean?"

"I'm not thrilled at the idea of driving today, Mom."

"I can understand that," Jan told him, "but it might make it easier for you to drive tomorrow, and all the tomorrows after that, if you get behind a wheel today."

What was she saying?

Before she could backtrack she added, "Why don't you go over to Doug's and see what he wants to do."

"Maybe that might be the best idea," Chet conceded, and a few minutes later he set out for the cottage.

Jan tried to assess her priorities for the day. But she was still too shaken by the previous night's events to get her thoughts in any kind of coherent order.

She finally yielded to an impulse, dialed Chocolate Fantasies and got Nancy on the phone.

"Could you do without me today?" she asked bluntly.

"Got something good going?" Nancy teased. "Like maybe an outing with your handsome tenant?"

"No," Jan said, then described what had happened last night as briefly as she could.

When she'd finished, Nancy said, "Why didn't you call me? I'd have come right over."

"At that hour of the morning?"

"You've stood by me at all hours, Jan," Nancy reminded her. "There are times when we all need someone to be there for us. I'm glad you had Doug."

Nancy added quickly, "Don't even think of coming in for the next couple of days. I've got the orders under control, and I'll keep an eye on the production. We're doing fine, Jan. I think this is going to be our best year yet. So just relax and stay home and take care of yourself and the twins, okay?"

"Thanks," Jan said, and hung up before she started to cry.

Her eyes were still glistening when Chet came back from the cottage. "It's all set, Mom," he said. "Doug says they have a rental car for him. This shouldn't take long."

"Where is Doug?" Jan asked.

"Waiting outside," Chet said. "I asked him to come in for coffee but he passed."

Jan didn't wonder Doug had decided not to come in when she thought of her behavior last night.

She followed Chet out to the back porch. Doug was standing at the foot of the steps, looking toward the cottage. Jan followed his eyes, and the simple beauty of the scene made her suddenly catch her breath. It had been so long since she'd really looked at it. Maples and oaks were interspersed among the pines in the woods back of the cottage. The sun, riding high in a cloudless bright blue sky, shone upon the trees, gilding their natural brilliance so that the autumn colors seemed twice as intense. The cottage itself fit perfectly against the sylvan background. Gray shingles, white trim, deep green shutters, orange-red geraniums still blooming in the dark green wooden boxes under each front window. Jan suddenly understood why Doug was so attracted to the place.

"Hi," she said softly.

At the sound of her voice, Doug turned sharply. She became aware she hadn't even brushed her hair yet this morning. The long, dark copper strands straggled around her shoulders. She'd had her pale blue flannel robe for years and it looked it. But right now appearances didn't matter. What Jan wished was that she could put how she was feeling into words. But there was no chance to speak to Doug with Chet heading for the car, ready to go.

Doug, his voice as soft as hers, said, "Hi. I hope you had a decent night's sleep."

"It was okay. Vicky's still asleep."

"When she wakes, tell her I checked with the hospital will you? Visiting hours start at two. I thought we might leave here around one forty-five."

"I'll tell her."

"I won't keep Chet long," Doug promised and headed for her car.

Chet turned to her to say, "Mike or Al might call. You can tell them I'll be back soon."

"I will." Jan added, the words meant for both Doug and Chet, "Take it easy."

IT WAS AFTER ELEVEN when Vicky came downstairs. Jan wondered if maybe they'd given her a tranquilizer in the hospital to calm her nerves.

Vicky had no telltale bruises, but she was very pale. Her voice faltered slightly as she said, "No one's called, have they, Mummy?"

"About Jim, you mean?"

"Yes."

"No one's called, and I'm sure he's doing fine, Vicky. By the way, Doug said to be ready by a quarter to two. Visiting hours start at two."

"That late?" Vicky asked, dismayed.

Jan smiled. "It's only a couple more hours," she said.

Vicky nodded, but she looked so miserable Jan's heart ached for her. She said, "Mummy, I'm afraid Jim's parents are going to hate me."

Jan was astonished. "Why in the world should they?"

"Because I was driving, and Jim got hurt."

"Vicky, it wasn't your fault," Jan said. "I've heard from the police that it wasn't your fault. Also from Chet who was right in the car with you. I'll bet you anything Jim's going to tell you the same thing."

"Maybe Jim won't even want to see me."

"Darling." Jan went over to her daughter and put her arms around her. "Stop to think," she said, "and you'll know that's not so. Jim loves you, for one thing. Also, he's an intelligent, fair-minded person. He's not going to hold you responsible for what was without doubt an accident."

"I never thought you liked Jim," Vicky murmured.

Jan started to frame a half-truth, then decided to level with her daughter. "It isn't Jim I haven't liked, but the idea of Jim," she said carefully. "What I'm saying is—I admit I've been upset by the closeness of your relationship because you seem so young to me. But," she added with a slight, sad smile, "I know you don't seem young to you. I've been there. I remember."

"You and Doug were lovers a long time ago, weren't you?"

Jan didn't know how she would have dealt with that question yesterday. But this was today. She said softly, "Yes, we were."

"What happened?"

"Doug went away to college, to California. He had an uncle who was willing to put him through college, otherwise he'd have had no chance to go. We drifted apart, once he'd left Ellis Falls. Distance doesn't always lend enchantment, Vicky. No matter how much you miss a person, it's human nature to pick up the threads of your own life and go on with it. After a time, I met your father and fell in love with him and we married..."

Her words drifted off, but they left an echo. What she'd just told Vicky was what actually had happened twenty years ago. It was as simple as that. Doug had not contrived to break her heart. He'd been the one to go away, she'd been the one to stay home. What had followed was inevitable.

Vicky said, "I don't think Doug has ever gotten over loving you."

"He got over loving me a long time ago, darling. Life goes on. His life went on, so did mine."

"When he came back here and saw you, I think he fell in love with you all over again," Vicky persisted. "There's a certain look on his face when he talks about you. And sometimes when he's watching you, and you don't know it, his eyes tell a whole story."

Jan laughed softly. "Vicky, my dearest, you are an incurable romantic."

"Maybe. But you and Doug would make such a wonderful couple."

Jan was too stunned to say anything. She quickly changed the subject.

"About Jim," she said. "I think I'll give Mrs. Farrish a call a little later. I want her to know we all feel very badly about what happened. But that we're so thankful Jim is going to be all right."

"Suppose she tells you she blames me," Vicky said nervously.

"I doubt she will."

"Suppose she does, Mummy. Will you tell me?"

"Yes," Jan said, and met her daughter's eyes honestly. "Whatever Mrs. Farrish says, I promise I'll tell you."

JAN WAITED to call Jim's mother until after Vicky had left the house with Doug. Chet had tagged along with them, asking to be dropped off at Mike's house, which was on the way to the hospital.

As she dialed the Farrishes' number, Jan wondered herself what Jim's mother was going to say to her. She didn't know Helen or Tod Farrish well. They'd moved to Ellis Falls from Pittsfield only a few years earlier.

She was relieved when Helen Farrish said, "I was going to call you, Mrs. Grayson. But this has been a topsy-turvy morning. Tod went down to his insurance office a couple of hours late. Since he left, I've been wandering around the house trying to decide what to do with myself."

"Am I keeping you from going over to the hospital?" Jan asked.

"No. We talked to Jim's doctor earlier and he's doing very well. We plan to go over to see him later in the afternoon."

"I might as well tell you Vicky is on her way now."

"I rather imagined she might be," Helen Farrish said. "Poor child. Such a terrible experience for her."

"She's afraid you and your husband may blame her for what happened, Mrs. Farrish."

"On the contrary, Officer Evans said that if Vicky hadn't been driving carefully, if she hadn't been in full control of the car, the results could have been so much worse for all three of the youngsters. When I see Vicky I'll make that very clear." She hesitated, then said, "I suppose you've probably felt like I have about Jim and Vicky. That they're awfully young for such deep involvement."

"Yes, I have," Jan admitted.

"I guess one of the main things we have to learn as parents is that we can't lead our children's lives for them," Jim's mother said. "Jim is devoted to Vicky. I would say she's equally so to him. Who knows if their love will endure? But, meantime...I know what a busy person you are, Mrs. Grayson, but once Jim's home from the hospital could you and your twins come for dinner one night?"

"We'd love that," Jan said, and she meant it.

Last night's accident was changing her thinking in a number of ways, she thought as she straightened up the kitchen, then went to take a shower. Doug was right. Life was both precious and precarious. There were no guarantees. What mattered was how you lived each day....

Doug appeared at Jan's back door around three-thirty. "Just wanted you to know I left Vicky at the hospital," he said. "Jim's parents came over and they'll give her a ride back here later."

"How is Jim?"

"Collecting autographs on his cast. I think half the kids in Ellis Falls High have stopped by to sign their names. I told him he's going to run out of space."

"What about his head injury?"

"It's not bad," Doug said. "He'll have a scar, but not a bad one. He's young. It'll fade. If it doesn't, he can consider plastic surgery. But the doctors doubt very much that will be necessary."

He eyed her closely, "How are you?"

"All right," she said. There was something else on her mind and she had to voice it, "Having the Farrishes drive Vicky home sort of botched your plans, didn't it?"

"She's promised to go with me for a drive before dinner tonight," Doug said. "Provided that's all right with you," he added hastily.

"It's all right with me."

"As you can see," he said waving toward a large sedan in the driveway, "I rented sort of a clunker of a car—appearance wise, anyway. I wanted something big and solid and safe, I wasn't going for aesthetics."

"No red sports jobs?"

"Not just now, no."

"Doug...that was very thoughtful. To rent that kind of car, I mean."

"It seemed more practical."

"Maybe." Jan was trying so desperately to find the right words to say to him that she was becoming tongue-tied in the effort. "How about coming back for dinner after you and Vicky take your drive?" she managed.

"Thanks, but I'm going to settle for something quick, which I'll share with my word processor," he said.

She persisted. "I really wish you'd come for dinner."

He misread what she was trying to say. "Look, the twins will be fine," he said. "They won't need my moral support. Once Vicky saw Jim, and he gave her that grin of his she was a new kid. And Chet's already driving like the accident never happened."

"I wasn't thinking about the twins," Jan said.

Doug's raised eyebrows gave away his surprise. "Are you saying *you* want me to come to dinner?"

"Yes."

"I admit that makes me curious," he said. "Why?"

"I didn't think you were very happy with me, Janny."

"I was tired last night," she said. "In fact, I was wrung out." She smiled. "At least, in the end, I admitted you were right."

Doug chuckled. "I confess all day I've felt like I have a laurel wreath on my head," he said. He smiled that lopsided smile. "But I've really got to go," he told Jan. "I have a ton of work to do."

Jan wanted to tell him that whenever he wished to resume their talk sessions, she was ready. Ready and more than willing, she thought wryly.

"If you change your mind about dinner," she said, "come on over."

VICKY CAME HOME in the late afternoon, and she fulfilled her promise of going for a drive with Doug.

But when they returned half an hour or so later, Doug didn't come into the house with her.

Jan was preparing a special chicken dish for dinner in case Doug decided to join them. Vicky got a soft drink out of the fridge, then turned to her mother to say, "It felt so weird, getting behind the wheel of Doug's car, Mummy. I thought I couldn't do it. I felt sort of paralyzed for a minute. I was afraid to even turn the key in the ignition. Then Doug said, 'It's all right, Vicky, just take it easy,' and it was like magic. I drove okay, no problems at all."

She drew a deep breath. "I'm glad I did that," she said. "It would have been a lot harder later on."

Not so long ago, Jan knew she might have felt a twinge of jealousy at Vicky's confidence in Doug. Now, she only felt sad—because she hadn't realized long before now how much Doug had the twins' interests at heart.

She asked Vicky, "Did Doug say if he was coming to dinner?"

"He mentioned you'd invited him," Vicky said, "but he said he has to work tonight. He has a lot to get done because he has to go to New York next week. He's going to be on the *Today* show. Didn't he tell you?"

"No," Jan said slowly. "No, he didn't mention it."

"He says he doesn't especially want to be interviewed right now," Vicky reported. "But his publisher has been pressing him to get some exposure for the book, so he decided he might as well go for it. You know, Mom, you were great to help him get started on the book. I think he really appreciates it."

Vicky finished her drink and set the can on the sink board. "He says after he got through transcribing all the tapes he made with you he sort of got the hang of communicating with the computer. That's the way he puts it. So, the whole thing's a lot easier for him. Thanks to you, he says.''

"He's being too generous," Jan said.

A few minutes later Chet arrived with Mike in tow. Mike promptly said, "Something smells good," and Jan invited him to stay for dinner. She felt their ranks could use a little swelling tonight.

Later, as she shooed the kids off to watch TV and started cleaning things up, the thought of Doug being on the *Today* show next week eclipsed everything else. It wasn't an unusual occurrence for him. Over the years, she'd seen him as a special guest on many TV talk shows, usually in connection with some specific issue he had covered. But she couldn't help but think this appearance meant that Doug was edging back toward his own world. The book was going along well; soon he would finish it. And there were less than two months left till the end of the year.

CHET SAID, "Mom, you absolutely have to give Vicky and me notes to excuse our being late tomorrow morning. Al and Mike both have notes from their parents, and they're coming over here to watch Doug. So's Cathy, and a couple of the other kids. If it was afternoon, we'd all go to the hospital and watch the show with Jim on his TV. But I don't think they'd let us in his room at that hour of the morning.''

Jan wrote notes for the twins and they went off to school. She wondered how many high school students would be bringing in notes from their parents, giving them an excuse to be late tomorrow morning. There had been a lot of teenagers at the twins' birthday party, and Doug had been popular with all of them.

The next morning the twins insisted that she take the armchair right in front of the TV—the best viewing position. They, and their friends, crowded around, most of them sitting on the floor. Suddenly the screen was filled with Doug's face, and a couple of the kids let out expressive, "Wows!" Jan leaned forward slightly, her eyes fixed on this image of the man she loved.

He was wearing a dark blue suit, a striped tie, his hair was combed perfectly and he had a nice ruddy tinge to his complexion from being outdoors so much over the summer and fall. He looked incredibly handsome. Jan was astonished by the sudden surge of desire she felt for him. It was disconcerting—to understate the case—to think that he could do this to her from the other side of the TV screen.

She watched his manner. He was charming and gracious. He spiced his remarks with a nice sense of humor. The interviewer appeared to be genuinely sorry when they ran out of time. Doug faded from the screen and the station took a break for a commercial.

Chet got up and switched off the set. "Fantastic," he said.

Some of the other kids looked faintly stunned. Even Vicky said, "I knew he was famous but…gosh, he could as well be a movie star."

"He's good-looking enough to be a movie star," Cathy Ferguson observed.

"Far as I'm concerned, he's just Doug," Chet said with a certain degree of smugness. "That's what he does for a living, so he has to project an image. But

I'll bet you he'd rather be lounging around here in old, comfortable clothes, puttering with something out in the cottage or making a pot of that famous beef stew of his."

Regardless of Chet's comment, some of the students still looked dazed as they left the house. And Jan, closing the back door after them, felt slightly dazed herself.

She was thoroughly familiar with Doug's TV persona. But this was the first time she'd seen it since he'd returned to Ellis Falls.

Suddenly she felt like he'd leaped light years ahead of her, and she didn't see how she could even begin to catch up with him.

CHAPTER EIGHTEEN

THE NOVEMBER WINDS blew the last of the leaves off the trees. The bare branches etched stark silhouettes against daytime skies that already had the pale flint quality of winter. Night came faster. It was dark by five in the afternoon; sooner, on cloudy days.

Jan tried not to let the drab weather get her down. She'd always loved winter. But this year, its advent had a new meaning. Doug would be going away right after Christmas, if not sooner. And she dreaded to think of the void he was going to leave. There would be no way—no way—to fill it up.

She hadn't seen that much of Doug since Halloween, but at least she knew he was there. She could look out her window at night, when she was getting ready for bed, and see lights burning in the cottage. She could picture Doug at his word processor, working on his book, and she wished she were curled up in the big old armchair by the window in his study. She'd read, she'd snooze, she'd be quiet, as long as she could be near him. But Doug never invited her, and she felt too uncertain to invite herself.

Perhaps, Jan mused, Doug thought the proximity would be too much for both of them? The attraction between them was as potent as ever; Jan could see it in Doug's eyes every time they got near each other. And her own desire for him intensified each time they met. Jan had long since given up branding her body a traitor. It was her body that was being truthful.

Pride prompted her to try to conceal her feelings when she was around Doug. The result was that she tended to behave like a polite stranger. When he asked her how things were going, she gave standard replies. Chocolate Fantasies was doing a fantastic business. Town politics were running on an even keel. The twins were doing well in school. What more was there to say?

She'd complimented Doug on his appearance on the *Today* show. He'd shrugged it off. "I'd rather have done that later, after the book is out," he said.

"Well," Jan suggested, "you'll probably be asked for a return appearance."

"Possibly," he conceded, without much interest.

Most times when Doug was around her, Jan had the impression he was impatient to get away. She noted that he didn't go out much, except to shop. Now and then, she'd see him heading for the trail to the cottage, each arm clutching a brown paper grocery bag. But much of the time the car he'd rented was parked right out there at the edge of the driveway.

With Christmas orders to be filled, Jan put in longer and longer hours at Chocolate Fantasies. Hundreds of delectable Yuletide confections were being molded. There were baskets of red chocolate poinsettias, to be used as centerpieces on holiday tables; each "flower" was individually wrapped so that at the end of the evening a hostess could offer a candy poinsettia as a gift to a departing guest. Chocolate Santas, chocolate jingle bells, holly wreaths, and all the other symbols of the season, were produced in the kitchen at the back of the shop by people who took pride in their creations. The candies were packed in the silver-foil boxes that were a trademark of Chocolate Fantasies. The star-studded blue ribbon they used the rest of the year was substituted, during the Christmas season with bright green-and-red striped ribbon, and a sprig of holly embellished each bow.

"Packaging is important," Jan had emphasized early on. "Look at Godiva. You see a gold box, and you know it's full of luscious chocolates."

The cost of the boxes and ribbons came high. But even Nancy, dubious at first about this added expense, now agreed that the packaging was worth every cent they spent on it.

"The silver boxes, the florists' boxes filled with tinted chocolate roses, and all the other packaging gimmicks you've thought up are what have helped me make my sales," she told Jan as they lingered in the shop one evening after everyone else had left.

She added, "You've been right about so much, Jan. You showed me I had to let Bob go. Now, thanks to you, it's clear to me that we'd long ago reached the point of no return."

"Don't be silly, Nancy," Jan protested, embarrassed. "It was just a matter of time before you figured those things out for yourself."

"Maybe. But, except for you, I might have been in a sanatorium drying out before I came to the right conclusions," Nancy said. "I no longer begrudge Bob the divorce. I'm glad it can be 'no-fault,' so neither of us has to rake up anything against the other. I actually feel at this point that Bob is a friend. A few weeks ago, I wouldn't have believed that could ever be possible."

Nancy then changed the subject so suddenly Jan wasn't ready for her question. "What about Doug MacKenzie?"

"I haven't seen too much of him lately," Jan said. "He's busy with his book. He has a first-of-the-year deadline."

"What will he do once the book is finished?"

"Go back to his network, I imagine." Jan wished they hadn't gotten onto this subject.

"You really think he's going to leave Ellis Falls right away?"

"Yes. There's no reason for him to stay." As Jan said that, she felt as though a heavy lump had settled in the middle of her chest. She tried to sound casual as she voiced some of the fears that had been haunting her. "Matter of fact, I wouldn't be surprised if he decides to leave before Christmas, if he can finish his book by then," she said. "I'm sure there are places other than Ellis Falls where Doug would have a better time spending the holidays."

Nancy eyed her narrowly. "Naturally I've heard that you and Doug went out together in high school," she said. "I think a lot of people around town thought the two of you might pick up where you left off, especially after he moved into your cottage."

Jan smiled rather wanly. "Time's not reversible," she told Nancy. "You can't go back. It's the height of folly to ever think you can go back."

"Then how about going forward?" Nancy suggested.

As she drove home that evening, Jan made a real effort to push Nancy's question out of her mind, but it kept repeating itself.

It had started to rain during the afternoon. Now, with the temperature dropping after dark, the rain turned to sleet. The driving became treacherous. Jan skidded going around a curve she'd negotiated thousands of times, and realized how easy it had been for Vicky to sideswipe a tree in order to avoid the object that had been tossed in front of her headlights. She nearly skidded into a tree as it was, without anything to distract her.

Both twins were home. Before starting dinner, Jan changed into a comfortable old wool housecoat. She was pinning her hair into a bun on top of her head when Chet called her.

"Phone, Mom," he said.

Jan didn't expect to hear Doug's voice. "I wanted to be sure that was your car that just drove in," he said.

"Why?" she asked.

"Just wanted to be sure you're home safe. It's such a rotten night out."

"It was bad driving," Jan admitted. "I'm glad to be home."

"Janny..."

"Yes?"

"Look, I'm just about finished the book. I should be able to take it down to New York next week. I want my editor to read the manuscript as is, before I start on my revisions. But after that—"

He broke off, and Jan waited. But then Doug said, "If I don't see you before I leave, I'll be in touch when I get back."

Thanksgiving wasn't that far off. Jan had already invited Nancy for Thanksgiving dinner, and now she nearly issued the same invitation to Doug. But then she decided to wait till he got back. Chances were, he'd only be gone a few days...

She was wrong about that. Each night, when she glanced out at the cottage before going to bed, all she saw was darkness. And the darkness translated into an emptiness that hurt.

Thanksgiving week came, and Doug still hadn't reappeared. At that point, Chet and Vicky began to get edgy.

"Don't you have any idea how to reach him?" Chet demanded one night after he got home from a basketball game.

"No, I honestly don't, Chet," Jan said.

"Did you ask him for Thanksgiving dinner?"

"I intended to, as soon as he got back. I didn't think he'd be gone this long."

"Mom, you know someone like Doug would get a raft of holiday invitations. He's probably accepted someone else."

"I can't help it if he has," Jan said defensively. "Anyway, I was thinking of asking the Farrishes to dinner. There are just the three of them, and they might welcome a chance to go out for Thanksgiving this year. Vicky says that Jim's getting around pretty well on crutches."

"Yeah, Jim's getting around fine on crutches," Chet agreed. "But what does that have to do with Doug?"

"Nothing, I suppose."

"Even if the Farrishes came, there'd be room for Doug, wouldn't there?"

"Of course."

"Don't you have any idea who his publisher is, Mom? You could call—"

"No, I don't have any idea who his publisher is," Jan said, beginning to get impatient with Chet. "Doug mentioned names occasionally, but I don't remember any of them."

"Why didn't you ask him for a number where you could reach him, before he left here?"

"Because he didn't say goodbye," Jan said. And suddenly, her words sunk in, leaving her feeling more desolate than ever.

Doug had left the morning after his phone call when she was at a selectmen's meeting. Later, when she arrived at Chocolate Fantasies, Nancy had reported that Doug had called. "He wanted you to know he's taking off for New York," Nancy said.

Since then, Jan had remembered something. Thanksgiving Eve, this year, was also Doug's birthday. He'd be thirty-nine.

She kept the knowledge of his birthday in the back of her mind. She didn't even tell the twins. But she wanted to do something to celebrate. Something special. She couldn't put on a luau for Doug, but maybe she could think of something that would be memorable.

Rather, maybe she could have, if he'd given her half a chance. Now she had no idea where he'd be, come the day before Thanksgiving.

Now Chet looked at her disgustedly. "The two of you should learn to communicate better," he said, and strode out of the room.

Jan looked after him, and didn't know whether to laugh or to cry.

But she did know Chet was right.

THERE WAS STILL NO SIGN of Doug the day before Thanksgiving.

Chocolate Fantasies was giving their employees two days off for the holidays, and the town office was closed, so Jan was free to get started on the dinner preparations.

She baked pumpkin pies and minced pies and squash rolls, and made a special walnut cake that was a family favorite. She fixed the creamed onions and put them in the fridge; they could be reheated the next day. She prepared the butternut squash, and made a string-bean-and-mushroom casserole.

Early Thanksgiving morning, she'd be getting up before anyone else, as she always did, to stuff the big turkey and put it into the oven. That would give her the rest of the day to finalize the food preparations and set a beautiful table. Dinner was planned for four o'clock, and the Farrishes had been more than glad to accept her invitation.

Since Chet had been old enough to do some cooking, he'd taken on the task of fixing hamburgers for Thanksgiving Eve supper, to spare Jan that particular chore. He did his stint that night, and Vicky did the cleanup. Then the twins went into the living room to watch television, while Jan waited for the walnut cake to cool enough so she could turn it onto a cake plate and store it overnight in the pantry.

Once that was done, she went to her room, curled up on the bed and tried to lose herself in a mystery novel she'd picked up at the library. It was a suspenseful book, but Jan could not concentrate. She lowered it to her lap as she stared at the floral pattern on the bedroom wallpaper, her thoughts on Doug. Where was he tonight?

The twins' movie ended and they came in to say good-night to her. After that, Jan spent some time soaking in a hot bath spiced with a pine essence that was supposed to be relaxing. But as she got out of the tub, she still felt as if her body was tied in knots.

She slipped on her nightgown and robe, and pattered back into the bedroom. It had become automatic to glance across at the cottage and now, as she did so, she blinked. There were lights twinkling in every window.

The first snow of the season had fallen during the evening. Now the moon was out, highlighting the snow blanket with silver-white radiance. Stars glittered in the midnight sky. Jan drank in the scene, but mostly she focused on those lights in the cottage windows.

After a time she went to her closet and took out the present she'd wrapped for Doug two days ago. She tucked the card that went with it under the ribbon bow, then went out to the kitchen and put on her boots, and a full, heavy coat. Seconds later, she was carefully negotiating the back steps and making the second set of footprints in the freshly fallen snow on the path to the cottage.

Why hadn't she heard his car drive up? she wondered. Probably because of the din of the TV. Why hadn't he come to the house to tell her—and Chet and Vicky—that he was back?

She knocked at the cottage door and, when there was no answer, knocked again. She wondered if Doug had gone to bed with all the lights on, and was so fast asleep he didn't hear the noise she was making. Or, maybe he was taking a shower, and the rushing water was drowning out other sounds.

The door opened so suddenly Jan took a step backward. She started to stammer out an explanation, to tell him why she'd come over. But then their eyes met, and Jan knew there wasn't any need for words.

She reached under her coat for the package she'd been protecting from the elements, and handed it to Doug. His eyes flashed questions, and she said, "Happy Birthday."

He drew a long breath. "I didn't think there was anyone in the world who would remember this was my birthday," he said unsteadily.

She smiled. "I doubt I could ever forget."

Doug moved into the room and Jan followed him. He put the package down on the coffee table and picked up the card. But then a rather strange look passed over his face, and he put the card down and picked up the package again.

He tore off the wrapping paper, and let it fall to the floor. Jan watched him as he stared at her copy of their high school yearbook, and she saw him swallow hard.

She said softly, "Read the card, will you please, Doug?"

Doug looked at her apprehensively, and she urged, "Go ahead."

Slowly, carefully, he slit the envelope open and withdrew the birthday card she'd gotten him. Inside she'd written:

There are a lot of wonderful memories between the pages of this yearbook. Cherish them . . . as I do.

That was then, Doug, and I loved you as much

as an eighteen year old girl could ever love anyone. But this is now, and I love you as much as a
thirty-eight year old woman could ever love
anyone.

Happy birthday, my dearest

Jan had never seen Doug cry. But now his eyes became glazed with tears, and he didn't try to blink
them back.

He said huskily, "Oh my God, Janny!"

He covered the distance between them in a single
step. She went into his arms, and for a long moment
he clutched her close. Then he kissed her. Never before had Jan been kissed like this. Its depth, its inten-
sity, went beyond measurement.

Jan lost herself in Doug's kiss, let it go on and
on . . .

When Doug finally released her, he looked at her
as if he couldn't believe he really was seeing her. "Am
I dreaming all this, Janny?" he asked, and smiled that
lopsided smile that always plucked at her heart-
strings. "Make me a promise. If I am dreaming, don't
wake me up."

"You're not dreaming." Jan's voice was unsteady
and inside she was trembling.

She'd never seen Doug look so uncertain. "I don't
know," he said. "Are you sure you didn't write your
message in an emotional moment?"

She smiled. "I was emotional, yes. But no more
emotional than usual, where you're concerned."

He shook his head. "I can't believe I'm hearing
this."

Jan took a deep breath. "Then I guess maybe we're
even. I can't believe I'm really seeing you."

"I don't understand."

Jan sat down on the edge of the couch and looked up at him. "I was so afraid you weren't going to come back."

He frowned. "How can you say that?"

"Because it's so. I wasn't sure you'd come back, Doug. And, I couldn't blame you if you didn't. Except, Vicky and Chet never would have understood it."

"But you would have?"

"Yes, I would have."

"Because you'd feel it would be history repeating itself?"

"That's not what I meant," she protested.

"Isn't it?" Doug sat down in his armchair, his face expressionless. "For all of what you wrote on that card, you still have no faith in me, do you, Janny?"

"It's not a question of having faith in you."

"Then what the hell is it? I walked out on you once, and you've obviously convinced yourself that as soon as I'm finished here I'm going to walk out on you again. If that isn't a lack of faith, what is?"

"I don't expect you to stay in Ellis Falls," Jan said quietly.

"Just what do you expect me to do?"

"It seems inevitable to me that you'll be going back to your own work, your own world."

"My work, my world. You make that sound pretty dramatic," Doug said angrily. "Damn it, I don't understand you, Janny. You tell me you love me one minute, then the next minute you seem to be ready to wave goodbye."

"What I was trying to say," Jan began, "was that for as long as you're here . . ."

"For as long as I'm here, we can make love to each other, because that happens to be something we do very well. Is that what you're saying, Janny?"

"Doug..."

"Well, that is what you're saying, isn't it? What do you take me for? Do you think I can possibly keep on making love to you and then up and leave you some morning because I have a sudden irrepressible urge to dart off to some far corner of the globe?"

"That's your work."

"Sure, it's my work," he agreed. "Work I've lived, eaten, breathed, for more years than I like to think about. Does it occur to you that while I was devoting myself and my life to my work I was missing out on a lot of other things? It's occurred to me...from the moment I got up on the reviewing stand at the Fourth of July parade and took a good look at you. About some things, I'm a quick read, Janny. It didn't take me long to begin to realize what I'd lost."

"Doug..."

"Listen, will you. I want more than I've ever had, Janny. Do you want to hear what I want?"

Jan waited.

Doug said, "I want a home. I've never had a real home."

She held her breath.

"I want to make that home with you, Janny."

"Doug..."

"No, no, hear me out, Janny. All I ask for is a little show of faith from you. I know I'll have to earn your trust. But give me that chance, will you?" Doug sighed, and his voice was ragged as he went on, "If you don't...I can't blame you. You told me yourself, after all, that I'm not worth one of your husband's little fingers."

He looked up, his blue eyes dark, his pain all too evident. "I love you more than I ever could possibly tell you, Janny," he said. "But that's a hell of a hard image to have to try to match."

Jan winced. "I was angry, angry and hurt when I said that, Doug," she protested. She stared at him helplessly. "You don't have to match anything where I'm concerned," she said. "I loved my husband, yes. I'm not going to be trite and minimize that love. But . . . you were my first love and there's no doubt in my mind or in my heart that you're going to be my last. You say you want me . . ."

"Oh, Janny," Doug said. "How can I ever possibly make you know how much I want you, how much I need you?"

Jan looked at Doug, and she suddenly felt as if her life was beginning all over again.

Her eyes sparkled. She teased, "I can think of ways."

Doug looked at her, momentarily startled by her mood change, by the exaltation and hope he saw written on her lovely face.

"As a starter," he asked, still not entirely trusting what was happening, "will you marry me, Janny?"

"Mmm," Janny said, "don't you think we should consult the twins about this?"

"What are you talking about?" Doug growled. "The twins started matchmaking the Fourth of July, when you drove me back to the inn."

"Smart kids," Jan began, and was about to go further when Doug, effectively, stopped her.

For a long time he held her in his arms, held her tight. Then he drew her down on the couch, still holding her close, and she was content to just sit there with him, resting her head against his shoulder.

She felt warm, she felt loved. She felt wonderful.

After a time, Doug said, "I can't believe you could have thought I might not come back."

"Please, let's not talk about that again."

"We won't," he said. "Because I'm never again going to give you a chance to doubt me. This time... well, the consultations in New York took longer than I expected they would. Then I started back here yesterday so I'd be home in plenty of time for Thanksgiving, but that car I rented developed a problem. I couldn't get a substitute rental in the town I stopped in—everything had been booked for the holiday. So there was nothing for it but to spend the night in a flea bag of a motel, then limp home today.

"I thought about calling you, then I thought it would be better to wait till I got back. Talk about being uncertain... hell, I didn't even know if you were going to ask me to Thanksgiving dinner."

"If I hadn't managed to ask you to Thanksgiving dinner, I think the twins would have stopped speaking to me," Jan confessed.

Doug smiled. "They're great kids, Janny. I'll do my damnedest with them."

"All you need to do is to continue to be yourself."

"Janny... you spoke about my work."

"Yes." Remarkable, but Jan didn't feel even the slightest flutter of alarm as she thought about his work.

"I'm not ready to give up what I do," Doug admitted. "Probably I won't be for a long time to come.

But I can pick and choose the assignments I want at this stage of my career. And sometimes you could go with me, now that Nancy's back in stride. Provided, of course, that you could straighten things out with the town hall."

She laughed. "I think I could straighten things out with the town hall."

"I wouldn't dream of letting you travel in seriously troubled areas," Doug said. "But there are great hotels in London and Paris and Cairo and Athens and lots of other places where we could stay while I'm on assignment."

He stared down at Jan. "I want you in my life as much as possible...whenever it is, wherever I am."

Suddenly he grinned, a downright wicked grin. "I was going to ask you if you'd stay here with me tonight, but I think we'd better make it your place," he said. "Then I'll be there in the morning to help get our turkey in the oven."

Tomorrow morning and all the mornings after. That promise sang in Jan's heart as she and Doug walked out the door of the cottage together.

EPILOGUE

"VICKY," Jan said, "will you kindly get over here with the rest of us so we can have our picture taken?"

Chet, Jan and Doug were standing in front of the mantel in Jan's living room. The mantel had been decorated both for Christmas and a wedding. Real red poinsettias, in this instance, and clusters of green holly, were threaded among rich white satin ribbons.

A tree whose star touched the ceiling stood in the corner of the room. This was Christmas Eve. There were brightly wrapped packages under the tree to be opened tomorrow, a mixture of Christmas and wedding presents.

Earlier, there had been a short, beautiful service in the old, vine-covered church in town where Jan had been baptized. Now, the special people who had been invited back to the house for an informal reception stood around beaming. Even Bartlett Folger looked benevolent today, Jan thought. Rose Ladue appeared to be moonstruck, and she and Tom Prentice were holding hands. Nancy, who had acted as matron of honor, was beautiful in bright red velvet. Maybe her brilliant smile was a bit too fixed, but she was doing a good job of keeping the shadows away.

Someday, there would be someone special for Nancy, Jan thought. Her wish was also a prayer.

Leona Martin looked like a different person, dressed in a stylish dark green suit.

The Farrishes were present, and Mike, Al and Cathy, as well as several of the twins' other friends. And Jim, at moments, vied with the bride and groom as a center of attention. He was sitting in an armchair, his crutches thrust to one side. His cast had been changed a couple of days ago, but the new one was already heavily inscribed with signatures. The bandages had long since been removed from his head, and Jan had been glad to see that Doug was right about the scar. It slanted close to Jim's hairline and wasn't disfiguring. In time, people probably wouldn't even notice it.

Floppy and the cats were also in attendance, and—obviously realizing this was a special occasion—had let Vicky tie red satin bows around their necks.

Jan began again, "Vicky, will you please..."

Vicky tore herself away from Jim and joined her mother, her stepfather and her twin brother, in front of the mantel.

Bert Collins, the photographer, had been a classmate of Doug and Jan's at Ellis High. Now he said, "All right, let's get it together. Chet, you look as if someone put a straitjacket on you. Vicky, stop posing. Jan, loosen up a little, will you? Doug, will you kindly try to relax? I'd think you, of all people, would be used to this sort of thing."

Bert suddenly made a face at his subjects, and all four of them burst out laughing. A moment later, he was taking pictures.

Jan was sure they were going to look like grinning Cheshire cats when the film was developed. But their wide smiles were justified. Bert wasn't merely taking pictures of a wedding party.

They were a family.

Harlequin Superromance®

Available in Superromance this month
#462—STARLIT PROMISE

STARLIT PROMISE is a deeply moving story of a
woman coming to terms with her grief and gradually
opening her heart to life and love.

Author Petra Holland sets the scene beautifully, never
allowing her heroine to become mired in self-pity. It
is a story that will touch your heart and leave you
celebrating the strength of the human spirit.

**Available wherever Harlequin books
are sold.**

Harlequin Superromance®

CHILDREN OF THE HEART
by Sally Garrett

Available this month

Romance readers the world over have wept and rejoiced over Sally Garrett's heartwarming stories of love, caring and commitment. In her new novel, *Children of the Heart,* Sally once again weaves a story that will touch your most tender emotions.

You'll be moved to tears of joy

Nearly two hundred children have passed through Trenance McKay's foster home. But after her husband leaves her, Trenance knows she'll always have to struggle alone. No man could have enough room in his heart both for Trenance and for so many needy children. Max Tulley, news anchor for KSPO TV is willing to try, but how long can his love last?

"Sally Garrett does some of the best character studies in the genre and will not disappoint her fans."
Romantic Times

Look for *Children of the Heart* wherever Harlequin Romance novels are sold. SCH

PENNY JORDAN

Sins and infidelities...
Dreams and obsessions...
Shattering secrets
unfold in...

THE HIDDEN YEARS

SAGE — stunning, sensual and vibrant, she spent a lifetime distancing herself from a past too painful to confront... the mother who seemed to hold her at bay, the father who resented her and the heartache of unfulfilled love. To the world, Sage was independent and invulnerable— but it was a mask she cultivated to hide a desperation she herself couldn't quite understand... until an unforeseen turn of events drew her into the discovery of the hidden years, finally allowing Sage to open her heart to a passion denied for so long.

The Hidden Years—a compelling novel of truth and passion that will unlock the heart and soul of every woman.

AVAILABLE IN OCTOBER!
Watch for your opportunity to complete your Penny Jordan set.
POWER PLAY and SILVER will also be available in October.

This August, don't miss an exclusive
two-in-one collection of earlier love stories

MAN
WITH A PAST

TRUE COLORS

by one of today's hottest
romance authors,

Now, two of Jayne Ann Krentz's most loved books are
available together in this special edition that new and
longtime fans will want to add to their bookshelves.

Let Jayne Ann Krentz capture your hearts with the love
stories, MAN WITH A PAST and TRUE COLORS.

And in October, watch for the second two-in-one
collection by Barbara Delinsky!

Available wherever Harlequin books are sold.